Hamra and the Jungle of Memories

Also by Hanna Alkaf:

The Girl and the Ghost

Hamra and the Jungle of Memories

HANNA ALKAF

HARPER

An Imprint of HarperCollinsPublishers

ISBN 978-0-06-320795-0

Typography by Alice Wang
23 24 25 26 27 LBC 5 4 3 2 1

First Edition

Sometimes it seems like the world breaks, and through the cracks slip in grief, anger, frustration, anxiety, and so many more feelings that seem far too big and too scary to handle all at once.

If you're struggling with those feelings: I see you.

This book is for Malik, and for Maryam, and for you.

Sometimes people leave you, halfway through the wood.

Do not let it grieve you.

No one leaves for good.

—Stephen Sondheim, "Children Will Listen/Finale,"
  from *Into the Woods*

1

THERE WAS ONCE a girl named Hamra who lived in a crooked house on the edge of the tangled Langkawi jungle, with a mother and father who told her what to do, a grandfather who told her stories, and a grandmother who told her truths. In time, she would come to discover that all of these things were equally important.

In fact, if Hamra could go back in time, she'd tell herself three very important things:

1. Listen to Atok.
2. Listen to Opah.
3. Listen to your father and for goodness' sake, tie your shoelaces.

Of course, without the ability to go back in time, all you can really do is wait until all the fun stuff's over before understanding the potentially life-changing consequences of your actions. Which, of course, is the reason why when Hamra went into the jungle on Tuesday, she was completely unprepared for what lurked there in the deep green shadows, waiting.

And watching.

And hungry.

But we're getting ahead of ourselves.

Since Hamra had no idea about the thing that was waiting for her in the jungle, at 6:57 a.m. on Tuesday, she lay in bed after Subuh prayers and counted down the seconds until the big hand of her Minnie Mouse alarm clock moved once more.

5 . . . 4 . . . 3 . . . 2 . . . 1 . . . tick.

6:58 a.m. "Happy birthday to me," Hamra whispered. Minnie only smiled her wide plastic smile in response.

Hamra was an only child, and for this reason, her birthday had always been a—capital B, capital D—Big Deal. "You came with the dawn," her mother told her, "just after Subuh, as if you wanted the world to be fresh for your arrival."

Hamra stared at the cracks on her ceiling and wondered what surprises awaited her today. The clock had been a birthday present the year she turned seven. That had been the year of everything Minnie Mouse, her absolute favorite cartoon character; she had worn a red dress with a skirt that twirled and a big red bow in her hair, and Opah had produced a magnificent cake in the shape of Minnie herself, a wonder of icing and deft knife work. Opah's cakes had always been the best part of birthdays back then. But back then was a long time ago, long enough to be a whole other world.

Ten had brought her own guitar and the promise of lessons, the inevitable conclusion to a year of hardcore flailing over Taylor Swift's *1989*; the cake was an Oreo cheesecake hastily bought from the bakery in town because Opah had forgotten the cake she was baking in the oven and it had burned all black, filling the house with acrid smoke. They'd laughed, then. "A silly mistake," Opah had said, tears in her eyes from giggling over it all. "Just one of those things." That was the year her grandmother began using sticky notes to remind her of things. "I'm a little forgetful these days," she'd say with a wave of her hand. "Ala, you know lah how it is with us old people."

But as the year turned it was clear the burnt cake was only a glimpse of what was yet to come.

Hamra's eleventh birthday was the year everyone forgot about presents, because in the middle of laying the table for her favorite meal—nasi ayam, and if she tried hard enough she could still smell the chicken roasting in the oven bearing the faded sticky note instructing: *This is HOT, do not TOUCH when light is ON*, just one note in a forest of notes—they realized that Opah was missing. She'd walked right out of the house, with the cake Hamra and her mother had helped her bake, without her shoes. They found her at the edge of the jungle, feet covered in mud. "I'm taking it to my mother," she'd said crossly. "It's her favorite, Victoria sandwich." At that point, Opah's mother had been dead for over a decade.

They brought her home and cleaned her feet, placing Band-Aids carefully over half a dozen tiny cuts from where Opah had stepped, unseeing, on rocks or thorns. Later, Hamra dug a fork into the cake and ate one single bite. It was delicious, and somehow that made her cry even more.

For her twelfth birthday, Hamra got a generic grocery store chocolate cake and her very own phone. Her parents did not explain why, only that "you're old enough to have one now." But twelve-year-old Hamra understood things that eleven-year-old Hamra might not have; twelve-year-old Hamra knew adults said things even when they didn't really say them. The phone was so her parents could make sure they always knew where Opah was. It was so that they knew she was taking care of Opah properly when they weren't home to do it.

Hamra thought about all of this. She thought about the pandemic, and about her parents and their worried faces, pale with exhaustion. Then she looked over at Minnie. Some of the black had rubbed off her nose. Hamra *had* spent the past year or so lobbying hard to have it thrown out so it could be replaced with something sleek and cool, something befitting an almost-teenager. But all her impassioned reasoning had fallen on deaf ears; Ayah had merely said "We don't waste money replacing things that still work perfectly well." And so that was that.

"Maybe we don't need any surprises this year," Hamra said to Minnie.

Minnie just smiled her wide plastic smile.

Tick.

At 7:34 a.m., Hamra sat, washed and dressed, at the breakfast table, nibbling on toast slathered in Nutella and waiting for someone to wish her a happy birthday.

The waiting and the nibbling occupied her enough so that she paid no attention at all as Atok talked about . . . something. There was a time when Hamra would have listened eagerly as her grandfather told his stories, no matter

5

how many times she'd heard them before. But that was before the virus, and the lockdown that had kept them all in their homes for the past month.

Well, all of them except for her parents.

". . . and so, to this day, the tiger still seeks his revenge!" Atok raised his arms and grimaced, baring his teeth in what would have been a decent impression of a tiger's fierce snarl, if not for the fact that his dentures chose that precise moment to slide out of his mouth and fall straight into his mug. Hot milky tea puddled in the creases and curves of the plastic lace-printed tablecloth that never would lie flat no matter how many times Hamra smoothed it down.

Great. Without saying a word, Hamra got up to get the rag they always kept by the sink, a tiny flame of irritation shooting up from deep within her belly and nipping away at her chest. *It's adults who are supposed to clean up kids' messes,* she couldn't help thinking. *Not the other way around.*

Opah muttered sharp, waspish things under her breath as she wiped flecks of tea off the back of her hand with the faded sleeve of her baju kurung, which happened to be inside out. Opah's words were the kinds of things that Hamra wished she could say aloud, the kinds of things that, if Hamra were to say them, Ayah would have washed her mouth out with cilipadi.

On good days, you could almost pretend that she was the Opah Hamra remembered from her childhood, sharp and generous and funny, with the warmest hugs and an unerring habit of pointing out the most inconvenient truths. There were days when Hamra would wake up to the scent of fresh baking, or walk into a room to hear music playing as Atok and Opah danced like they were teenagers again, or listen to Opah reciting the Quran so beautifully, so melodiously that it could make you weep. On bad days, when the dementia loomed over them all like a shadow, nibbling away at her memories, stealing away the things that made Opah herself, Opah snapped at the edges of everyone else's nerves, and was crabby and belligerent and stubborn as a little kid who's just been told it's bedtime.

Today was . . . well, let's just say, today wasn't one of the good ones.

"Can't trust tigers," Opah announced at the end of Atok's story, staring pointedly at her as Hamra leaned over to mop up the tea.

"Sure, Opah."

"I mean it! Nasty, slippery things."

"All right, Opah." Hamra slid back in her seat with a sigh, trying not to cringe at how Atok shoved his tea-soaked teeth straight back into his mouth.

"What?" he said, noticing her glare. "It was still hot! Heat's a great way to kill germs, you know. They're practically sterile now . . ."

A sharp ping from her phone was a welcome distraction. "Your mother?" Atok asked.

"Yeah." Maybe Ibu would be the first one to wish her a happy birthday.

Good morning, my sayang. How's everything at home? I'm doing okay. Tired from a long shift last night, about to head to my room for some rest. How are the old folks doing?

Hamra gazed at her grandparents, wondering how to answer this question. Opah was sitting with her arms crossed, glaring at her bowl of porridge with the world's most mutinous expression. And as she watched, Atok farted, sighed, grabbed the newspaper, and headed straight for the bathroom, grabbing a can of air freshener on the way.

Ibu, tired from another long day of nursing in an overworked, overcrowded hospital far away from home, surrounded by death and disease, probably didn't need to know any of this.

8

We're all fine, Hamra typed carefully. *Miss you.* And then, hesitating for only a second, she typed: *Will you come home soon?*

I don't think that's possible, sayang. The same reply, every time.

"Morning." Ayah wandered into the kitchen, hair all messed up, rubbing the leftover sleep out of his eyes. He pressed kisses to their heads on his way to the coffeepot. Opah flinched at his touch. Hamra smiled, but it didn't feel like her usual wide, easy grin; it felt forced and thin, like there wasn't quite enough of it to reach her eyes or heart. She tried again. *Better.*

"Late night?" she asked.

Ayah sighed as he rummaged around the drying rack for a mug. "Always. You know how it is. But we did manage to get food out to some families we've had trouble reaching for a while."

"That's good, right?"

"It's always good when kids don't have to go hungry."

The clock on the wall chimed its happy little chime, signaling eight o'clock. When the world was normal, Hamra would have been in school, trying her hardest to look like she was paying attention in science while surreptitiously passing notes to her friends. Ibu would have been at the

9

clinic, dispensing smiles and medicine in equal measure. Ayah would have been out of the door by now, ready to fire up the van or boat to take the crowds of tourists that flooded Langkawi all year long on their next exotic, natural adventure: a cycling tour that meandered along riverbanks, through paddy fields, and on jungle paths; floating through the still mangroves at sunset, the sky painted in strips of pink and orange; an island-hopping trip, the boat scything frothy waves through deep blue seas.

But the world was not normal; the world was sick, with an illness nobody really seemed to understand. So Hamra sat at the dining table at home instead of her desk at school and worked on housework instead of homework. Ibu nursed virus-struck patients back to health in a far-off hospital and went back to a box of an apartment to rest between shifts instead of being home with her family, where she belonged. And instead of laughing, rowdy tourists, Ayah used his van to run volunteers and supplies up and down the island to reach the poorest families, the nursing homes, the refugee communities so loath to receive government aid. The boat stayed moored at the dock, just as Hamra stayed home with her aged grandparents, all of them bobbing in place and gathering dust.

Hamra's world was full of sickness. There was dementia,

a thief that stole Opah from them in the cruelest way, letting her come back to visit, making them believe she would stay, letting them get comfortable before snatching her away again. There was the virus, a thief that stole her mother, shipped off as she was to a red zone where they needed more medical personnel; stole her father, focused as he was on the plight of the less fortunate; stole Hamra's freedom. And it stole any attention she might have otherwise gotten for Extremely Important Occasions like, say, leaving childhood behind and becoming a teenager.

Which nobody seemed to have realized had happened more than a whole entire hour ago.

"I'm going to have to sort out some PPE deliveries today," Ayah said, slurping noisily on his coffee. "We're getting a shipment in from KL. Finally! Shortages everywhere, those factories must be working double-time . . ."

"Okay."

And then there was a crash.

Hamra whirled around, her heart pounding. From behind the closed bathroom door, she heard Atok's voice exclaiming "YA TUHANKU, WHAT WAS THAT??" But Hamra could see what Atok couldn't. At the table, Opah sat with bottom lip sticking all the way out, her pale pink bowl—plastic, not ceramic, Hamra had learned this lesson the hard way—upturned on the floor beneath her feet. The rice porridge Hamra had ladled into it earlier smeared across the peeling green linoleum, looking like how Hamra felt: grayish, lumpy, spread too thin.

"This is garbage," Opah told her. "GARBAGE. I want nasi ulam."

Hamra sighed. Nasi ulam was a favorite of her grandmother's. It was a dish Opah had grown up with, rice delicately flavored with a medley of fresh herbs and leaves and memories. "All right, Opah."

"Now."

"All *right*."

"Don't sass your grandmother," roared Atok from behind the closed bathroom door.

"And none of that supermarket nonsense either. It's full of nasty chemical things that poison your insides."

Opah always insisted nasi ulam tasted best with leaves plucked fresh from the tree or bush. Hamra glanced at the kitchen window, where the sun was already streaming mercilessly through the blinds, and sighed. "Okay, Opah."

"Why are you calling me Opah? I don't even know you." Opah frowned. "And when are we going home? We've stayed too long."

"This is your home, Opah."

Atok emerged from the bathroom, newspaper under his arm, satisfaction written all over his face. "Pays to be regular," he said right on cue, slapping his belly.

Ayah groaned into his coffee mug. "I was about to shower! You can't trap me in there with that smell . . ."

The chemical tang of lavender air freshener filled the room, and Hamra felt her irritation gather into a ball of flame and lodge in her stomach, its heat moving restlessly just beneath her skin. *So this is thirteen.*

Ayah turned to Hamra. "You think you can handle some nasi ulam? The clinics really can't do without that PPE."

"I guess so." Ayah's face fell, and Hamra's insides squirmed with guilt. *No, Hamra, you can do better than that.* "I mean . . . yes. Of course I can. Don't worry about a thing, Ayah, I can take care of everything."

He smiled at her. "That's my girl."

That's me, she thought morosely. *Good ol' dependable Hamra. Ready to do anything her parents ask, ready to be the perfect daughter, the perfect granddaughter. And not even a "happy birthday" in return.*

Atok squeezed her shoulder gently. "I'll clean up, sayang. You go get ready."

"Thanks, Atok." Hamra's smile quickly slid into a gaze of pointed suspicion. "Wait. Did you wash your hands?"

"Of course I did!" Atok put on an injured expression. "Why must you think the worst of me? Children these days . . ."

"With soap?"

He paused for just a little bit longer than she was entirely comfortable with before grabbing his cane from where he'd hooked it on the back of his chair and brushing past her. "Of course. Now where's that rag?" Then he turned his attention back to Opah. "Come, my love, let's listen to some music, eh?"

The soft strains of P. Ramlee followed Hamra all the way to her tiny room at the back of the house. To call it a room was really quite generous; it was more of a glorified closet that happened to fit a single bed and a chest of drawers and not much else. In fact, it pretty much just had two redeeming features: the door, which allowed her to shut out the rest of the world, and the single square window that looked out on the deep green of the jungle and the miles and miles of sky beyond. At night, you could throw open the shutters, focus on a distant point past the tiny squares of the screen meant to keep out bugs and mosquitoes, and pretend you were freewheeling through the stars.

From down the hallway, over the sound of the running

shower, she could hear her grandfather singing tunelessly along to the music. "Engkau laksana bulan . . ."

Stop it, Hamra. The last thing she needed was to be caught up in memories. The past, as far as Hamra was concerned, was nothing but a minefield of inconvenient feelings. Far better to focus on nice, concrete tasks than things you can't change. *Concentrate.*

Hamra tugged open her bottom drawer where she kept her neatly folded pile of hijabs and ran her hand down the row of soft cotton until she landed on her favorite one. Red, like her name. "I named you Hamra so you would always have a fire burning inside here," Ibu had told her once, pressing her hand to Hamra's heart. The problem, really, was that her parents hadn't defined specifically what that fire was supposed to be. Hamra figured it was supposed to be passion, like the thing that makes you want to *do* things and *be* things and *create* things. But lately, creativity had been impossible. And the fire burning inside her was something else entirely.

The fire burning her up now was anger.

Hamra was tired of wiping up messes and cooking and listening to Opah say things that didn't make sense, and always having to be nice and good and polite and responsible. She was tired of seeing her friends as little squares on screens. She was tired of waiting in long lines just for some bread and eggs. She was tired of all the masks she had to wear, the real ones and the ones you couldn't see. And worst of all, Hamra was really, really tired of her grandparents.

"Kau tinggalkan diriku . . ." P. Ramlee drifted from the kitchen.

Hamra had always hated this song, because it made her feel like an abyss was opening up in her chest, and the darkness inside was suffocating. His deep voice comparing his love to the moon and crooning plaintively about loss, about pain, about sorrow . . . it was hard enough to hear it, but worse still thinking about Atok singing it to Opah. That just made her even angrier.

There you go again. Focus, Hamra.

Quickly, she pulled her dark curls into a ponytail, slipped on a plain black inner cap that in theory was supposed to keep any hair from escaping—although this was often a losing battle, since Hamra's hair was almost as stubborn as she was—and wrapped and folded the scarf deftly around her head. She'd just started wearing the hijab this year, and it had taken hours of practice to master the exact way she liked it pinned, the way she wanted it to drape just so.

Then she grabbed her big brown canvas bag, slung it over one shoulder, and stared at herself in the mirror: the neat hijab, the round cheeks, the pointed chin, the dark shadows under darker eyes. Resentment shot out of those eyes like cartoon superhero laser beams. Did she want to spend her thirteenth birthday sweating in the oppressive heat of a Langkawi midmorning and being bitten alive by mosquitoes? Not exactly. But she was good, dependable Hamra, and so that's what she was going to do.

In the living room, her grandparents sat side by side on the two stuffed armchairs, which, like them, had seen far better days. Opah's eyes were closed, and Atok held her hand, caressing it gently as he continued to sing. The way he looked at her made Hamra's eyes prickle. "I'm going," she said loudly.

Atok nodded at her. "Remember the Rules."

"Fine." You could hear the capital R when any of the grown-ups talked about the Rules.

"Don't just say fine! You young people, fine this, fine that." Atok sniffed. "Nothing good ever comes from forgetting the Rules."

"How could I ever forget them?" Hamra sat down to pull on her socks, printed all over with tiny sloths. "You've only told me about them every day since I could walk . . ."

Atok poked her with his cane. "I may be old, young lady, but I still recognize sass when I hear it."

"Sorry."

"Make sure you tie those shoelaces properly!" Ayah's voice boomed from his room. "Don't just shove your feet in like you always do, you'll ruin the backs, and I have no money for new shoes for you!"

The irritation in her belly flickered again, fluttering at the base of her heart, tickling an eye-roll out of her. "O-kay." That earned another poke of Atok's cane.

Opah started awake and stared straight at Hamra, and her expression was a mixture of sadness and fear. "Sudah masuk ke dalam mulut harimau," she said softly, her eyes never leaving Hamra's face.

"What, Opah?"

"Don't say what!" Atok reached over to smack the back of her legs lightly with his cane. "Say pardon!"

"You're in the tiger's mouth now," Opah said, shaking her head sadly. "No going back. No going back."

"What? What are you talking ab—ow!" Another smack to the legs.

"Say pardon!"

"You're both impossible!" The words came flying out

18

before she could stop them, edged with fire, hot and biting. "I can't wait until all this is over and I don't have to be home with the two of you."

Then she slung on her face mask and shoved her feet into her shoes—and no, she would not tie her laces, she just *wouldn't*, that's all, and *nobody could stop her*. Slamming the door shut behind her, she tried to ignore the twin expressions of hurt and disappointment on her grandparents' wrinkled faces.

It was 8:37 a.m., and in the jungle, the thing in the shadows sat up and grinned a knowing, wicked grin.

She was coming.

2

THE RULES ARE simple. If you're a child who grew up near Malaysian jungles, you've probably heard them all your life. The grown-ups say them often, drilling them into your head so you won't forget.

1. Always ask permission before you enter.
2. Don't challenge what you can't even see.
3. Never use your true name.
4. Never take what isn't yours.
5. If you hear someone calling your name, never, ever look behind you.

And usually, Hamra was careful. Usually, she listened.

Unfortunately, this year was not a usual year, and today was not a usual day.

Later, she would say it was the fire in her heart spreading slowly, burning under her skin and making her brain itch so she couldn't think straight. Later, she would say she should have listened—to Atok, to Opah, to everyone. Later, she would be a lot smarter about a lot of things. Regret tends to have that effect.

But as we've discussed, time doesn't really wait around for you to figure this stuff out.

When Hamra broke the first Rule, it was an accident.

She'd walked a good five steps into the jungle before she realized she'd forgotten to ask for permission, forgotten to whisper, as she usually did, "May I enter, if that's all right with you?" (Grown-ups never said who you were asking permission from, mind you, only that it was important to ask. Hamra felt this was a rather big thing to skip over, but then again, adults rarely asked for her opinion on these things.)

The realization that she'd forgotten, though, made her stop in her tracks. It felt unsettling, like putting her (untied) shoes on the wrong feet. She wavered, uncertain. *Should I go back? Should I start over?*

Her grandmother's hurt, haunted eyes flashed in her mind. The fire moved under her skin, flared up in her chest. *NO*, she told herself. *Don't be silly, Hamra. You're thirteen, almost grown up. You know better. The Rules are just things adults say so you do what they tell you to do. They don't mean anything.*

And so she walked, carefully scanning the ground all around for snakes—Hamra *hated* snakes and kept a healthy distance from them if she could help it. She kept her scissors in hand, snipping herbs and leaves wherever she spotted them among the foliage and slipping them into her bag: turmeric leaf, smooth to the touch; heart-shaped daun kaduk with its mild, peppery taste; the faint, minty smell of daun kesum; the rounded edges of daun pegaga; and above all, ulam raja, the king of the salad leaves, which folds its leaves primly at night so it can get its rest away from prying eyes. Opah herself had taught Hamra all this long ago, showing her where the leaves liked to hide themselves away, how to pick the best ones, how to snip the stems just so. It was familiar, soothing work, the cool green a balm to the fire in her chest. *Snip, snip* went her scissors; leaf after leaf made its way into the dark recesses of her bag.

Later, she would say that she never even noticed how far she was going into the jungle, that she never realized how the sunlight filtering through the trees deepened and cooled until all around her was dim.

This was a lie. When Hamra broke the second Rule, she knew perfectly well what she was doing.

"I'm not afraid," she spoke aloud, startling herself with the sound of her own voice—how loud it was, how clear through the fabric of her mask. Saying the words made her feel dizzy and reckless and wild all at once. So she said them again. "I am NOT afraid. I don't care about your dumb old rules. There's nothing here that can scare me."

This was another lie. And because she knew it, she said it again, but this time as a yell, because if you can't be convincing, you can at least be loud. "THERE IS NOTHING HERE THAT CAN SCARE ME."

The words hadn't even finished echoing through the trees when she heard a rustling behind her.

She stopped in her tracks. *Please let that not be a snake, please let that not be a snake . . .*

Then there came another sound: the faint snap of a twig.

The only thing that moved was her chest, which could barely contain the frantic thumping of her heart. *It's nothing,* she told herself. *Just an animal making its way through the jungle. Like you. Just passing by, nothing to see here. It's probably just a squirrel. Or a monkey. Or . . . or a slithering, slimy, poisonous snake . . .*

As she was debating how she might survive an encounter with a snake—lie down and play dead? Scramble up a tree? Throw a shoe at its head and run?—there was a rustle somewhere in the trees behind her.

Hamra crouched low and eased off one of her red sneakers, trying to ignore the dampness of her palms, the thundering in her ears.

Then, closer still, the crunch of leaves.

Then, at last, just as she thought she might pee in her blue jeans, a voice said: "Are you hallucinating or something?"

All at once, her panic receded like the tide. Hamra straightened with a sigh. *I know that voice.* "Come on out, you idiot."

A minute later, he was in front of her, red-faced and panting through his mask, his glasses sitting slightly askew upon his nose: Ilyas Chang Abdullah, who lived in the house close enough to her own that you could call him the boy next door, and was sometimes her best friend, but usually just a pain in her butt.

"What are you even doing?" Ilyas picked a stray leaf off his khaki cargo shorts and pushed his glasses up from where they'd slid down his nose. His mask was crooked; sweat made his round face glisten in the dim light. "I could hear you yelling from way over there."

Hamra shrugged. "I was picking ulam."

"What does that have to do with the yelling?"

"I do my best work at top volume."

Ilyas rolled his eyes but didn't bother asking any more questions.

She brushed some dirt off the seat of her pants. "What are you doing here, anyway? Are you following me?"

"Yes." Like Hamra, Ilyas never saw any point in going around in circles when straight lines got the job done so much faster. It was one of the reasons she . . . well, *liked* seemed like a strong word. She *tolerated* him. "I wanted to give you your birthday present."

"You did?" He'd remembered her birthday? For a moment, a wave of gratitude dampened the flames of her anger and irritation. *Someone thought of you. Someone sees you.* "What is it?"

He handed her a small, knobbly package wrapped in old newspaper and tied with a hot pink ribbon printed with the name of an ice cream store. "Sorry," he mumbled. "We didn't have any wrapping paper."

"That's okay." How enthusiastic were you allowed to be about presents when you were thirteen? Hamra weighed her options and decided that this being her only present this year outweighed any need to be cool, so she tore at the paper with uninhibited delight.

It was a little wooden bird, warm in the palm of her hand, delicately carved and intricately painted in shades of crimson and maroon, the details carefully picked out in black and gray. It looked as if it might fly away at any moment.

It was beautiful.

"Do you know what it is?" Ilyas asked quietly.

"A crimson sunbird," she said. Ilyas loved birds, and he'd taught her well, over many hours of peering at trees and lying on their backs just watching the sky. "Did you make this?"

He nodded, his eyes not meeting hers. "You know my dad's pretty into wood carving. I've been practicing so I can show him how much I've improved next time I see him." He coughed. "Whenever that is."

Hamra nodded. Ilyas didn't often speak of his father, who lived in Kuala Lumpur now with a whole other family, and whom he hadn't seen since the pandemic began and they'd cut off all ferries and planes in and out of Langkawi. But years spent in and out of Ilyas's house meant she remembered lots of things about him, like the fact that he snorted when he laughed, and that he dog-eared the books he read, and that he wore glasses too, and that he did in fact do wood carving as a hobby, and that when he'd left a year ago, Ilyas had been sure he was going to come back, and had waited by the window, watching, every day after school for a month.

Ilyas grinned. "Remember when we first spotted one of these? I thought: That's Hamra's bird. It flies fast and direct, no aimless soaring. It loves sweet things. You'll often find it in the jungle. And it's little, and red. Little Red. Like you."

There it was again, the heat flaring beneath her skin, swallowing up her gratitude, needling at her insides. Little Red was Ilyas's jungle nickname for her; the Rules said you were never to use your true name in here, so she was Little Red because she'd been tiny when she was little (still was, really, only nobody really dared say it to her face anymore after she'd punched the last kid who tried), and he was Buggy because his glasses had been too big for his face, making his eyes look like they were bulging out of his head, and also—though he tried hard to make her forget this part—because he'd had a tendency to try to eat bugs "just to see if they tasted good."

Little Red. Just another of the many things she'd outgrown. She had just turned thirteen, dammit—that's right, she'd used a bad word, so what?—and she didn't need childish nicknames any longer.

When Hamra broke Rule three, she was almost happy about it.

"Hamra," she said.

The trees shook. Just the breeze, Hamra thought, ignoring the sweat that dripped down her forehead, the tiny voice inside her head that whispered: *But Hamra, there is no breeze.*

Ilyas had taken off his glasses to clean them with the corner of his plaid shirt; when she spoke, he turned so quickly she thought he might pull a muscle. "What did you say?"

"My name is Hamra," she said, her voice calm and even, though the cold sweat on her forehead had nothing to do with the tropical heat. "It's a perfectly good one. You should use it."

When Ilyas spoke again, it was through gritted teeth. "You know why we don't—"

"No, I don't, actually," Hamra said, her words slicing through his as if they were knives. "Do you? They tell us all these nonsensical rules and expect us to follow them, but nobody ever actually explains anything to us. At all. About anything." She shoved the bird into her bag, wrappings and all, and turned to walk away.

"We're kids!"

"So?" She whipped back around so fast that Ilyas

stumbled back, his eyes wide. "That doesn't mean we're stupid. Or that we don't deserve to know." She pulled down her mask, threw her arms out wide, and tilted her head to the sky. Through the canopy high above, she could just make out a streak of blue. "MY NAME IS HAMRA!" she yelled, with all her might.

"Stop!" Ilyas wore the same expression of fascinated horror he had when she'd attempted to learn parkour by jumping off the roof of his family's storage shed and ended up with a cast on her elbow for six weeks.

"What?" She said in her snarkiest tone. "What could possibly happen now?"

It was at that precise moment that they learned why Rule two—don't challenge what you can't see—existed.

Because as soon as Hamra said this, a beam of light shone straight through the jungle canopy, slicing neatly through the darkness and illuminating a clearing in which there stood a tree bearing the most perfect jambu air Hamra had ever seen in her entire life. They were the stuff of picture books: shiny and fresh, with deep berry pinks fading slightly to a paler hue at the tips of their bell-shaped bodies. All she had to do was look at them to know exactly the way they would taste, the feel of them in her mouth, all crispy and sweet and refreshing.

Suddenly, there was nothing that she wanted more.

Then something snagged at her sleeve.

"Don't," Ilyas said softly, holding her back. Hamra blinked. She hadn't even realized her feet were moving.

"Oh please," she said, injecting as much scorn as she could muster into those two words. "You're being ridiculous. It's just a tree." She shook her arm free of his grip—a surprisingly strong one, to Ilyas's credit—and began to walk closer, keeping her eyes on those gorgeous fruit.

Later, she would swear that she never heard what he said after that point; later, she would say that all she heard was a voice, a low, rough voice, a curiously seductive voice, telling her one thing, over and over again: *Take the fruit. Take it, Hamra. Don't you want to taste one? Doesn't it look so good, so juicy? Just one, Hamra, what's the harm?*

And that was when Hamra broke the fourth Rule.

3

THE JAMBU FELT good in her hand, fitting neatly into the curve of her palm. Hamra didn't remember even plucking it off the tree, but now that she held it, she never wanted to let it go. It was almost as though it belonged there, in her grasp. As though it had always belonged there.

It looked even better up close, like someone had sculpted and painted it lovingly in the most perfect colors, like it belonged in a museum, like it should be declared the blueprint for every jambu that would ever grow again in the world henceforth. And when she brought it up to her nose, she inhaled a faint sweetness that suddenly made everything around her seem brighter, more vibrant.

"LITTLE RED." The old nickname finally penetrated the gentle pink fog in her head. "WHAT. ARE. YOU. DOING."

"Hmm?" Hamra looked up and smiled dreamily at Ilyas, who, it slowly dawned on her, looked absolutely horrified. "What is it? What are you talking about?"

"You can't just take your mask off! And you can't just take things that CLEARLY aren't yours from the jungle!" Ilyas gesticulated so wildly he almost knocked the glasses from his own face. "Especially when those things are CLEARLY MAGICAL THINGS!" He grabbed her by the arm and began to tug. "Come on. We have to get out of here. We have to—"

But Hamra didn't move. She couldn't. She also couldn't seem to tear her eyes away from the fruit in her hand.

That is, until the roar came.

Hamra had been to the local zoo before, a tired place full of tired buildings and tired animals, including a distinctly indifferent-looking tiger that seemed more accustomed to yawns than roars. In fact, the only roars she'd heard had come from movies and TV shows: bears on the attack in nature documentaries, the lion in that MGM Studios logo at the beginning of the old Tom and Jerry cartoons they still showed on TV sometimes, CGI dinosaurs in your Jurassic movie of choice.

But she'd never heard anything like this.

This roar was deep and ferocious and so loud that it

shook the trees and silenced every birdsong and bug screech in its wake. It was wild and wicked and utterly, completely terrifying.

In the stillness it left behind, they both heard it: a wet, heavy panting. Then, from the darkness beyond the trees, a low, menacing growl.

Hamra turned to look at Ilyas, who was staring at her with an expression she could only imagine was a mirror of her own, somewhere in between "What the heck was that?" and "I'm about to pee my pants."

"Time to go?" she asked.

"Time to go," he said.

And at almost exactly the same time, they turned and began running, running, running past the trees and thickets as familiar to them as the paths on their own palms, running as if their lives depended on it, trying their hardest to ignore the rustling of leaves behind them, the way the sound of their own heavy footfalls and labored breathing did nothing to mask the swift steps growing closer and closer behind them.

"Don't—look—back." Ilyas wheezed the words out between breaths.

But it was too late. Because just as they reached the edge of the jungle, she tripped on the shoelaces she'd never bothered to tie and went sprawling to the ground. And as she struggled to get up, she heard that voice, that familiar seductive voice, growl out one word: *"Hamra."*

And so finally—maybe inevitably—Hamra broke the last Rule. At the sound of her true name, she glanced over her shoulder and saw it for the first time.

The tiger.

Only this one was nothing like the bored old tiger at the Langkawi Zoo. This one was at least three times larger, its coat of orange and black thick and luxuriant, its sharp, wicked teeth bared, its face so close she could feel the mist of its breath on her skin.

It looked at her with a knowing gleam in its golden eyes, and spoke her name once more. *"Hamra."*

Then she heard nothing more, because Ilyas grabbed her arm and yanked her back to her feet, and together they ran and ran until they collapsed to their knees, safe in the garden of her crooked house.

Which was when she realized she still held the jambu, so tightly that her hand was starting to hurt.

It was at this point that Ilyas turned to her, an accusing look in his eyes, and asked her the same question she'd been trying her best not to ask herself.

"Hamra, WHAT HAVE YOU DONE?"

4

THERE ARE TWO ways your brain can cope with having just seen something completely impossible, like, say, a talking tiger in the depths of the Langkawi jungle. It can:

a. Accept that impossible things sometimes just . . . exist, or

b. Try to find a way to make the impossible thing somehow make sense.

Hamra's brain chose option B.

"I don't know what you're talking about," she said defensively, getting up and wiping dirt from her palms. "That was clearly just a . . . a . . . a panther who was hungry and wanted to make us his dinner."

"It was striped." Ilyas squinted at her.

"Those weren't stripes," Hamra snapped. "It was the way the sun was shining through the trees that made him look all . . . stripy." The jambu was still in her hand; for some reason, she didn't want to let it out of her sight.

"Panthers hunt at night! It's not even noon!"

"Then call it brunch!"

"HE SAID YOUR NAME!" At this point, it was possible that Ilyas was going to choke on his own outrage and spit.

"No he didn't! He . . . he . . ." Hamra racked her brain for a reasonable explanation. "He coughed."

Ilyas let out a sigh that seemed to echo from the very depths of his soul. "You are impossible."

Since he said this at least twelve times a week, Hamra didn't take it personally. "At least we made it back safe and sound. And I got the ulam for Opah."

"And something else." Ilyas's eyes were trained on the jambu in her hand. It made Hamra uncomfortable. "What are you going to do with . . . that?"

Hamra blinked. "I don't know yet, actually."

"You should get rid of it."

"What? No way." For some reason, Hamra's hand clenched around the fruit just a little bit tighter. "Times are tough. We don't waste food," she said, parroting one of her father's favorite maxims. "And anyway, I can give it to Opah. As a special treat. You know she loves jambu."

Hamra knew this would get Ilyas off her back; his own grandparents lived in far-flung states and even before the pandemic, he usually only got to see them on special occasions like Eid, or Chinese New Year, or at the odd wedding or funeral. Opah and Atok had spent years being their stand-ins, and he loved them like they shared the same blood.

"Okay, fine." Ilyas inspected a cut on his arm and scowled. "I gotta go. My mom is making me take extra online classes from some lady so I won't fall behind when school reopens, whenever that is. I told her she didn't understand the stress of trying to study in a pandemic. She told me that she'd understand my stress better when I understand how to correctly apply the Pythagorean theorem." He sniffed. "She thinks she's so funny. You're lucky to have parents who don't value your education *that* much."

Hamra wasn't sure whether to be sympathetic or insulted.

Ilyas rubbed his nose absentmindedly through the mask. "Or two parents who are still together at all, I guess."

Sympathetic, Hamra decided right then. The divorce was still too fresh for Ilyas. You had to feel bad for him, no matter how annoying he was.

"Heard from your dad lately?" she asked, as gently and

casually as she could manage. "We could send him a picture of that bird you made for me. You're getting really good, I'm sure he'd love to see how hard you've been working at it . . ."

He shook his head, not meeting her eyes. "Nah. He probably wouldn't reply. Too busy with his new wife *kot*. Or at least, that's what my mom mumbles under her breath when she thinks I can't hear her . . ."

As if on cue, from the house next door came a shrill cry, getting progressively louder as it went on until it ended in a triumphant climax: "IIIIIIIIIIIIIIIILLLLLLLL-LYAAAAAAAAAAAAASSSSSSSS!"

Ilyas's shoulders slumped.

"You'd better go before she—"

"ILYASSSSS   CHANGGGGG   ABDUL-LAAAAAAAAAAAH!"

"Too late." She'd pulled out the full name card; he was a goner now.

Ilyas trudged off toward the direction of his house. "Good luck," Hamra said to his retreating back; he merely waved wanly in response.

The first thing Hamra did once she'd entered the house was pull down her mask and take off her hijab, sighing with relief at the way the air from the ceiling fan whirring lazily overhead cooled her sweaty scalp.

"Back so soon, love?" Atok was still sitting in the chair where she'd left him, shirt off, his checkered kain pelikat tied loosely around his waist.

"Got everything I need," she replied, somehow unable to make herself meet Atok's gaze. She was suddenly acutely aware of the words she'd thrown at her grandparents before she'd left, the bitter aftertaste they'd left on her tongue, the wicked little stab of relief she'd felt at saying what she really meant, for once.

"Anything exciting happen?" This was Atok's favorite question to anyone who had just come back home, his way of seeing a world he could no longer take in on his own. The first blow had come when he'd hurt his leg long ago—before Hamra was even born—and had walked with a cane ever since; the second came when he crashed his car, an old blue Wira, while driving Opah home from the market. Ever since, he'd been summarily forbidden by Hamra's own father from ever driving again. The car was sold, and Opah's mind began to play its cruel tricks on her, and now Atok rarely ventured beyond the confines of the house.

Hamra stood at the kitchen counter, unloading her wares. Her guilt shimmered in the air between them, making every word fall awkwardly from her tongue. She wondered if she should tell Atok about the tiger. *No, panther, Hamra.* She didn't think this was the wisest idea—grown-ups did tend to overreact about such things—but she didn't want to lie to her grandfather either.

"I ran into Ilyas," she said instead carefully. "We came home together."

"And what's new with our young man?" Atok leaned back in his seat and folded his hands over his protruding belly. "He hasn't been to see us in a while."

"Aunty Linda is making him take mathematics lessons while they're still figuring out the whole schooling thing," she explained, washing the dirt and grime from the daun kadok.

Atok shuddered slightly. He was all too familiar with Aunty Linda and her aggressive efficiency. "That woman," he muttered. "She's terrifying."

Hamra remembered Aunty Linda and her many kind-nesses: the food she dropped off ("Don't worry, I buy from the halal place, okay? You just enjoy!"), the countless rides she'd given back and forth across the island to get Atok and Opah to their doctor's appointments, the way she dropped by to take their rubbish to the communal dumpster every time she went to throw hers out ("Very hard for you to bring such big bundles on your bicycle, girl, you just give to me, I take for you"). It was hard to think of her as anything but a blessing—even with the booming voice and the overbearing flavor of her instructions. "She's doing her best," she said. "They both are."

"You're right. So are we all, at the end of the day," Atok said gently. "All of us. And if things sometimes get a little too much, well, that's only understandable, don't you think? We're all going through this huge, once-in-a-lifetime event together. The least we can do is extend some grace to the people we care about."

Hamra knew this was Atok's way of letting her know it was okay, and that he understood, and that they didn't need to talk about it if she didn't want to, and it made her both want to cry and also be annoyed at herself for wanting to cry at exactly the same time.

"Where's Opah?"

He jerked his head in the direction of her bedroom. "Back there, taking a nap." He coughed and closed his eyes. "Rough day, you know."

"I know." Hamra picked up the jambu where she'd left it by the sink and rolled it around in her palms. The light from the kitchen window seemed to bounce off its sides and make the whole room glow with warmth.

Atok peeled one eye open. "What's that you've got there?"

"A treat," she said quietly. Grabbing her favorite knife—the one with the bright yellow handle that fit perfectly in her grip and the blade that could slice through anything—she set the jambu on her chopping board and cleaved it in two.

The effect was immediate. You know after one of those heavy monsoon thunderstorms, when it feels like the rain has washed the whole world clean and the sky is bright blue and the air is fresh and bright? It was kind of like that. Hamra suddenly felt lighter, as if nothing could really be that bad. And Atok, who had managed to fall asleep in an instant, let out a little snore and then suddenly smiled, as if he was dreaming the most wonderful dreams.

Deftly, Hamra cut the jambu up into thin slices, admiring the delicate pale green at its edges fading into white at its center, drinking in its strange light. Then she arranged the slices on a plate and made her way quietly to Opah's room, treading carefully so she wouldn't wake her grandfather.

Opah's room used to be Opah-and-Atok's room. But dementia is a thief, after all, and it loves nothing more than to steal your memories—even of the people you love best in the world. And so, after several instances of Opah waking up in the middle of the night and screaming at the top of her lungs at the presence of an intruder in her bed, Atok resigned himself to the sofa in the living room. Hamra had tried multiple times to offer him her own bedroom, but he'd said no every time. "Much better out here," he'd explained, patting his belly. "It's closer to the snacks."

Now Hamra stood staring at her grandmother, who lay with her eyes closed and her mouth open, a thin line of drool making its way from one corner and puddling on the pink pillow beneath her head. Opah always slept the same way, flat on her back, her mouth puffing out gentle little snores—nothing like Atok's, who sounded like a hacksaw and could be heard from every room in the house. In the old days, Hamra would take afternoon naps snuggled up next to Opah, their legs entwined, and she would fall asleep to the sound of her grandmother's voice softly crooning zikir, over and over and over again: *Subhanallah, Alhamdulillah, Wala ilaha ilallah, Allahuakhbar* . . .

As she stood there, Opah opened her eyes just a crack. "What?" she mumbled.

Hamra had had warmer welcomes, but she'd take it over screaming and crying. "I brought you something."

Her grandmother struggled to sit up; the loose T-shirt

she wore had ridden up during her sleep, exposing the curve of her ribs, all lined up like a xylophone. The sight of them made tears sneak up suddenly right behind Hamra's eyes, so that they itched and ached. In her memories, Opah was big and warm and soft and squashy; she was belly laughs and cooking smells and sharp raps on the knuckles with the pointer when you yawned over your Quran recitation; she was random joget dance parties when old songs came on the radio and too many hours spent making too many Eid delicacies for everyone and the sting of a comb being pulled through the snags in your hair as she scolded you for "looking like you were raised by monkeys."

Hamra tried very hard to hold on to those memories. This was easier on some days than others.

"What is it?" Opah squinted at her suspiciously.

"Jambu."

The effect was like turning on a light in a dark room. Opah's face lit up all at once, bright and break-your-heart beautiful. "My favorite!" she said, clapping her hands like a child.

Hamra went to sit beside her on the bed. "Open," she said.

Obediently, Opah opened her mouth and Hamra placed

a piece of the fruit on her outstretched tongue; she'd been careful to cut it into small, delicate pieces to make it easy to chew. Immediately another memory welled up—a composite of memories, really, a tapestry of all the times Opah had made her and Ilyas sit cross-legged before her and fed them both from her own hand, out of the same bowl loaded with rice and lauk.

"Good?" she asked as Opah chewed, slowly, silently.

Hamra prayed five times a day—on most days, anyway, and she really did try, it's just that sometimes she forgot, you know how it is—and recited the Quran like every other Muslim kid she knew, but she'd never given much thought to miracles until the exact moment that Opah turned to her and smiled that big, warm smile that she remembered so well. "Hamra?"

It was hard to speak past the sudden lump in her throat, but somehow she managed. "Hi, Opah."

Opah opened her arms and Hamra slid in for the hug she'd been missing for so long.

"Why are you crying, silly girl?" Opah pulled back and smiled down at her, that miracle of a smile. "You'll get my clothes wet."

Hamra sniffed loudly. "Sorry."

"Now, where's your grandfather?" Opah got up and retied her batik sarong so it sat firmly at her waist. "That man. Always sleeping when you need him. ABANG!" And she strode out with the plate of jambu in her hand as if it was perfectly natural, as if they hadn't waited for this moment for the longest time.

Because of course, sometimes Opah, the real Opah, came back. Sometimes it was as though she'd never left. But they knew, all of them, not to pin their hopes on those times. "They're like she's visiting," Ibu had explained to a tearful, bewildered little Hamra, who didn't know why Opah had gone from teaching her how to play Batu Seremban to sauntering off and forgetting her name. "She'll come back for a little while to be with us, and then she goes off somewhere else. She still loves us. It's just that sometimes it just takes her a little while to find her way back."

It had been a long stretch this time, so long that Hamra had almost lost hope Opah would come back at all.

She wiped the tears away with the back of her hand and was about to walk out of the room when Opah poked her head in the door. "Oh, and Hamra . . ."

"Yes?"

Opah smiled, and it was like the rays of the sun caressing Hamra's skin. "Happy birthday, sayang."

It took Hamra a while to swallow the lump in her throat. By the time she made it back to the living room, Opah and Atok were swaying along to the music, arm in arm, as he crooned softly into her ear. "Engkau laksana bulan . . ."

Hamra was the happiest she'd been in ages.

5

IT IS AN unfortunate truth about rules that they must, by design, exist side by side with consequences, and that you can't break the former without triggering the latter.

To Hamra's credit, she did try terribly hard to avoid those consequences for as long as she could—which, being as stubborn as she was, was an impressively long time. Every time Ilyas began a sentence with "Remember what happened that day, in the jungle?" or brought up any mention of tigers at all, she did her best to distract him, once by "accidentally" spilling an entire glass of orange juice in his lap, once by smacking his leg hard in an attempt to squash a nonexistent mosquito, and once by saying "Is that Atok calling me?" before he could finish his sentence and then running away very, very quickly. It got to a point where it was simply easier to just hide from him, which she worked on as if she was training for a sport she was determined to win, even squeezing behind the ixora hedge when he came looking for her, biting her lip to keep from crying out when she was stung by a bee, indignant at her intrusion. She stayed well away from the jungle, only running the most necessary errands before returning straight home to her grandparents. At night, she shut her window so she wouldn't have to see the line of trees where the jungle began, and watch, and wonder, and worry.

She missed the stars.

But there were so many other things to think about, to busy herself with, so many things to cram into her head that there was no room for her own fears. So when the consequences did come, they almost surprised her.

So it was that she woke up one night, tumbling headlong out of a pleasant, hazy dream of her mother and her father, the whole family together and happy, to a sound that reached into the recesses of her chest, gripped her heart with icy cold fingers, and squeezed.

It was the sound of scratching against the walls.

Hamra lay in bed listening for a long time to the scrape, scrape, scrape of nails against concrete. *It's a squirrel*, she thought to herself, desperately trying to calm her racing heart. *Or rats . . . Or a cat hunting for prey.*

That did it. Hamra turned over, pressed a pillow firmly over her ears, and began to recite Ayat Qursi aloud. The scratching may have continued well into the night, but she couldn't hear it any longer.

Or so she told herself.

That was the first thing.

The second thing happened days later. Hamra was struggling to complete her math homework—did anyone *really* need to know the value of x? Who cared if x wanted to remain anonymous? Why couldn't they all just give x the privacy it so *clearly desired* anyway?—when she heard a loud BANG, and then Atok's voice uttering a string of swear words that made her ears turn bright red.

"What is it, what is it?" she called, running out of her room. "What's going on?"

She found Atok in front of the front door, scratching his head. It seemed fairly anticlimactic for all the ruckus he'd been making.

"Well?" she asked. She was suddenly irritated, embarrassed even, by how worried she'd been just moments before. "What?"

He said nothing, merely gestured at the door—the door which now boasted four long scratches gouged painfully into its worn wooden surface. Hamra reached out a hand to touch the ragged edges of one scar with trembling fingers. "What could have done this?" she whispered.

Atok just shrugged, but Hamra could see how tense his bony shoulders were as he surveyed the damage. "A parang, maybe. A sharp enough knife . . ."

Claws, Hamra thought, and shivered. "They're so deep."

Atok nodded. "There was a lot of power behind it, I'd say." He sighed. "Suppose I'd better figure out how to fix this. Who does one even call to fix doors? Cuba Hamra goggle."

"Google, Atok."

"Same thing." He paused slightly before clearing his throat. "Maybe . . . maybe check how much it would cost to replace the lock with a different one. Something . . . stronger. And maybe call your father and ask him to have a word with Din down at the police station. You know, I used to threaten that boy with my slipper for picking mangoes from my mango tree, and now he's some big shot officer over there . . ."

His voice trailed off as he walked away. Hamra watched his retreating back for a while before turning her attention back to the door.

There was a lot of power behind it, I'd say. Sure, Hamra

thought, power fueled by anger. The kind of anger that comes from a creature unused to doors being closed to them. The kind of anger that that comes from a creature tired of waiting. The kind of anger that means it will not wait anymore.

The third thing hid in the garden and waited for Hamra to find it.

Opah wanted prawns that day, stir-fried in butter with cereal and curry leaves and bird's-eye chili. So Hamra was sent outside with an order for the glossiest leaves she could pick from her father's garden below the window.

It had rained the night before, and the air felt like a sponge that hadn't been properly wrung out; it was heavy, and hot, and sat uncomfortably on Hamra's skin. The garden sloped gently downward, away from the side of the house, and mud squelched under Hamra's slippers when she reached for the leaves. Of course, she slipped and had to reach for the wide lip of a nearby heavy stone pot to stop herself from falling . . .

. . . which is when she saw them.

Paw prints. Two of them, each the size of a Frisbee, embedded neatly in the mud. Hamra took in the sight of them, noting the rounded pad in the center, the way each digit tapered off into a point: the sharp tip of a wicked claw. She reached down and held her hand close to see how it measured in comparison; two of hers could easily fit into one of them.

On a hunch, she stepped into the paw prints, fitting one foot neatly in the center of each one. The slope made it hard to get her balance; instinctively, she reached for the windowsill to steady herself, and her fingers sank into something soft, and cool, and disconcerting.

Hamra looked down.

Mud? On the windowsill?

Then she looked up.

Oh.

From inside her room, with her shutters open, there was a perfect view of the jungle and the sky and the stars. From the outside, even though her shutters were closed, there was a tiny sliver of space through which one could get a perfect view of Hamra's bed, and, she imagined, of Hamra herself as she slept.

He's been watching me, she thought, and the blood froze in her veins.

One might have been a coincidence. Two felt like a

sign. Three, and Hamra knew them for what they were: a warning.

It became harder to fall asleep at night, even with one of Ibu's batik sarongs tacked over her window to cover the crack in the shutters, and in daylight she felt as if she were constantly looking over her shoulder, straining her ears for the soft padding of a cat on the prowl.

Then the dreams began.

In every one, Hamra was running, always running, trying to escape the beast behind her, so close she could feel his warm breath on her neck, smell the wild smell of him all around her, feel the earth shake beneath her feet as his great paws thundered behind her. Every time he caught her, every time she felt the nip of his wicked teeth around her ankle, she woke up drenched in sweat, her heart pounding, with a dull ache in her legs. This was no longer a warning. This was an invitation—no, a command.

In the wee hours of the fourth night, Hamra could no longer take it. She threw open the shutters, drew in a deep breath, and bellowed out toward the jungle: "ALL RIGHT, FINE, YOU WIN. I'M COMING."

In the living room, Atok let out another choice string of particularly colorful expletives. "Hamra! Apa kejadah—"

But Hamra ignored him. Instead, she lay back on her pillow and stared out at the stars, and thought of wicked teeth and wicked claws, and the thing that waited for her in the deep, cool stillness of the Langkawi jungle.

6

MONTHS AGO, THERE had been a story on the news of mat salleh hikers who lost one of their own, somehow, as they made their way out of the forest. Hamra remembered seeing their sweaty pale faces on the TV, skin burned red from the equatorial sun, brows furrowed in confusion. "I don't understand it," one said to the camera earnestly in American-accented English. "I really don't, he was right there behind us and then . . . and then . . . and then he wasn't." They found the missing hiker days later, just steps away from the path he'd wandered off of. He looked at his rescuers, dazed, and asked if it was them he'd heard whistling in the shadows.

Hamra remembered the hard, disapproving click of her mother's tongue as she folded the pile of clean clothes before her. "These people never listen to locals, that's why," she'd said. "What do I always say?" And Hamra had singsonged back at her dutifully: "Never go too deep in the forest, ask permission before you enter."

"Pandai pun," she'd said. Clever enough. Clever enough to know the limits, clever enough to understand that there were some things you shouldn't mess with.

Somehow, Hamra doubted her mother would think she was being clever enough now.

She started today's journey into the dense green with jaunty, confident steps, so sure that she knew this jungle like the back of her own hand. But the deeper she went, the more it seemed to stretch on forever in a tangled, verdant mess, and what used to be familiar and safe suddenly began to feel wild and sultry and dangerous. Hamra thought of the hiker, stumbling around unseeing in a forest full of sunlight, and shivered.

Then, suddenly, there it was: the clearing and the jambu tree, the golden ribbons of sunlight slicing through the canopy and making everything glow . . . including the burnished velvet orange fur of the tiger, who lay by the tree with his paws folded neatly before him, staring straight at her as if he'd been waiting for her all his life.

"Sit," the tiger rumbled, gesturing before him with a massive velvety paw.

"I'd rather not," Hamra said shortly, trying to make her voice bigger and braver than she was really feeling. She didn't add, *because I may need to run*—at least not aloud.

The tiger narrowed his eyes. "Stubborn," he muttered.

"My mother tells me the same thing." Hamra scratched at a mosquito bite on her elbow and scowled. "Well, I'm here. What is it you want to tell me?"

"Tell . . . you?"

"Well, yes." She crossed her arms and tapped one foot impatiently. "You clearly wanted me to come here and see you. So what is it? An invitation would have worked just fine, by the way, no need for such dramatics. We had to replace our door and everything."

The tiger looked slightly discomfited, as if this wasn't quite what he had planned. "What?"

"It's fine, I suppose you wouldn't know any better."

The tiger now wore the expression of a creature who recognizes a fast-unraveling situation and must stop it at all costs. He drew himself up in all his majesty and growled, in a voice like thunder: "Hamra of the Islands, you have been summoned to the jungle to face me and pay for your crimes." His words were oddly stiff and stilted, as if he hadn't used them in a while and all their joints needed oiling.

Hamra clenched her hands into tight fists by her side to

keep them from trembling. The face mask she wore made her breath sound even louder and more labored than it was. "And what might those crimes be?"

"You know very well," the tiger snapped. "You have stolen from me."

"Stolen? From you?"

The tiger gestured to the tree beside him. "You took my fruit!"

"And how was I to know it was yours?" she returned, hoping he didn't notice the way her voice shook. "There were no signs, no fences. How am I to see one tree in a jungle full of them and recognize who it belongs to?"

"*You dare argue with me?*" This time, the voice was almost a roar, so loud that it made the ground beneath her feet shake, and though she had to bite her tongue to do it, Hamra did not dare utter another word. "You know the Rules. And you broke them. In this jungle of all jungles, on this island of all islands, you must understand that your actions have *consequences*."

Hamra cleared her throat. She had spent years being capable, dependable Hamra, always able to find an answer or a solution, always taking care of everyone else. She wasn't used to feeling as scared and wary as she felt now, and she didn't particularly like it, if she were being a hundred percent honest. "Fine. You're right. I'm sorry. I won't do it again."

The tiger glared at her. "And you think this is *enough*?"

Hamra blinked. "Well. I mean. What else can I do? What's done is done."

The tiger got to his feet and began to pad gracefully about the clearing. "Because you are a mere child, and because I am so very kind and benevolent and . . . and . . ."

"Generous?" Hamra supplied hopefully. *Oh please, let there be a way out of this. Oh please, let me go home.*

"Generous, yes, I will give you a chance to make things right." The tiger stopped and peered down at her from his great height. "Merely return what you stole, and all will be forgotten."

Hamra's heart sank. "Er. About that . . ."

The tiger's eyes narrowed. "Is that a . . . problem?"

"Very slightly." Hamra gulped. "You see, it has sort of . . . possibly . . . definitely been . . . eaten."

"Eaten? EATEN?" The tiger looked as aghast as a tiger can possibly look. "You dared to eat the fruit of my tree? You had the audacity, the sheer . . . the . . . a magical fruit . . . you are not even *worthy* . . . how could you *do* such a thing?"

Hamra's heart pounded so loud in her chest that she

could barely get the words out. "I'm sorry. It's my grandmother's favorite. I didn't think . . ."

"No, you did not." The tiger came closer and closer, bending down until his face was mere inches away from hers. "Did your grandmother also teach you to steal?" he rumbled softly, menacingly.

"No," Hamra whispered. He was so close she could feel the fine mist of his breath on her cheeks.

"Certainly you've at least been *taught* the Rules?"

She nodded, unable to speak.

"Then you dishonor your teachers." The tiger straightened himself and whipped around. "No matter. The laws of the jungle are explicit. If you cannot return what you stole, then you must pay for it by other means. An eye for an eye, as it were."

"You want my *eye*?" Hamra sputtered.

"No thank you, it's hardly my favorite part," the tiger demurred. "Much too squishy." He ignored the fact that Hamra had turned a sudden sickly shade of green and went on. "No, you have taken something of great value to me, and if you are unable to return it, you are in my debt. And the laws of our world mean that debts must be repaid."

"But I'm a kid. I have no money, and nothing worth anything to sell either."

"What use is human money to a tiger?" The tiger continued to prowl back and forth through the clearing as he contemplated her. "No, what I want is far more valuable to me than money."

The thrum of anxiety that had been vibrating through Hamra's chest grew even stronger, so loud she could hear a humming in her ears. "What is it?"

With one sudden leap, he was in front of her, his amber eyes gazing directly into hers. Then he smiled, a slow, wicked smile, one that showed off every last one of those sharp, sharp teeth. "You will make me human again," he said softly.

Her eyes widened in shock. "What?"

"You heard me." He slunk away from her, movements as liquid as only a cat's can be. "It may have escaped your notice that I am far from being an ordinary tiger . . ."

"You can say that again," Hamra muttered under her breath.

"And the reason for that is simple," he went on, sweeping her remark aside. "It is because I was born a man. Well, a baby, but you understand me."

Hamra frowned. "And how does a man end up a tiger?"

The tiger paused, as if to think. When he finally spoke again, his voice was so soft she had to strain to hear him.

"By doing some dark things. Unspeakable things. Things I try not to think about, even now."

She swallowed back the painful lump that suddenly appeared in her throat. "Then why would you do them?"

His smile was almost sad. "Because I craved power. And to be a weretiger—what power that was! To be able to shift my form, from human to tiger and back again at will . . . you cannot understand how intoxicating that was. How addicting. The way that strength rippled just beneath your skin, the way you knew it was there, and that only you could control it . . ."

"So what happened?"

The tiger mumbled something.

"Pardon?"

"Stuck, okay? I said I got stuck." His bottom lip stuck out mutinously. "I kept staying longer and longer in my tiger form and one day I just . . . forgot how to turn back. And then as time passed, I forgot I'd ever been human at all." He sighed, and it came out as a low growl. "That's how it is. You wear a new skin long enough, and it becomes part of you, until it was as if I was never anything else. And then you came along and something . . . changed."

"Changed?" Hamra felt as if a thousand ants were crawling along her skin. "I . . . changed you?"

"You made something inside me shift. You made something inside me . . . *remember.*" The tiger began to pace up and down restlessly. "I was content before, when I thought I was simply a tiger. But since I remembered . . . I cannot rest. I cannot go back to ignorance." He stopped and stared directly at her. "I tire of this existence. I want to be human again."

She stared right back. "And how am I supposed to help you with that?"

"I am depending on you to figure that part out." He smiled at her and twirled one whisker with a velvety paw.

Hamra thought she might cry, which was a feeling she absolutely hated. She dug her nails into the palm of her hand to keep the tears back. *Stop it, Hamra. Focus.* "Sir, I respect your desire to become human again. Really. I get what it means to want to return back to a time when things felt . . . good and right and normal. But this seems like . . . a lot." She rubbed her face with her hands, suddenly weary. "All I did was take one fruit. One little jambu. Surely my payment doesn't need to be this . . . complicated? And also kind of . . . dangerous-sounding? Is there no other way? Can't I just . . . find some money and pay you back?"

"No."

"Why not?" She crossed her arms, suddenly feeling that

familiar anger. "Why can't there be another solution?"

"Because a thief does not get to dictate the consequences to which they are subject," the tiger said smoothly.

"I don't—"

"And because I can give you back your grandmother."

Every muscle in Hamra's body froze. "You . . . what?"

"You heard me." He grinned at her, displaying rows of sharp, white teeth. "You'd like that, wouldn't you? And you believe that I ask for too much in return for just one little fruit? So why not sweeten the deal? She enjoyed that jambu, didn't she? Helped her find her way back through the fog, didn't it? Like a light in the darkness. Suddenly she was there again, just the way she used to be. There for you."

Hamra remembered Opah's warm hug, the way the smile spread over her face, and her heart clenched. "You can do that?"

"I am the weretiger of Langkawi," the tiger said matter-of-factly. "There is little I cannot do." He leaned close, whispering the words in her ear: "Do you ever wonder what it would be like? Never having to miss someone who was right there beside you?" He stepped back then, regarding her with those amber eyes. "Do we have a deal?" he said, his voice like silk, as he extended a paw toward her.

Opah, bustling in the kitchen. Opah, belly jiggling, eyes

squeezed shut, as she laughed and laughed at one of Atok's terrible jokes. Opah, reciting the zikr as they lay together side by side in bed. *Subhanallah, Alhamdulillah, Wala ilaha ilallah, Allahuakhbar . . .*

You'll never have to miss her again.

Hamra searched his face, trying to find any signs of malice in his expression. But all she saw was a hunger in the tiger's eyes that made her stomach flip.

"Well?"

Slowly, she reached out her hand to grab the paw and shake it firmly.

"We have a deal," she said.

And all around them, invisible insects screeched as if they knew what she had done and mourned her fate.

7

WHAT DO I *do? What do I do? What do I do?*

The words crashed around in her head as she trudged home, barely noticing the path she was taking, barely noticing the footsteps that drew gradually closer behind her, barely noticing anything at all until she felt something grab her hand from behind and yelped so loudly that a bird resting idly on a nearby branch let out a surprised squawk and flapped off hastily.

"It's only me," Ilyas said mildly, as Hamra tried her best to quiet her pounding heart.

"DON'T. DO. THAT."

Ilyas shot her a pointed look. "Between the two of us," he said, crossing his arms, "I think *I'm* the one who has earned the right to tell *you* what not to do, frankly."

Hamra turned on her heels and began stalking back

toward her house. She was still rattled, but she'd be darned if she'd let Ilyas Chang Abdullah see that. "I'm absolutely capable of handling things on my own," she tossed over her shoulder as he scurried along behind her. "I always have been. You know that." The effect of her grand statement was only slightly marred by the fact that she tripped over her untied laces right as she finished making it, but she chose to believe he didn't notice.

"I think a weretiger might be just a teensy bit outside your realm of experience, Hamra!"

Her heart sank. "So you were spying on me, you little . . ."

"Well, someone needs to look out for you!"

"I don't need you to babysit me, Ilyas!" There it was again, that fire coursing through her veins, that anger burning her up from the inside out.

"I'm not trying to babysit you!" He'd finally caught up with her and tried to grab her wrist to hold her back, but she wrenched it away and quickened her pace. How dare he. *How dare he.* "I want to help you!"

"I don't need your help!"

"Oh yeah? So what are you going to do, then?"

Hamra paused. She didn't quite want to admit that she hadn't gotten that far yet.

Ilyas smirked and pushed his glasses more firmly up his nose. "That's what I thought."

Oh, how she longed to wipe the smug look off his face. "Okay, smarty-pants," she snapped. "What's your bright idea, then? Since you're so dying to help?"

"Well." He cleared his throat. "I thought we'd ask Atok."

She couldn't believe what she was hearing. "That's it? *That's* your brilliant suggestion? Ask my grandfather, the man who has barely left his house in the last five years, that one? Never mind the fact that once he hears what I did, he'll never let me out of the house again! And then that tiger thing will come EAT US."

"*Eat* you?" Ilyas gaped at her. "I didn't know that was on the table!"

"You saw what he did to our door! Imagine what those claws do to *bodies*!" She shuddered. "It may be even worse than *snakes*."

"Okay, but think about it." Ilyas's ears had turned bright red, so frantically was he trying to get the words out. "The weretiger, that's a creature from our legends, right? From our stories. And nobody knows this island or its stories better than Atok."

There was a long silence as Hamra tried to process this. Much as she hated to admit it—and oh, did she hate to admit it—Ilyas actually had a point.

"Fine," she said eventually, as the house came into view. "Fine. Maybe you're right. Let's go ask Atok."

"Together?" he said brightly, going full-on puppy-dog-eyes at her.

Hamra sighed. "I suppose you could be somewhat useful . . ."

"If Malaysian people had middle names, Somewhat Useful would be mine!"

"Then fine, yes. Together." She kept right on walking. "But if I have to waste any time saving your butt while we do this, I'm going to force you to eat cilipadi right off the tree. Five of them."

From somewhere behind her she thought she heard him mutter "rude" under his breath. But his footsteps never wavered, and just for a moment the anger that simmered in her chest became a different kind of warmth altogether.

They heard the booming of the TV long before they reached the front door. Atok would never admit that his hearing was no longer what it used to be, and always turned the volume up to a level that made the walls vibrate like they were in a nightclub—or at least, whatever version of a nightclub Hamra had managed to cobble together in her head from the bits and pieces she'd seen on TV or in movies Ibu and Ayah probably weren't aware she'd watched.

When they entered the house, they found Atok and Opah sitting side by side on the worn wooden chairs in front of the TV, her hand on his knee, his thumb lightly tracing mazey pathways on the papery skin of her palm. Her eyes were closed; his were glued to the screen, where a heavily made-up actress with flawless skin and a hijab draped so perfectly its creases looked as if they would cut you was staring, lips trembling, at someone just off camera. As Hamra watched, a single, perfect tear traced a path down her cheek. *Mira tak sanggup, abang . . . Mira tak cukup kuat . . .*

Ilyas cleared his throat loudly, and Atok jumped so that Opah startled awake, blinking at them owlishly. "What?" she rasped. "What is it?"

Mira masih sayang abang . . . tapi . . .

"Just the children, bulan," Atok said, scrabbling around beneath his slowly loosening sarong for the remote. "Nothing to worry about." Finally, he found what he was looking for and pressed the red button, and the tearful Mira disappeared from the screen with a sorrowful little bleep. Then he turned his full attention to Ilyas, a wide grin cracking his face in two. "Ilyas! Why haven't you been to see us in so long?"

"I was just here last week, Atok."

"Ya, so long lah, like I said. Come, come, it's lunchtime, we eat." Atok bustled toward the kitchen, thankfully retying his sarong enough so that Hamra didn't have to contemplate what she'd do if it fell. "What do you want? We have some leftover nasi goreng kampung that Hamra cooked yesterday, some mee goreng mamak your grandmother wanted but didn't finish, that kuih your father brought back from the market the other day pun kita tak habis, kan Hamra? And that laksa too . . . Bulan, you want laksa?" As he talked, he contemplated their open fridge, the rows of plastic containers bearing their unfinished meals lined up like sentinels in its cool depths.

"No," Opah said, rubbing the sleep out of her eyes like a little kid. "I want char kuay teow."

Atok clicked his tongue as he peered through the clear walls of each container. "That's the one thing we don't seem to have, beloved."

Ilyas looked slightly bemused by this barrage of hospitality. "I'm okay actually, Atok . . ."

"Nonsense! You are a growing boy. Growing boys must eat." Atok smacked his belly for emphasis, as if this was what it would take to convince Ilyas to take some food: a magnificent specimen of stomach. "And take off

72

your masks lah. You're inside now."

"I . . . uh . . . that is . . ."

Hamra decided to put him out of his misery. "Actually Atok, I wanted to—ow!" She shot Ilyas a murderous glare and rubbed the tender spot where his elbow had dug into her ribs. "I mean, *we*—we wanted to talk to you about something."

"And what might that be?"

Hamra took a deep breath and launched into the speech she'd been rehearsing in her head all the way home. "I know this is going to sound completely ridiculous, and I won't blame you if you don't believe a single word of what I'm about to tell you. I can barely believe it myself. But Ilyas was there and he can vouch for everything I say, and I'm sorry if it makes you mad or upset or worried, but I don't think I really have a choice, and OW! CAN PEOPLE STOP DOING THAT!"

This time the interruption came in the form of a sharp rap to the head from the wooden spoon in Atok's hand. Hamra winced. "You guys can just interrupt me with actual words, you know," she muttered, trying to rub the sting away. "It would hurt less."

"Get to the point," Atok said crisply. "And don't mumble."

"Fine." *Go on Hamra, you can do this. What's the worst that could happen?* "I . . . may have taken something I shouldn't have from the jungle, and as it turns out it belonged to a weretiger and now I have to help him turn human again or else he won't . . ."

"Who's talking about tigers?" Opah was sitting straight up now, eyes wide and staring, clutching the arms of her wooden chair so hard Hamra could see her hands tremble. "Are there tigers about? You can't trust them, you know, you just can't trust a tiger . . ."

"Shush, bulan," Atok said soothingly, and Opah slowly sank back into her chair. "Shush. There are no tigers coming near us, believe you me. I won't let them." He turned back to Hamra. "He won't what? Spit it out, my girl. Quickly."

What if it doesn't work, Hamra? What if you do all of this, and it doesn't work? If you tell Atok now, won't you just disappoint him? Hamra thought of the hope draining from her grandfather's eyes every time Opah didn't recognize him, or on her bad days when she yelled and swore and they could barely remember who she used to be, and she didn't think she could bear to give him hope of something so big as Opah's return, only to snatch it away again if she failed.

"Or else he won't . . . forgive my debt," she said instead. "That's how it works over there, right? You take something, you have to give something back."

Atok stood very still, squinting at Hamra's face for so long that she began to feel distinctly uncomfortable. In the living room, Opah still stared at them, tense and watchful, the way you wait for an explosion you know is about to come.

"Do you think he heard you?" Ilyas said in a too-loud whisper. "Maybe you need to say it again. Louder. ATOK. HAMRA SAID—"

This time it was Ilyas who got the smack of Atok's spoon on his head. "Ow!"

"I heard her lah, bangau," Atok growled.

"Oh," said Hamra. "Um. So. Ya. Err, what should I do now?"

"Well it's obvious, isn't it?" Atok turned abruptly and bent down, disappearing from view as he began to rummage around in the fridge.

"It is?" Hamra and Ilyas exchanged bewildered glances as Atok emerged, bearing an armful of plastic containers.

"Ya." Atok's voice was muffled behind a mountain of leftovers.

Ilyas cleared his throat. "Would you mind . . . explaining a little . . . to those of us who aren't quite seeing things as clearly as you?"

"She made a promise," Atok said simply, grabbing a bunch of bananas from the wooden bowl on top of the microwave. "And she must keep it. So you're about to go on a quest, my dears, and I'm making sure you have provisions."

"Provisions?"

"Can't have you going hungry." Atok grabbed a jar of iced gem biscuits off the counter and frowned as he contemplated the now-full countertop. "Quests are hard enough, you've got to keep your energy up. And I don't trust that fancy-shmancy fairy food." He snorted. "Nectar this, magic potion that, next thing you know, you're a talking cicak looking for true love's kiss. No thank you! Good honest human food, that's what you need." He opened another container unearthed from the back of the fridge and sniffed its contents, then grimaced. "Maybe that one wasn't so honest," he mumbled, hastily shoving it aside. "Remind me not to go to that seller again."

"Don't give them the char kuay teow!" boomed Opah from her chair, making Hamra jump.

"We don't have any char kuay teow, bulan, I told you."

Hamra's head was beginning to hurt. "Atok," she said finally. "What are you doing? Why aren't you trying to . . . to stop me?" In her heart, she was beginning to realize, she'd been hoping that he would, that he would make her stay home, that he would keep her safe.

His face softened. "Hamra sayang," he said tenderly. "You've lived here your whole life. This island, its legends, they're in your blood. Surely you can recognize when a story chooses you? What happens in every tale you've ever been told?"

"The hero saves the day."

"That's you, love." He went back to rummaging among the containers. "Time to save the day."

Hamra felt the sting of inexplicable tears behind her eyelids. "But what about you and Opah?" she said softly. "Who will take care of you?"

Atok drew himself up. "I rather think I can do a decent job at that. I've had a lot of practice. A whole lifetime's worth, in fact, which is at least—" His mouth moved silently as he did the math. "At least six of yours." He leaned forward. "Now what you'll want to do is make sure you bring two or three pairs of extra socks. Too easy to get them wet or muddy or torn. You want to keep those feet comfortable, take care of them for the times you'll need to run or climb away from things. Bring a jacket, you never know when you'll get cold, and maybe an umbrella for the rain. It's also good for jabbing at naughty creatures. Some of these non-human things don't know how to behave." Atok drummed his fingers on the counter, frowning. "What else, what else? Try to eat your own food as much as possible, as I said. Tricky things, these supernatural beings, you don't want to eat their food, you'll find yourself in a dreamy fog and then wake up walking halfway to Johor in just your underwear, singing Rasa Sayang . . ."

Hamra frowned. "Why does that sound so *specific* . . . ?"

"Right," Ilyas was scribbling furiously. "Right. Any other tips? What are your thoughts on appropriate foot-wear? Because I have some ideas . . ."

It was too much. It was all too much. "Atok." It came out smaller than she'd intended, more helpless, more bewildered.

He stretched out a hand to rest on her head, warm and comforting. "You can do it, Hamra," he said quietly. "Remember Puteri Gunung Ledang, Cik Siti Wan Kembang, Puteri Saadong? Our history is littered with young girls who found themselves thrust into the heart of the story and fought their way through. And you can too." Atok straightened up and set his sarong more firmly around his waist. "Now. You'll want to go to the night market first. It's Wednesday, yes? So it'll be in Kuah town."

"Good." Opah nodded enthusiastically. "Go. Then you can buy me char kuay teow."

"Is it even open?" The pandemic, as Hamra understood it, meant closed everything: closed businesses, closed schools, closed doors, closed ranks.

At the same time, Ilyas frowned. "You think they'll have the right kind of shoes? Because I was thinking . . ."

Atok waved their words away as if they were so many annoying mosquitoes. "Not our night market. Theirs."

Hamra blinked. "Where do we—"

"What do they call the night market? Uptown, yes? The fae world is a mirror of our own. And where there's an Up, there must be a Down." Atok began stacking up containers to make more space on the counter. "You'll have to find the entrance to Langkawi Down Below on your own, though. It changes every time. I tell you, these supernatural fellas, they do like making things difficult, don't want random humans finding them I suppose. . . . Anyway, once you're in, look for the Seer of Fates and ask for what you need."

"The Seer of Fates?" Hamra's head was starting to throb. "Who is that? Atok, how do you even *know* all of this?"

He paused and glared at her. "My dear girl, do you

think you're special? You're hardly the only one in this family that's been chosen by a story." He tapped his bad leg. "How do you think I got *this*?"

This was too much to take in. "I don't know! Because you've never, you know, TOLD ME?"

"No time now," he said. "Get packing. Take only what's needed. You're going to have to move fast. I'll tell you some other time."

"But I—"

"Now, Hamra."

"I'll go get my stuff," Ilyas said, and he quickly slipped out of the door as Hamra made her way to her room. As she grabbed things out of drawers and shoved them into her backpack: socks, underwear, a long-sleeved T-shirt printed with tiny foxes, a heart-printed pouch that held lip balm and sunscreen and an emergency pad, her second-comfiest pair of jeans (she was wearing the comfiest ones), a foldable rain jacket in eye-watering neon green, a spare portable USB charger for her phone, and a small white towel with VISIT LANGKAWI 2020 that her father had gotten for free. What irony, huh? Considering how nobody could visit Langkawi now? Her mind was a jumble of mixed-up thoughts that went something like: *What do I pack? Can my grandparents really take care of themselves? Should I even be doing this? Do I have a choice? Who is the Seer of Fates? What actually happened to Atok? What kind of hijab style is best for a magical quest? Isn't this an incredibly weird question to have to ask yourself?*

Eventually she selected five different hijabs, both shawls and pull-ons with no need of pins, and stuffed them in as neatly as she could. Then she slung her backpack over her shoulder, checked that her phone was safe in her pocket, and stood in front of the full-length mirror that hung on the back of her door, staring at herself. Her face was pale beneath her usual tan. She looked the way she felt: haunted, and terrified.

"Puteri Gunung Ledang, Cik Siti Wan Kembang, Puteri Saadong, Hamra," she chanted to herself. "You can do this."

And then she wrenched open the door, trying very hard to ignore the feeling that this might be the last time she would see her room ever again. But if she did—if she was successful . . . the thought pushed her out into the living room.

There, Ilyas was packing the containers of food into his own backpack. "I think this is more than enough, Atok, honestly . . ." Hamra could see the gleam of sweat on his forehead as he tried to jam a plastic bag full of mangoes

("Not ripe yet, but they'll be perfect to eat in a day or two!" Atok insisted) between what seemed to be an umbrella and a pair of slippers. His mission successful, he picked up the next container, which made an ominous sloshing sound. "And uh . . . we probably shouldn't take anything that might spill."

"But Hamra loves laksa!" Atok protested, taking the container from Ilyas's outstretched hands.

"You told us to be practical," Hamra reminded him. "Remember?" She went over to the coffee table, now strewn with whatever Ilyas hadn't managed to pack in his bag, and began slipping things into her own: here, a bright pink container filled with yesterday's fried rice; there, a clear tub with a sky blue lid that held slices of her grandmother's famous fruit cake, which they'd made the last time she'd had a good day. Hamra had kept it in the fridge, loath to eat more than the tiniest slice at a time, wanting to make it stretch for as long as possible—both the cake and the memory. Her hands shook slightly as she put away all these small, tangible portions of her grandparents' love.

When they'd taken as much as they could, and turned away offers of more ("What about this?" Atok kept saying, waving everything from large unopened packets of rempeyek to a half-eaten piece of apam balik to a jar full of

cherry tomatoes. "What about this? This one, maybe?"),
Ilyas and Hamra exchanged looks.

"Ready?" he asked her softly.

"No," she said. "But let's go anyway."

They stood awkwardly, hoisting on their now-overstuffed
backpacks, not sure what to say now that the time had
come. Atok cleared his throat. "Tie your shoelaces and be
careful out there," he said hoarsely, patting Hamra on the
head and knocking her tudung askew. "I know you'll be
successful. It's in your blood."

"Atok, if my mother asks . . ." Ilyas trailed off as if he
wasn't quite sure how to continue, and Atok held out his
hand for a firm handshake.

"Don't worry, boy," he said gruffly. "You just leave her
to me." He stood back and sighed. "You are very quickly
going to find out each other's strengths and weaknesses.
Don't be afraid to lean on each other, you hear me? You
will need each other in the days to come, I know it."

Hamra hugged her grandfather tight. "We will, Atok."

Opah hadn't stopped staring at them from her chair, her
eyes beady and wary. "You make sure you bring my containers back, you hear me?" she said finally. "Covers also.
Don't go losing my things goodness-knows-where. Otherwise I'll whack you with the feather duster." She gestured

to where it lay on the coffee table next to her chair, where Atok had left it, as usual, after his cursory dusting that morning. Atok never remembered to put it back where it belonged.

"Okay, Opah." Hamra wondered how much she understood, how aware she was of what they were about to do.

Opah considered her for a moment. "On second thought, take it with you," she said, grabbing it from the table and thrusting it into Hamra's hands. The brown chicken feathers felt soft beneath her fingers; as she clutched it, one detached itself and floated slowly, slowly, slowly to the floor. "You never know when you might need it. Useful things, feather dusters."

"I don't know how much cleaning we'll actually—OW!" This time it was Hamra's turn to dig a sharp elbow into Ilyas's ribs.

"Thank you, Opah," she said, looking straight into her grandmother's eyes. "I'm sure it will come in handy."

"And mind you be careful of tigers," Opah said sharply. "Dangerous beasts. Can't trust them, not one bit."

"Okay, Opah."

"And remember." Opah paused, as if she was about to impart something particularly important, and Hamra found herself leaning closer, waiting, waiting . . .

"I like extra cockles in my char kuay teow," Opah pronounced grandly.

It almost made Hamra smile. Almost. "Got it, Opah."

And they both put their face masks on, turned around, and walked away, back toward the forest, pretending not to see the worry etched in every line of Atok's face, or the tears in Opah's eyes, as they held hands and watched them walk into the jungle.

8

HAMRA AND ILYAS grabbed their bikes and wheeled them toward the jungle, matching each other step for step along well-trodden, familiar paths to a future that was anything but. Hamra was silent because she was still trying very hard not to burst into tears. She suspected Ilyas, blinking fiercely behind his glasses, felt the same.

Just as they got to the edge of the jungle, Ilyas tugged Hamra to a stop.

"What?" she said, anxiety lending a sharp edge to her voice that she didn't really mean.

Ilyas pushed his glasses up his nose. "What's the plan?" he asked.

"We go in there, we get the tiger, get to Uptown, and, I dunno, figure it out from there."

"It doesn't seem wise to rest our lives on 'figuring it out from there'!"

"Do you have a better idea?" Hamra snapped. "Look, it's not like I've done any of this before either, okay? But just imagine what we get at the end of this. We get Opah back, Ilyas. Don't you realize what that means? For all of us? For Atok?" Ilyas's face softened, and she pressed on. "So we're just going to have to get real comfortable with the idea of not knowing what we're doing and . . . and . . . making it up as we go along." She hoisted her backpack higher on her shoulders, and the duster, now tied on securely with twine, waved its brown feathers in the wind. "Now let's leave the bikes here while we go get him. Come on."

And on they walked, as the birds trilled and the monkeys whooped as if heralding their arrival.

In the clearing, by the lush jambu tree, the tiger stood waiting.

As they got closer, Hamra felt it again—that tug. *Take another, Hamra. A broken rule is nothing but an opening, after all, and there are so many interesting things on the other side. What's one more?* Before she could stop it, her fingers began to twitch, began to flutter, began to reach out. *Take it, Hamra, take it.*

"Shut UP," Hamra said firmly, pulling her hand back, feeling that familiar flame leaping through her chest. "Stop talking to me! You're the whole reason we're in this mess in the first place!"

Ilyas looked at her, aghast. "Don't talk to him like that," he hissed urgently. "Have you seen his teeth? Those are the kind of teeth you should be really, really polite to *all the time*."

"Her comments are not directed at me, boy," the tiger drawled, an amused glint in his amber eyes.

"Then who is she . . . who are you . . ." Ilyas turned his head from Hamra to the tiger and back again, bewildered.

"Let's go," Hamra said, ignoring him. "We have a Seer to find."

The tiger tilted his great head as he regarded her face. "An interesting idea. It has been many moons since someone has tried to discern my fate. Perhaps it is wise; no good sailor navigates into the unknown without a map. Lead the way, captain." He grinned, baring his sharp teeth.

Hamra heard a quick intake of breath from beside her and trod gently on Ilyas's foot. *Be cool, man.* Aloud, she said only: "All right then. Let's go."

The Kuah night market was held every Wednesday and Saturday, a bustling gathering of locals and tourists that stretched on from five thirty in the evening until at least ten or eleven at night—or at least, that's how it was. How it used to be. *Before.*

As Hamra, Ilyas, and the tiger walked through the streets now, she couldn't help but reach into her catalog of memories and pull out so many that featured slow walks past rows and rows of bright-colored canopies, red and yellow and royal blue, with banners that announced their owners' wares in bold technicolor: crispy fried chicken pulled fresh from deep woks of bubbling golden oil; row upon row of kuih and cakes in every color of the rainbow; butter-yellow roti jala served with piping hot curry full of chunks of meat and potatoes; every rice dish imaginable, from nasi lemak to nasi dagang to nasi ambeng. She and her family would make it a point to be there just as the vendors were setting up, and Hamra would tug on Atok's hand every time she wanted to pause to watch another delight, another wonder. Her favorites were the char kuay teow uncle, who expertly tossed the noodles and sauces and cockles and taugeh around in his wok, and the man who sold apam balek, so deftly folding the thin pancake filled with crushed peanuts and sweet corn with his bare hands, never flinching from the heat ("Doesn't that hurt?"

Hamra had asked him once. "I've been doing this since I was ten years old," he told her as he dipped his cup in a huge red bucket for more batter to spread on his round, flat pan. "And I'm forty now. These fingers are used to the pain.").

They would walk until Hamra's little feet began to hurt, and then they would buy the absolute best coconut shakes in the world from an aunty that Hamra swore added magic to her blender, and make their way to their favorite place. A little river snaked alongside the market, with bridges every so often that stretched across the water. Hamra's favorite was painted blue and white and had a roofed patio right in the middle that made the perfect spot to lean, and sip, and chat, and watch, as the skies began to darken and lights began twinkling one by one all over Kuah town. Then Opah would say gently, "Let's go home, dah Maghrib dah ni," and they'd head back, hands loaded with treats to savor in their own time.

And now?

Now the street stretched ahead, long, empty, the pavement filled with dead leaves that scattered and pinwheeled freely now that there was nobody there to sweep them away. The sun was setting, but there were far fewer lights; the storefronts were shuttered, and there was more than one "closed for good" sign in sight. This was now, and

Langkawi *now* was nothing but an island of used-to-bes.

At least no one would notice the weretiger walking along beside them.

As if on cue, her phone vibrated in her back pocket. A message from her mother. *Goodnight, sayang Ibu*, it read. *I miss you, and I love you.*

Hamra blinked back even more inconvenient, unwanted tears. *Stop it, Hamra. You don't cry. You get things done.*

They left their bikes by a wooden bench covered in dust and bird poop. Ilyas moved to lock his, and Hamra rolled her eyes. "You aren't serious."

"I don't want it to get stolen!"

"Who's around to steal *anything* right now?"

He gave the lock a tug and nodded in satisfaction when he was sure it was secure. "I don't like taking chances."

That was Ilyas all over, of course: prepared for everything. He could almost always produce the exact item you needed from his voluminous cargo pants pockets: Band-Aids, rubber bands, tape, safety pins, chewing gum, hair ties. It was like being friends with a more awkward, teenage boy version of Mary Poppins, except with a Steve Irwin aesthetic.

"Lucky for us, there's a pandemic right now," she mumbled from behind her mask. "Otherwise, walking around with a huge tiger might be a little, oh, I don't know, *obvious*."

Ilyas snorted. "We still need to be careful," he said. "Stick to the shadows. Let's not go looking for trouble. I heard the police can give out these huge fines for people who break the SOPs."

"Show me where in the list of standard operating procedures it says 'cannot walk around with a tiger.' Somewhere between 'wear a mask at all times' and 'no traveling beyond a ten-kilometer radius of your home,' maybe?" Sometimes Hamra felt Ilyas loved rules just a little too much.

"Hamra. They're the *police*. They can do what they like."

"Well maybe what they *should* do is mind their own business." She wasn't sure she really meant this, but the little gasp that came from behind Ilyas's batik mask was immensely satisfying.

"I would not worry too much about your law enforcement officials," the tiger said, his voice like velvet wrapped around a brick, soft and smooth and somehow still dangerous. "I have ways of . . . deterring them."

Hamra squinted at him. "Those ways better not involve claws or teeth."

The tiger sniffed. "I am not simply a wild animal," he said with great dignity. "Rather, the human mind is inclined to take many twists and turns to rationalize a reality that it thinks of as too absurd or surreal to be true—like, say, two young children accompanied by a large talking tiger—and I use my gifts to simply . . . encourage that inclination." His eyes lit up as he spotted something on the horizon. "Ah, what perfect timing. Observe."

Hamra's heart sank as she saw a police officer approach them, the shiny buttons of his dark blue uniform glinting in the dim light. He was frowning as he stopped in front of them. "What are you two kids doing out and about?" His eyes slid over to the tiger, whose smiling lips moved furiously, and though Hamra couldn't hear what he was saying, she recognized a wicked gleam in his eyes. The officer's own eyes began to water as they tried furiously to communicate to his brain exactly what they were seeing. "With this here . . . this here . . ."

She could practically see steam coming out from his ears. "Cat?" she supplied, not very hopefully.

"Cat!" he said gratefully. "Cat, that's it. No time to be out and about. You think the virus sleeps past seven p.m.? No! It doesn't!"

"Sorry, sir," Ilyas said quickly. "So sorry. But the restaurants are open until eight, right? We're just going to get some food."

"Right," Hamra said. "Because our mother will be home soon. And she'll be hungry. She's a nurse, you know. A front liner."

The officer's face softened. "Tough time for you kids, eh. I understand. Well, go on then, quickly. Cukup duit tak?" They nodded in unison, and he smiled. "Okay then. Make sure you treat your mother to something delicious. Take care of each other. And your . . . er . . . cat." It seemed to take enormous effort to get the word out, particularly with the tiger baring his teeth at him in a lazy, knowing grin. "Off you go."

"You see?" the tiger said as they walked away. Hamra's palms were sweating so hard she had to wipe them off quickly on her jeans. "People are so simple."

Hamra couldn't resist looking back. The police officer was still standing where they'd left him, his brow furrowed as he watched them walk away, as if he was still trying to figure it all out.

"Now what?" Ilyas asked.

"I don't know."

"What are we even looking for?" Ilyas mopped his sweaty forehead with his shirtsleeve. They'd walked the length of the empty street, Hamra taking great care not to look at the little blue-and-white bridge on her right. Memories could be such inconvenient things.

"The market, silly." Hamra swatted away a random bug flying past her nose. "Don't tell me you've forgotten our quest already."

"Can't we just ask him?" Ilyas jerked his head in the direction of the tiger, who winked back. He hadn't said much as they walked, preferring to silently prowl along beside them, sometimes melting into the shadows so that he almost disappeared from sight altogether.

"Come now," he said. "What would be the fun in just being supplied with answers? Have you not heard grand tales of quests and adventure? The heroes must make their own way. Besides, I want to see if you two are really capable of handling this quest, or if I should abandon this idea now, before it is too late."

Ilyas frowned. "We're doing this so you can get what you want. Doesn't that mean it's in your best interests to . . . help us?"

The tiger shrugged, and Ilyas scowled. "I bet he doesn't know either," he whispered to Hamra. "He's just pretending so he can be as irritating as possible."

Hamra sighed. "Whatever. Can we get back to the point, please? Focus. We need to find this entrance."

"Okay, but what are we even looking for?"

"Anything out of the ordinary, I guess." The night sky mirrored her own mood: dark. "You were there. You heard what Atok said. That's all we've got to go on."

Ilyas plunked himself on the curb with a sigh and rubbed his calves. "So much walking."

"I thought your middle name was supposed to be Somewhat Useful."

"I'm trying! I just . . . wait." He straightened up and fixed his gaze on a point just beyond Hamra's left shoulder.

"What?"

"That's weird. Is that . . ." He stood up and began to walk slowly toward something, as if he didn't want to be noticed.

"Ilyas, what are you doing?"

"Shh!" he hissed. "It's a Jerdon's baza."

"A what?"

"A decent snack," the tiger supplied, licking one paw daintily.

Ilyas ignored this interruption. "Jerdon's baza," he whispered. "They're a migratory raptor. Super hard to spot, and you definitely never see them in town like this. I mean, the last time I saw one I had to trek up to Gunung Raya, and the mosquitoes used me like a buffet . . ."

Hamra finally caught on. "Ilyas. Are you . . . bird-watching? Right *now*?"

"You said to look for anything out of the ordinary, and this is definitely out of the ordinary. Now be quiet." He gestured toward the bird, and Hamra bit back the sharp retort that perched right on the tip of her tongue. She knew Ilyas loved birds, but this was ridiculous. And what was so special about this bird, anyway? It was brown, and it had a crest of three little feathers atop its head that stood erect, like a crown, black with white tips. And all it was doing was . . . was . . .

Huh.

The bird was walking on its feathered legs, back and forth, its head swiveled only toward the bridge, pacing for all the world as if it were waiting for something to happen.

"Birds don't usually do that, do they," she said softly. She didn't really need Ilyas to answer. You didn't need to be a bird-watcher to know this wasn't normal bird behavior. "I wonder what it's waiting for."

There was a great whooshing sound, and a sudden gust of wind almost knocked Hamra off her feet; it picked up the leaves where they lay on the ground and made them dance and whirl, so many leaves that it was hard to see what was happening, until at last the gale died down and the leaves settled, and on the bridge stood the largest hornbill that Hamra had ever seen.

Ilyas let out a long breath. "I think we've just found out."

9

THE HORNBILL WAS as tall as a man, and terrifying in its magnificence; Hamra was sure that if it spread its great wings, it would be large enough to smother the moon itself. Even in this dim light, its glossy black feathers shone, and the white tips of them seemed to glow. It turned its head to look straight down at the little brown bird with its sharp, gleaming eyes, throwing the distinct yellow curves and points of its casque and bill into sharp relief against the moonlight.

The Jerdon's baza bowed a deep bow, its crest almost touching the ground.

"What are they doing?" Hamra whispered.

"Shhhh," Ilyas said, his eyes fixed on the birds.

The Jerdon's baza puffed out its chest as if it was taking a deep breath, and then began . . . speaking? At least that's what the high-pitched twittering seemed to be, and the great hornbill tilted its head to one side and nodded every once in a while, for all the world as if it was listening intently.

Then, when the smaller bird had finally stopped speaking—it took a while—the hornbill paused before opening its bill. When it spoke, its voice was deep, and the sounds it made were a variation of the familiar guttural *kok-kok-kok* Hamra was so used to hearing as she walked through the deep green of the jungle. The utterances bounced off the walls of the deserted buildings around them; in the quiet of the abandoned road, it seemed as loud as the foghorns of the largest ocean liners.

The hornbill didn't say much, but whatever it did say resulted in a long, long pause. The Jerdon's baza stood first on one feathered leg, then the other, looking around as if it was thinking deeply. When it finally answered, its twitters were short, and they trailed off on a questioning note. Hamra could almost hear the pleading tone; it sounded exactly like she did when she scrambled to give her teacher an answer to a question during one of those interminable, endless Zoom classes, praying it was the right one.

It usually wasn't. But perhaps the Jerdon's baza was

luckier or smarter than Hamra was, because the great hornbill simply bowed, then stepped aside to let the little brown bird pass.

Hamra knew this bridge. She knew that beyond it lay nothing but an empty parking lot and the backs of rows of shophouses, as regular and bleak a landscape as you could find in any town all over the country, probably all over the world. Yet the Jerdon's baza was so excited that it practically dashed past the hornbill, bowing deeply as it went, then breaking into a running hop before spreading its wings and taking flight, through the little archway and beyond where it . . . where it . . .

Where it disappeared, in a brilliant flash of peacock blue.

"Ah," said the tiger softly. "So that's how it goes now."

"What?" Ilyas and Hamra turned to look at him. "How what goes?"

"The hornbill is the gatekeeper," the tiger said. "And we must make it past him to get to the market." And with that, he rose from where he crouched in the shadows and began to walk to where the hornbill waited, looking straight at them as if it had been expecting them the whole time.

Hamra and Ilyas exchanged glances. Then, with no

other options that she could see before her, she got up and followed the tiger, and with a sigh, Ilyas shuffled along behind her.

The hornbill kept watching as they approached, head turned to the side to affix one red eye on them. When they arrived at the steps of the bridge, they stopped and waited, the tiger sitting on his haunches, flanked by Hamra and Ilyas, to hear what the bird would say.

Hamra wiped her damp palms surreptitiously on her jeans yet again and wondered how she would understand the bird when it spoke. She wasn't exactly fluent in hornbill.

As it turned out, her worries were unfounded. When the hornbill at last began to speak, they understood it perfectly. "Greetings, travelers. What brings you to the night market?"

Hamra swallowed; she couldn't tell if she understood the hornbill because it was speaking English or Malay—the words just seemed to appear in her head, perfectly formed, and the ease of it all was slightly unnerving. "We seek answers from the Seer of Fates," she said, as loudly and bravely as she could.

"And what questions do you bring for the Seer, young one?"

"I have a debt to pay," Hamra said. "And I need help to figure out how."

The hornbill tilted its head. "With companions such as these?" it said, sounding amused. "It is not often one sees human younglings in the company of a weretiger. Why are you here, old man?" This question it addressed to the tiger, who bowed his own head in acknowledgment.

"I come to claim what is owed and to find what has been lost," the tiger answered, his voice low.

"Very well," the hornbill said. "And now you." Here, it turned its gaze to Ilyas, who looked to Hamra as if he wanted the ground to open up and swallow him whole.

"M-Me?" he stammered.

"Why are you here?"

Ilyas thought about this a minute before pushing up his glasses and answering more firmly than Hamra thought would have been possible for him: "I come to help a friend."

"That is all?"

"That is all."

The hornbill nodded. "Then that is enough. More than enough." It looked up at the moon for a while, as if thinking about what to do next, then nodded. "Travelers often come to the night market to look for their heart's desire.

And we welcome them, however big or small those desires may be, because everyone deserves the opportunity to see a dream realized, and the night market is where you will find the means to do just that. However—" The hornbill bent low so that one eye, burning redder than ever, was mere inches from Hamra's face. "However. We cannot abide those whose desires are too dark, whose hearts burn black within their chests. For dreams to some are nightmares to others, and the Gatekeepers must decide your fate so as to not see our world burn." It straightened up again, gazing in turn at all three of the travelers before it. "He—" At this, he gestured to the tiger with one great wing. "He is one we would not usually allow into the market. For we know his past and know what he is capable of. Yet we acknowledge that even a weretiger may change and grow. And so, to pass, you must answer three riddles. The answer to each is a clue to your own heart." It stopped at Ilyas. "You. You first."

Hamra found that she couldn't stop tapping her foot against the ground, as if her nerves were trying their best to leave her body through its soles. Ilyas hated being put on the spot. But her old friend merely nodded slowly. "I'm ready," he said softly.

The hornbill opened its beak and sang the words:

"Ditutup sebesar kuku; dibuka sebesar alam.
When closed, the size of a fingernail; when open,
the size of the universe."

Beads of sweat dripped down Ilyas's forehead, his mouth moving furiously, silently, as he worked out the answer. Hamra's heart hammered as if it wanted to dive right out of her chest. *Does he know? Will we make it?*

"That's it," he murmured to himself. "That's it. Eyes!" he said loudly.

The hornbill nodded and Hamra felt the weight lift from her chest slightly. "Next. You."

It was the tiger's turn. "I am eager to appease you, my lord," he drawled. It sounded, to Hamra's ears, almost like insolence.

"Then listen." This time, the hornbill sang:

"Pagar orang kita tampak, pagar kita tiada tampak.
We see the fences of others, but not our own."

The tiger didn't pause. "Teeth," he answered in a growl, his own looking sharper and more wicked than ever.

The hornbill nodded and turned to Hamra. "Now you," it said.

She gulped. "What is my riddle?"

"Listen." When it sang, she felt the words in her bones.

"Pelita padam, rumah tertinggal.
The lamps blown out, the house abandoned."

Hamra closed her eyes. For a brief moment, she saw Opah, brows furrowed, living a life surrounded by so many unfamiliar people. "Death," she whispered. "The answer is death."

The hornbill looked at all three of them for a long time, the tiger longest of all. "Very well," it finally said, spreading its wings with a great whooshing sound, for just a moment blotting out the sky. "You have earned your passage to the night market." It moved aside. "Go in peace." It glanced briefly at the tiger before adding quietly under its breath: "Or else."

Hamra bowed; it seemed like the right thing to do. "Thank you." Then, trying to muster up all the courage she could, she stepped up onto the first stair and began to walk up and across the bridge, Ilyas and the tiger following closely behind her.

As she walked, Hamra reached out her right hand and ran it along the wall of the bridge, and the ghosts of old memories walked beside her: a younger Atok and Opah and little Hamra between them, holding on to their hands and asking a million questions. *Where does the river go, Atok? Can we have another coconut shake? Are there fish in there? Do fish like coconut shakes?*

She paused and shook her head, as if to clear away the thoughts that clung like cobwebs. *Stop it, Hamra. Your memories are no good here.*

"Coming?" Ilyas was looking back at her, one eyebrow quirked.

"Coming," she said. And she turned, tripped on her untied laces, and fell right on through to the other side.

10

THE FLASH OF peacock blue felt like being bathed in warm water, and then immediately being plunged into an ice cold bath. By the time they emerged from the bridge, Hamra was gasping, and the shock was so disorienting that it took her a minute to focus her eyes on what lay ahead.

The night market.

The scene before them glowed like an ember in the night. The perimeter of the entire marketplace was lined with rows of pelita, oil lamps set on posts lodged deep into the earth; their flames flickered in the breeze and the light they cast didn't so much fall as dance on everything it touched. The market itself was a riot of color: brightly striped canopies and tents of every hue, colorful glass lanterns that hung from tree branches stretching overhead, and the silken clothing of the people and creatures who wandered amongst the traders, gazing at the riches on display.

"Ready?"

"What?" Hamra turned to Ilyas, her eyes shining. It took her a while to realize that what she was feeling was excitement, a sense of pure anticipation that bubbled up inside her so that it drowned out the flames entirely and she felt almost giddy.

"I said, are you ready for this?"

"Are you kidding?" Hamra got up and began to run, and Ilyas and the tiger followed, her laughter trailing along behind them and dissolving into the inky blackness in their wake.

Before they could plunge into the crowd, the tiger bounded ahead, blocking their way with his body so that they ran headlong into his velvet flanks.

"Hey!" Ilyas pushed his glasses up his nose, indignant. "What are you doing?"

"I understand you are in a rush to explore, and I know firsthand how intoxicating the market can be," the tiger said, his whiskers twitching. "But be careful," he told them. "It is a lot to take in, your first time. Go slowly."

"All right, fine," Hamra said quickly. It felt strange to have this fearsome beast looking out for their well-being, and for a second she wavered. Could she trust this tiger?

Really, truly trust him? The hornbill had let him through, deeming the answer to his riddle sufficient to prove his worth, but he'd also told her plain as day that he'd done terrible things for power. What if this was yet another trick of his dark heart?

But the night market was not a place made for thinking—not for too long anyway. Hamra and Ilyas were distracted soon enough, greedily drinking in all the sights crammed back-to-back in this small space. This was nothing like the pasar malam Hamra knew. This market was filled with wonders and marvels of an entirely different kind. Here, the air was filled with strange, spicy scents mingled with exotic perfumes and the loud calls of traders begging visitors to sample their wares. And what visitors! And what wares! It had been so long since she'd been somewhere so teeming with unconcerned, unmasked life that Hamra wasn't even sure what to look at first. Stout orang kerdil yelled the benefits of strange fruit laid out enticingly on woven straw mats and smelling of honey and sunshine; a slender young woman eyed potential buyers from behind a diaphanous veil as she sat beside a table filled with bottles of bright-colored potions bearing labels like NAGA TEARS and LOVE POTION and ITCHY PANTS; two figures in painted masks and bright red robes chattered to each other in a language Hamra couldn't quite understand as they presided over large earthenware dishes piled high with plump white pau filled with all manner of strange jams and meats; in another corner, she spied a pile of shimmering bejeweled armbands "from the infamous cursed tombs of the Southern Isles," a gentleman boomed to a transfixed crowd, his dark skin shining with sweat as he worked, "guaranteed to make your enemy's arms turn black and wither away within one month, my lords and ladies, just one month, upon my mother's life!"

"Nobody's wearing a mask like us," Ilyas whispered. "Should we take ours off too? Blend in?"

"I guess so," Hamra whispered back. It felt strange, baring her face to the world like this, but she tried her best to quash her discomfort as she stuffed her mask into her pocket and turned her attention back to the wonders all around them.

In a large tank filled with blue-green seawater, two duyungs danced in a magical whirl of shimmering tails and long, long hair laced with seaweed, as onlookers tossed gold coins to a bored-looking attendant otter, who swam along the edge with a bucket held between its teeth and expertly caught all the money. On a nearby platform, an impossibly tall, impossibly thin man dressed all in black wailed keenly over the incessant chatter: "Manja, Manja, oh Manja . . ." For a price, he told his assembled audience, for a mere gold coin or two, he would present them with a ring from the many spread out on his straw mat, a ring that would help them find their way to their heart's desire.

"Maybe that's what we need," Ilyas said in a low voice, nudging her in the ribs. "Maybe if we buy one of those, we'll just find exactly what we're looking for, turn the tiger back to a human, and be done in time for dinner tomorrow."

"I don't think it's that simple," Hamra replied. "And I'm pretty sure that thing will just turn your finger green. Permanently."

"It is wise to exercise your skepticism," the tiger said from behind them, and they jumped as he padded past them on those soft, silent paws. "As wondrous as it seems, much of the market is built on the buying and selling of glamour and illusion, on slippery words and trickery. You must look for what is true and hold fast to it."

There it was again, that little flicker, that flare of irritation burning under her skin. She knew the tiger was right, but somehow it grated on Hamra's nerves to hear him make these pronouncements, as if he was her father or friend instead of . . . whatever it is he was to her. "We can handle ourselves," she retorted. "You don't have to keep watching out for us as if you care what happens to us."

"Of course I care," the tiger said blandly. "I must, until our bargain is sealed. Beyond that, I will happily allow you to sell your soul to a sweet-talking fairy for a bottle of aged snail snot, or whatever other entrancements you desire. But for now, be a good girl and listen to me."

Be a good girl? Oh, now the flames were liquid heat in her veins. "I'm not your girl," Hamra snapped, "good or otherwise." And she turned on her heels and walked away.

"Hamra!" she heard Ilyas call frantically behind her. "Hamra!" And though uncertainty snagged at her skin, telling her to *go back, you don't know what you're doing, go back, Hamra, go back*, she ignored it and kept right on walking.

It took all of five minutes for her anger to clear and her steps to slow down, five minutes of wandering up and down the mazy lanes and through the crowds of creatures she thought only existed in the old tales her grandfather told—Bunian folk with faces so bright and beautiful she could barely look at them before turning away, eyes burning; orang kerdil that barely came up to her waist; gergasi towering overhead and sending the smaller beings at its feet scattering hurriedly away with every step; and all manner

113

of beasts, from dusky lemurs chattering to each other about their latest bargains at the tops of their voices to a pair of snakes hissing melodiously together atop stools in a tapai stall (Hamra gave them a wide berth, and tried not to shudder too obviously at the sight of them) to a grumpy tapir muttering under its breath about some bad bananas to—and at this, Hamra's breath caught in her throat—a brilliantly hued cenderawasih stretching its wings, ready to take flight. *Ilyas would love to see this*, she thought, and she half turned to point it out to him before remembering he wasn't right there beside her, the way he usually was.

The flames receded, and in their wake all that was left were ashes of regret.

Great, Hamra, brilliant. Now you're in a strange market full of fae folk and supernatural creatures and you have no idea where your friends are.

Hamra sighed. One day, she'd learn to stop giving in to the flicker of fire in her heart. One day.

For now, she had to figure out how to make her way back to Ilyas and the tiger. She frowned as she scanned the rows of market stalls and tents, trying to find something familiar, something to help her retrace her steps. *I need to find them,* she thought feverishly, her anxiety growing with every passing minute. *I need to get back, I need to find the Seer, I need . . . I need . . .*

WE KNOW WHAT YOU NEED, a sign appeared in front of her, and she blinked.

It was a simple wooden structure, the kind of food stall you often saw by the side of the road all over Langkawi—all over Malaysia, really—brightly lit inside, with neon fairy lights strung along the roof. Only where there were usually signs or banners advertising their wares—tom yam, or fried rice, or all manner of enticing dishes to be eaten with steaming hot rice—only one sign hung over the entrance: THE WARUNG BETWEEN WORLDS. And then, just below, in smaller block letters, the words that had caught her eye: WE KNOW WHAT YOU NEED.

Before Hamra realized what she was doing, she was walking slowly up the stairs and into the warung, propelled by a force she couldn't seem to control. *I'm hungry*, she thought to herself, *that's all*, and it was enough to mask the small tendrils of fear that blossomed in her chest, the surge of panic at having her feet move without her telling them to.

The inside of the warung was empty, and though steam and smells of all kinds drifted from the direction of what Hamra assumed was the kitchen, nobody came to greet her. Feeling vaguely silly—*what were you so afraid of, Hamra?*

It's just a warung, like any other warung you've ever eaten at—she was turning to leave when a hand tapped her lightly on the shoulder. She turned to find a face looming above her, so close that she had to muffle a scream of surprise.

"Where you going, little sister? Tak nak makan?" The aunty was tall and broad-shouldered, her salt-and-pepper curls cropped short, her voice raspy. She beamed at Hamra, and suddenly everything seemed a little brighter.

"She doesn't want food," another voice said, and Hamra whipped her head around to see another aunty at her elbow, looking her up and down with shrewd eyes. "I can tell." This aunty was thin, her voice sharp, her gray hair piled up into a loose bun on top of her head. Her sleeves were rolled up and she held a spatula in one hand; her apron was speckled with the remnants of whatever she'd been cooking.

"It's not about what she wants," yet another voice said. "It's about what she needs." This voice, melodious and warm, belonged to a round, short aunty, whose hair Hamra couldn't see because it was hidden beneath her worn, graying knit cap, the kind Opah wore beneath her hijab.

"What I need?"

"Why yes." The third aunty beckoned for her to take a seat, and Hamra sank into a red plastic chair, just like so many red plastic chairs she'd sat in at so many warungs before. "Now. Do *you* know what you need?"

"I . . . what?"

"No matter if not." Third Aunty waved one hand in the air as if to shoo away her concerns. "Few people who visit us do."

Hamra gripped the edge of the white plastic table before her; it felt a little bit like the room was starting to spin. "Is there a menu or something that I can look at, or . . . ?"

First Aunty broke into a laugh so loud it shook the beams. "Menus? Ada ke? No need for menus here, little sister."

"It's right there on the sign," Third Aunty said, smiling. "We know what you need."

"How can you know when I don't know myself?"

"It's our job."

First Aunty leaned in close, so close that Hamra automatically shifted away. But First Aunty didn't seem to notice. She took a deep breath. "Sadness," she said quietly. "A lot of it. Hard to tell what else is there under all of that sadness."

Third Aunty nodded. "Yes, quite unusual for one so young. I also detect some whiffs of . . ." She stopped and sniffed the air thoughtfully. "Rebellion? Undertones of anger. And a strong current of stubbornness there, interesting . . ."

There was a snort, and Second Aunty, who had spent all this time staring directly at Hamra without blinking, much to her discomfort, finally spoke. "You two. Hopeless. All these big words, all talk talk talk only. You wait, I know exactly what the girl needs." She bustled off into the kitchen, and soon there came the sounds of crashes and bangs and, somewhat ominously, a wild shriek. Then, finally, the whirring of a blender.

Hamra gulped. *Much of the market is built on the buying and selling of glamour and illusion, on slippery words and trickery*, the tiger had told her. Was that what this was? Tricks and illusions?

First Aunty smiled at her as if she could hear Hamra's thoughts. "Don't worry, little sister. Second Aunty is very good at what she does."

"Maybe the best of us," Third Aunty said, nodding.

Hamra was almost afraid to look. But when Second Aunty emerged from the kitchen, she came bearing the one thing Hamra least expected: a clear plastic glass of coconut shake, droplets of condensation already forming along its icy cold walls, the creamy white liquid topped with a perfect dome of vanilla ice cream.

"Tu diaaaa!" Second Aunty set it on the table and Third Aunty added a striped red-and-white straw with a flourish, while First Aunty clapped her hands in excitement.

"That," Third Aunty said with satisfaction, "is exactly what you need."

Hamra gazed at them in wonder. "How did you *know*?"

"We just do."

"Aunties always know," Second Aunty said waspishly. "Even in your world. Now drink up."

Hamra knew that Atok had told her to be careful and avoid fae food. She knew the tiger had told her to find what was true and hold fast to it. She knew all that. But now that the drink had been placed before her, she was suddenly, achingly, painfully thirsty. Her throat felt parched and dry, and her tongue was as rough as sandpaper. There was nothing, absolutely nothing in the world that she wanted more than this coconut shake; no, not wanted. *Needed.* There was nothing in the whole world that could soothe her thirst now except for this, she was sure of it.

And so she grabbed the cup and she began to drink.

She was careful at first, hesitant, taking only the smallest taste—but as soon as the first creamy sweetness hit her tongue, she was done for. Hamra slurped the whole drink down as if her life depended on it. It was the most delicious thing she'd ever had, and with every sip, she thought about her worries less and less. She was lighter, as if everything that was weighing her down was gone. She was free. And she was happy.

When she was done, sucking up the last remnants with a loud, satisfying slurp, she looked around at the dark wooden walls of the Warung Between Worlds as if she was in a daze. "What was in that?" she asked quietly.

"What you needed," Second Aunty said, pointing to the sign. "Just as advertised."

"And now we'll be needing your payment," rumbled First Aunty, and all three stood and looked at Hamra expectantly.

Hamra gulped. "P-Payment?"

Third Aunty narrowed her eyes. "You didn't expect to get this for *free*, surely?"

"Magic comes with a price."

"Especially ours."

The lightness was beginning to disappear and in its place, Hamra felt the cold weight of dread. "I'm sorry, I . . . I have nothing to pay you with."

"Now that's just not true." Third Aunty smiled, a wide, benevolent smile, and it seemed to Hamra that the lights in the warung flickered just then, casting strange shadows on her face. "You only think that. But there's plenty you have that we would like, you see, plenty."

Hamra licked her lips, which had gone dry again. "Like what?" she asked.

The three aunties exchanged glances. "A feeling, perhaps?" First Aunty said. "We haven't had one of those in so long."

"Or maybe a sense," Second Aunty pondered. "Sight, fr'instance. Could give us some interesting new points of view. Geddit?" And she let out a guffaw.

"No," Third Aunty said, and they both looked at her. "A bird."

Hamra blinked. "A what?"

"Why, the little bird you have in your bag, of course."

Hamra's hands trembled as she rummaged in her bag and pulled out the little red bird Ilyas had made her for her birthday. Again, the lights flickered and dimmed, and Third Aunty's face seemed stranger than ever. "It's so small. So useless. You'll never miss it."

"And if I don't give it to you?"

First Aunty stood over her, tall and strong and more menacing than ever. "Nobody leaves the warung without paying for their share."

"Trust us, little sister," Second Aunty said.

"You'll never even know it's gone," Third Aunty said.

Hamra hesitated. More than anything, she wished now

that she'd listened to Atok, and to the tiger, and that she was back beside Ilyas where she belonged. But there was no way out—First Aunty blocked the way to the door—and it was three against one. And really, wasn't this better than giving up her senses or feelings? It was just a little bird. What harm could it do? Surely Ilyas would understand.

"Fine," she said. "Take it."

In a flash, it was in Third Aunty's calloused hands, and she smiled a toothy, unsettling smile.

"Pleasure doing business with you," she said brightly.

Hamra suddenly felt thin hands grip her shoulders tightly. "Have a nice day," Second Aunty whispered in her ear.

And then there was darkness.

11

"HAMRA! HAMRA!"

She stirred. *Go away,* she thought. *Go away and let me sleep a little longer.* But the voice persisted.

"Hamra! Hamra, wake up!"

This time it was accompanied by vigorous shaking, and she groaned irritably. "Stop."

"Not until you open your eyes!"

When she finally, begrudgingly pried her eyelids open, it was to the sight of Ilyas's and the tiger's faces looming disconcertingly close to hers. "Get away, I can smell your breath," she grumbled, struggling to sit up. They were, it appeared, in a little clearing behind a blue-and-gold striped tent, away from the crowds that still strolled through the night market. "What are we doing here?"

"You tell us!" Ilyas placed his hands on his hips as he

glared at her, doing a very good impression, she realized, of his mother. "You ran off, and we were looking for you for ages, and when we finally found you, you were just lying on the ground between two tents! Snoring!"

"I do not snore!"

"Snoring like *Atok*!" Ilyas added firmly, and Hamra bristled.

"You take that back!"

Throughout this exchange, the tiger was staring intently at her. "What happened?" he asked finally, his voice a low rumble.

Hamra frowned. "I was at this food place. A restaurant. The Warung Between Worlds, it's called." The tiger sat back, his mouth a thin line. "You know it?"

"I know it," he said. "And you ate their food." It wasn't a question.

"She wouldn't," Ilyas said confidently. "Atok told us not to."

Hamra hesitated. "I did," she said reluctantly, hating herself just a little for betraying his faith in her. "I knew I wasn't supposed to, and I did it anyway."

"Hamra!" Ilyas looked aghast. "How could you?"

"I don't know! I don't know. It just happened."

The tiger looked at her. "And what did they ask of you as payment?"

He looked at her with knowing eyes, and her heart sank even further. "You know, don't you?" she whispered.

The tiger sighed. "Of course I do. I hear all."

"What is he talking about?" Ilyas looked bewildered. "What did you give them?"

"It's not a big deal. Just something small." Still, the tiger's eyes bore holes into her, and it took a long time to muster up the courage to reply. "They asked me for my bird."

"Your bird?" Ilyas's face was scrunched up in confusion.

She couldn't look at him. She just couldn't. "Your birthday present," she said, and guilt wrenched at her insides.

Hamra aged a million years in the time it took Ilyas to speak again. "Oh."

You could read a million different emotions in that "oh." Hurt, and understanding, and disappointment, and frustration, and each one stabbed at Hamra's heart like a knife.

"I'm sorry, Ilyas," she said, hating herself for feeling like wanting to cry. "I didn't have a choice. They weren't going to let me go if I didn't give it to them, and—"

"You had a choice," the tiger said quietly. "The choice was not to take what was offered. You have given up a piece of yourself for a moment's pleasure. Have a care, Little Red, for there are only so many pieces you can give away before you lose yourself altogether." He turned away, but she still caught the last words he spoke. "Trust me."

You must look for what is true and hold fast to it.

The tiger's words echoed. *I should have listened to him,* Hamra thought. *I should have trusted him.* Her stomach was a jumble of hard knots. "You guys weren't there," she said, scowling to try to cover up her own discomfort. "You can't blame me for doing what I needed to do to save myself."

The tiger sighed and got back on his feet. "Never mind. There is little to be done now. Ilyas and I have found the Seer's tent. Let us get on with our quest."

And Hamra, still wrestling with the disappointed look on Ilyas's face and her own tangled feelings, could do nothing but get up and follow.

Finally, the tiger stopped. "There," he said, nodding in the direction of a tiny, nondescript tent. Plain gray, and adorned here and there with velvet ribbons and hanging mirrors, it looked much less exciting than the tents on either side (SHOEMAKER AND REPAIR, said the sign on the vivid teal tent on the left, WE CAN PUT SHOES ON ANY-THING, with images of stylish shoes on a satisfied-looking grasshopper and a giant foot whose owner was so large that the picture of it standing beside the tent ended at mid-ankle).

THE SEER OF FATES, the sign on the outside proclaimed in large curling script. Below that, in smaller block letters: FORETELLER OF FORTUNES, DEMYSTIFIER OF DESTINIES. And below that, in smaller letters still: THE MANAGEMENT IS NOT RESPONSIBLE FOR ANY HURT INCURRED AS THE RESULT OF SEEING INTO THE FUTURE, WHETHER EMOTIONAL, SPIRITUAL, OR PHYSICAL. And below that, someone had scrawled in cramped, messy handwriting: ABSOLUTELY NO REFUNDS. The NO REFUNDS bit was underlined three times.

"Refunds?" Ilyas frowned. "We have nothing to pay them with." He addressed his comments to the tiger, since he was still ignoring Hamra entirely.

Hamra sighed. "It's no use turning back now. Might as well ask and see if they'll help us anyway."

"Few fae offer their services for free," the tiger rumbled. "As you have now found out for yourself."

He *had* to bring that up. "Fine, then we'll offer whatever we have in return. Maybe they'll settle for something other than money."

Ilyas snorted. "Like what? Half a pack of stale bahulu? Cold karipap? A used jar of Tiger Balm? Or do you have any other useless presents you'd like to off-load?"

Ouch. Maybe it was better when Ilyas was ignoring her. "We'll think of something."

Ilyas sighed. "Why do I feel like this is going to get us into trouble?"

"Look at it this way," Hamra said. "We're already in trouble. What's a little more at this point? Now come on, let's go see our fates."

12

INSIDE, THE TENT was stuffy and dusty and smelled strongly of lemongrass. The tiger sneezed and wrinkled his nose, but to Hamra, the smell was warm and comforting, like the ghost of a dozen meals prepared in the kitchen of her crooked house.

In the middle of the room stood a little round table covered in red velvet that was so old and worn it was pink in patches where the velvet had rubbed off, and the only light came from two rusty oil lamps that burned on either side.

There was a seat on the side of the table opposite them. It was empty.

The trio looked at each other. "What do we do?" Hamra said. "Are we supposed to summon the Seer somehow?"

"Allow me," the tiger said. He walked over to where a heavy gold silken cord hung from the ceiling and, grabbing it between his teeth, yanked hard, twice.

From above them came the harsh jangling of a hundred little bells, so loud that Hamra and Ilyas immediately clapped their hands over their ears, though not loud enough to mask a distant screech of "Coming! Coming! No need to deafen the whole neighborhood!"

Out of the back of the tent shuffled an old woman, her cloud of pure white hair barely covered by the royal blue scarf she'd wrapped haphazardly around it. She was dressed in robes of gray and black. In one hand, she carried an intricately carved wooden birdcage that contained a plump pillow of deep green, upon which sat a little bird. In the other, she carried a cane, which she used to prop her along as she walked; Hamra heard the *tap-tap-tap* of it against the ground as she approached and suddenly missed Atok with a strength that made her chest hurt.

The old woman set the cage down none too gently on the table, plunked herself on the chair, leaned the cane against the table, and then swore loudly when it slipped and fell with a loud clang, just narrowly missing one of the oil lamps. "Almost set the whole place on fire, didn't I? Though that would probably have been for the best, if you think about it. . . . Thank you, boy," she said to Ilyas as he handed back the cane that he'd rescued from where it had fallen. "Now," she said, squinting at them after she'd settled herself down properly. "What do you want?"

"Umm." Hamra looked around uncertainly. "You are the Seer of Fates, right? We're . . . we're here to see ours. See, we're on this quest . . ."

"Yes, yes, you and every young upstart who comes here these days," the old woman said, waving away Hamra's words like so many mosquitoes. "Quest this, beautiful princess that, next thing you know she wants barrels of tears and hearts of germs and you're in for nothing but a world of pain, let me tell you."

"Is . . . sorry, it's just . . . is any of that actually written in our destinies?"

The woman sniffed. "No," she admitted. "Not exactly. Haven't seen them yet, have I? But I've seen enough to know."

"Er. Right." This situation quickly felt like it was slipping out of control, and if there was one thing Hamra hated, it was feeling out of control. "So can we get our fates seen, please? Our real ones."

"Not up to me, is it?" The old woman fussed about with the scarf on her head. "Have to check with the powers that be."

"Ah yes," Ilyas said wisely, pushing his glasses up his

nose and leaning in closer. "Consult the mystical powers, that does seem like an important part of the process . . ."

"She means the bird," the tiger said wryly.

Ilyas stared. "What?"

The woman shot the tiger a furious look. "There you go, ruining the mystique of the whole thing! You know the customers like the illusion, the magic, the . . . the . . ."

"The sham?" the tiger supplied, and she scowled and swatted him on his rump with her cane.

"We sell the *experience*," she said stoutly. "It's part of the package . . ."

"Enough." The voice was high and bright, and had a ring of authority to it; it was a voice that simply did not allow you to disobey. Everyone fell silent. "Open the door and let me see them."

The old woman subsided, though not without another dirty look in the tiger's direction. She reached over and swung open the door of the cage she'd placed on the table, and out hopped the little bird. ("A long-tailed parakeet," Ilyas breathed out beside Hamra—not to her, of course—as he leaned forward to get a closer look, "a bayan.") Its finely groomed feathers gleamed in the light cast by the lamps, the yellow-green at its crest gradually darkening to the blue of its long tail feathers; its bright red beak shone as if it had been polished; its eyes, set in a rose-red strip on either side of its beak, were bright and intelligent and at this moment, fixed on Hamra and Hamra alone.

The room was still, and quiet.

"What would you ask of me, Little Red?" it said.

"Someone told me that you could help me," she said as calmly as she could, trying to ignore the way the blood pounded through her veins, red as her name, hot as her heart. "I am trying to fulfill my part of a bargain. I would like to know: How can I help him—" And here, she gestured at the tiger beside her. "How can I help him turn back into who he used to be?"

The bayan turned its sharp eye to the tiger, who stood perfectly still and stared right back. "You want to be transformed?" the bayan asked him, and Hamra thought she heard a note of surprise in that creamy voice.

"I do," the tiger rumbled.

"After all you have given up, all you have done to get to this point?"

The tiger shrugged. "I grow tired of this form."

"Hmm. You ask much of them. Her especially." The bayan scratched its breast with one foot as it contemplated the tiger. "They are just children, after all." Hamra fidgeted from one foot to another, trying to quell the growing flames of her irritation. She hated being treated like she wasn't there. Hated being reminded she was a child in a world of adults, even magical ones.

"I ask only for what has been agreed to," the tiger retorted. "And nothing that they are not capable of. *Her* especially."

The bayan contemplated the tiger, its head tilted to one side. "And your side of the bargain?"

"She agreed to what was put on the table."

"As you say." The bayan turned back to Hamra. When it spoke, its tone was gentle, kind. "And you. Are you sure this is what you want? Many come to me believing that they truly do wish to see what lies before them, then leave with bruised hearts and bitter tongues."

Hamra thought about this for a moment. She thought about the anger that rippled beneath her skin, the way she ached to beat her own path. She thought of Atok's hand over hers, explaining the wonders of the world in his scratchy voice, telling her familiar, comforting stories; she thought of Opah and the way she used to whirl around the kitchen, making her own kind of magic.

She looked at the bayan. "I'm sure," she said simply.

The bayan smiled. "You are an interesting one, Little Red. Give me your hand."

Hamra lowered her hand to the table, wincing slightly as the bayan hopped onto her index finger and dug its little talons into her flesh.

"Bring me closer," it said, and she brought it up so that it was inches away from her face. "Now listen closely," it said quietly, and she did. "The only way to help the tiger is to strip him of all the powers his form brings. What big eyes he has! What big ears! What big limbs! What big teeth! Each of these elements combine to make him the dangerous beast that he is: his powerful eyesight, his ears that never miss a sound, his supernatural strength, and of course, those teeth. Always those teeth." The bayan spoke low and firm, and each word echoed in Hamra's head like a slap. "You must rid him of these gifts, one by one, until there is nothing left for him to hide behind. And then, to summon him out of this body and return him to his true form, you must call him by his name. His true name. For names have power here, and his soul only recognizes that which it used to be called. And it is his soul you need returned to him, for he lost or traded away pieces of it long ago."

There are only so many pieces of yourself you can give away before you lose it altogether. He'd tried to warn her.

"His true name?" Hamra whipped her head around to look at the tiger. "But what is it?"

For once, the tiger seemed confused. He shook his head so that his whiskers waved wildly. "I don't know," he said. "I . . . I don't remember."

"You don't remember your name?" Ilyas asked in disbelief.

"It is hardly surprising," the bayan said. "Just as we leave most of our childhood memories behind us as we grow older, so too did the beast shed his old skin when he put on this new one. It is, in a way, a kind of death, just as the loss of our old selves are a kind of death."

The answer to the hornbill's riddle, Hamra thought, *death*. A clue to her own heart. She couldn't shake the feeling of fear that reached out its cold fingers to grip her heart. Was *she* supposed to take the tiger's teeth and limbs and eyes? Was *she* supposed to kill him? "But how can we do this? Any of this? We're just . . . kids."

The bayan bent to caress its beak gently against her palm. "Oh, Hamra. As the tiniest seed grows into the mightiest tree, as the smallest nail brings down the most powerful stallion, so too can a child change the shape of the story and in doing so, the shape of the world."

Hamra swallowed the lump in her throat. "You can see the future. Do we succeed?"

There was a silence. "My visitors so seldom understand

destiny," the bayan said quietly. "They view it as a fork in the road, where one choice determines the outcome. In truth, destinies are as many-forked as the branches of a tree, where each decision, small or large, brings you to one of a hundred fates. For you, Hamra, I see light. But only if you make the right choices. Do you see?"

"No," she said honestly.

The bayan nipped her finger gently. "You will," it said. "Now put me back on the table."

She did as it asked, and it hopped over to where the old woman had put its pillow, right in its center. It settled itself down on its plump depths and sighed, as though the conversation had tired it. "Now listen," it said, addressing all three of them, and they drew closer. "I cannot tell you the exact path you must take. But I can tell you five things that will be of use to you on your journey. The first: Ask the lady why she screams. The second: Ask the praying man why he prays. The third: Ask the bones why they weep. The fourth: Trust another, no matter how unlikely. And the fifth: Trust yourself."

"Wait, wait." Ilyas, prepared as ever, had whipped out a notebook and pen from his backpack and was scribbling away, muttering to himself as he did: "Lady . . . praying man . . . bones . . ."

Hamra swallowed hard. "I don't know what any of it means."

"It is rare that anyone who asks to see the hand that fate has dealt them understands immediately what they are seeing," the bayan said. "Things become clear in the doing. I wish you well, Little Red; this is all I can tell you. And now, I must rest. Jamilah!"

The old woman rose from where she'd seated herself in the shadows and scooped up the bayan, cushion and all, to place it gently back in its cage. Then she turned to the trio before them. "Right. Now pay up."

Hamra cleared her throat. "About that . . ."

"I told you we needed something to pay them with!" Ilyas hissed.

"We have nothing of value," Hamra explained quickly. "But maybe we can . . . we can trade you? We have clothes, food. Umm. A feather duster . . ."

"I have an umbrella!" Ilyas supplied hurriedly.

"And what use would I have for such human trifles?" the bayan asked, amused.

"It's all we've got," Hamra said.

"That," the bayan said, "is not true." And its eyes took on a curiously hungry gleam.

Beside her, Hamra felt the tiger stir, and an answering

138

pang in her stomach—a warning. *Have a care, for there are only so many pieces you can give away before you lose yourself altogether.*

"No," Hamra agreed. "But it's all we're willing to give."

The bayan glanced at the tiger, who remained where he was, still and calm. "I see she has learned from you already."

"She has learned herself, through her own mistakes," he growled. "But she is learning, nonetheless."

Jamilah grunted. "Talk, talk, talk in circles, but still no talk of payment. That there was some quality fortune-seeing you did, and for what? Tiger fur all over the rug, that's what, and that's a pain to clean off, let me tell you . . ."

"Jamilah makes a fair point," the bayan said. "A service has been rendered, and payment must be made. You do not want to incur any more debts, Little Red."

Hamra felt her hands tremble and clenched them into hard fists to make them stop. "What do you want from me?"

"I will not ask of you the things that make you who you are," the bayan said. "But whatever powers I have, I am not immortal. And so I ask for your time."

Hamra frowned. "We've already been here for like, twenty minutes—"

"No." The bayan shook its head. "I am not asking for time spent with you. I am asking for your time, time gleaned from your own lifeline, that I may use to extend mine."

First the bird, and now her time? Hamra glanced at the tiger, who scowled. "Now it is you who are asking too much, Seer," he said.

"Am I?" The bird cocked its head. "What difference does it make to you? Ten minutes skimmed out of the top of her life, when would she even miss it?"

The tiger bent his head close, so close Hamra could feel his breath mist on her face as he spoke. "Listen to me, Hamra," he said urgently. "Every minute of your life is precious. Every single one. Even a minute can mean a tighter hug, a longer goodbye, a lingering glance at the stars, one last chorus in your favorite song. Please. Think about this."

"What choice do we have?" Hamra whispered. "Debts require payment. You taught me that." And though the tiger looked away, she still caught the sadness in his amber eyes.

Hamra took a breath. "Ten minutes is too much," she said. "I am young, after all. There's so much ahead of me. I don't know yet when I'll need that time."

"Ten minutes is my price."

"Then take some from me," Ilyas said suddenly, and

Hamra whipped her head around to stare at him.

"What are you doing?" she hissed.

Ilyas ignored her. "There's two of us. So take five from me, and five from Hamra. And . . . and . . . and some bahulu, as a bonus!" Ilyas knelt down, rummaging around in his backpack until he emerged with the container of soft, flower-shaped cakes, holding them triumphantly above his head like a trophy.

The room was silent as they watched the bayan contemplate this offer, but it seemed to Hamra as if everyone could hear the thumping of her heart, so hard was it hammering in her chest.

"Thank you," the bayan said finally. "I will accept your offer."

Ilyas blinked. "Even the bahulu?"

The bayan smiled. "Especially the bahulu. Now go, and may favor shine upon your journey."

And though she still had a million questions, there was nothing more Hamra could do but turn around and walk away.

13

THE FIRST THING she did was smack Ilyas on the shoulder, hard.

"Ow!" He glared at her, rubbing the sore spot where her hand had landed with a satisfying smack. "What was that for?"

"Why did you do that?" Hamra was so mad that the flames were flickering even up to the tips of her ears.

Ilyas frowned. "Do what?"

"That!" Hamra was practically yelling by now. How could he not see? How could he be so calm? "Do you even realize what you've done? What you've given up?"

"I did what you did," Ilyas said mildly.

"You didn't have to!"

"Five minutes from each of us is better than ten from

one of us," he said, and for some reason the matter-of-fact way he said it, so calm, so collected, made her even angrier. The flames leaped higher and higher, until she couldn't control them anymore, until they had to explode out of her. How *dare* he be so nice? How *dare* he be so kind when she'd just given away his gift to her? How *dare* he be so . . . so . . . *Ilyas*?

"I don't need you to save me!"

Ilyas shrugged, maddeningly calm as ever. He'd never known how to fight her properly; it was one of his worst qualities, in Hamra's opinion. "I know you don't," he said. "I didn't do it to save you. I did it to *help* you. Accepting help isn't the same as being weak. Berat sama dipikul, ringan sama dijinjing, or whatever it is Puan Ramlah tried to teach us in BM that time."

"This isn't BM class."

"No," he agreed. "This is real life, with real dangers, and if you don't start realizing you need to trust people to get to the end of this, we're not going to make it."

The tiger, who had been watching silently as all of this went down, padded over to Hamra and nipped at her sleeve.

"What?"

"Come," he said, and she followed him to a quiet

corner between tents, her face still red, her blood still boiling, stinging retorts still floating, unsaid, on her tongue. "Breathe. Collect yourself."

And though she longed to speak, she sat silent until the fever in her cheeks had cooled and she could think again. "He didn't need to do that," she said quietly.

"He already did," the tiger said. "You could not have stopped him. And I believe the custom amongst your set is to say thank you when someone has done something good for you. Not attempt to grievously injure them."

Hamra glanced sidelong at him. "What do you care, anyway?"

The tiger puffed out his chest. "I do not *care*. I merely do not want any delays on our journey due to your inability to control your temper. Humans are so easily distracted by their emotions."

"You," Hamra retorted, "are human too. Or at least, you were. And you want to be again."

The tiger sighed. "Well. Perhaps this quest will yet teach me what a mistake that desire is. And for all we know, all that awaits us is failure. After all, the most important piece of the puzzle is hidden in memories I no longer possess." He smiled, but it was a smile laced with bitterness so palpable Hamra could almost taste it. "Ironic, is it not? Here

I am, all these powers at my disposal and yet, I cannot remember anything of my past. I strike fear in the hearts of all who have the misfortune to encounter me with a single roar, fell grown men with one strike of my paw, and yet something as simple as my own name eludes me." He spread his paws out helplessly. "What good is power if you don't know who you are? And therefore, what to use it for?"

Hamra reached out a hand and patted the tiger awkwardly, his striped fur soft to the touch. "The good news is I spend all day, every day with old people. I've had a lot of practice at taking care of lost things." It was strange, to feel this sudden pang of sympathy for a creature she'd been thinking of as a monster all along.

"I hope so. For all our sakes." The tiger sat and looked at the night sky above them for a long time before he spoke again. "Do you hear that?" he asked her softly.

"Hear what?"

"Of course you don't." The tiger took a deep breath. "If all is silent and I listen hard enough, I can hear the stars singing to each other. And it is the most beautiful sound in the world." His voice dropped to almost a whisper. "I will miss their song."

Hamra wasn't quite sure what to say. So she decided it

was best to say nothing at all. They just sat in silence, staring at the stars.

After a while, the tiger stirred. "Enough of this foolishness. Let us keep moving, Little Red."

She smiled. "You know . . . until we find your true name, we should figure out something to call you. A temporary name."

He glanced at her. "Are we friends now? Do you not remember your grandmother's words? It does not do to trust a tiger."

"I wouldn't say we're friends, exactly," Hamra retorted. "I'm just saying that it's hard to talk to you without a name to call you by."

The tiger thought about this. "Those who walked in the jungles and did not want to say 'tiger' for fear of calling me to them used to refer to me as Pak Belang."

It wasn't quite what Hamra had expected. She called her uncles Pak, and older men who acted like uncles and were uncle-aged. The tiger really didn't seem to give off the same vibes. But who was she to judge? "Do you like the name?"

He shrugged a tiger shrug. "It is as good as any, I suppose."

"Then Pak Belang it is." Hamra stood up and dusted the dirt from the seat of her jeans. "We should go."

"In a moment," the newly christened Pak Belang said. "I must relieve myself."

"What does that mean?"

The tiger looked nonplussed. "It means I must . . . attend to some urgent business."

Hamra frowned. "What could be more urgent than—"

"I need," Pak Belang said desperately, "to pee."

"*Oh*. Oh. Okay, go ahead."

Hamra sighed as she rubbed her shoulders, which ached from carrying her stuffed backpack. She supposed it might be a good time to rest and eat (some human food) and puzzle out the bayan's clues so that they could work out their next move. "AAH!" She jumped as she felt a sharp poke in her side. Jamilah stood just behind her, a little wooden box in one hand, the cane responsible for the poke in the other.

"You young people," she sniffed. "So skittish. Nah, I brought you something. For you only. Don't show your friends."

"What is it?"

The old woman shoved the box into Hamra's hand, glancing left and right as if she were worried someone might see them. "Tu. You open and see."

Hesitating only slightly, Hamra pried open the box,

which was made of plain, polished wood, with a cover that hinged on one side.

It was a stone the size of a plum and a shimmering amber-gold; when held up to the light, it seemed to glow. It reminded Hamra of Pak Belang's eyes, and the way they gleamed.

"What is this?"

"Protection," Jamilah said. "Just in case. He's a crafty one, the old man-cat is."

Hamra blinked. "But he's been trying to help us."

Jamilah snorted. "Of course he is. Because helping you means helping himself get what he wants. You mark my words, once he's done with you . . . well. I'm just saying, it doesn't do to put too much trust in a tiger. You keep yourself safe, ya? Use that if you need to. Now give me that box back."

Hamra felt a shiver make its way down her spine as she handed it over and watched Jamilah shuffle away. *Can't trust them, Opah had told her. Not one bit.*

"Hamra?" It was Ilyas, his voice soft and uncertain, looking anywhere but at her as he spoke. "We should go."

"Yeah," she said hurriedly, stuffing the stone into her pocket. "Yeah, we should." *Add this to the dozen other things you're going to have to think about later, Hamra.*

They sat together just beyond the borders of the night market, on a waterproof sheet that Ilyas had fished out of his backpack and spread out on the ground carefully so they could avoid the damp and dirt, and slowly munched on cold fried noodles, day-old chicken rice, and a handful of iced gem biscuits for dessert. When Pak Belang returned, he took a look at the spread, illuminated by the flickering light of the oil lamps, politely declined, then disappeared in the darkness to "procure my own sustenance." Hamra didn't ask. She didn't think she really wanted to know, not when she was just starting to get used to having him around.

Their chewing sounded loud and unnatural in the silence, and with each moment Hamra grew more and more frustrated at the way Ilyas avoided her eyes.

Finally, she couldn't take it anymore. "Look, I'm sorry, okay?" she burst out, flinging down her plastic container and sending biscuit crumbs scattering across the sheet.

Ilyas blinked at her. "What?"

"I said I'M SORRY." She bit her lip, suddenly uncomfortable. She couldn't remember the last time she'd apologized for anything, much less to Ilyas. "I know you spent a lot of time making me that bird. I shouldn't have just . . . given it away like that."

"Oh." Ilyas paused to take this in, and Hamra could see how much of an effort it took him to shrug his shoulders oh-so-casually in response. "That's okay," he said. "It's like you said. In that moment, you didn't have a choice."

"Right," Hamra said. "Right. I didn't have a choice." *Except you did, didn't you, Hamra?* a tiny voice needled at her insides. *Just like the tiger said.*

Ilyas was silent for a moment, staring at the bright lights of the night market. "Do you still think this is all worth it?" he asked her quietly. "All these things we have to do. Do you think we . . ."

"Yes," she answered quickly. "Of course it is. Remember what he promised? We get Opah back, Ilyas. Back to how she used to be. And I miss her. I really do."

"Okay then." Ilyas smiled at her, and it was hard to describe the flood of relief she felt as she smiled back. He whipped out his notebook and flipped it open. "We should start working on these clues. Ask the lady why she screams. Ask the praying man why he prays. Ask the bones why they weep. Trust yourself. Trust another. What does any of it mean?" He leaned back and sighed. "I was always hopeless at puzzles. Why couldn't the bird just give us a nice numbered list of instructions instead?"

Hamra laughed. "What kind of magical quest would that be? Haven't you read any fairy tales before, you dungu? Working out the puzzle is part of the fun."

Ilyas tossed a twig at her. "Laugh lah some more! You figure it out then, smarty-pants. Since it's so *fun* for you."

"I will." She paused for the briefest of moments. "*We* will."

Ilyas glanced at her, the light glinting off his glasses. "We, huh?"

"Yes," she said simply, and his gratified smile was like a balm to her own guilt. "All right, let's take it one at a time." Hamra began to doodle shapes in the dirt with the twig Ilyas had thrown at her. "Ask the lady why she screams. Somewhere on Langkawi, there must be a screaming lady, right? Who—or what—could that be?"

Ilyas threw his hands up in the air. "I don't know! Someone who's in pain? Someone who's suffering? Someone who just stepped on a Lego? It could be anything! And anyway, I'm not sure I want to know to be honest. Screaming ladies, praying men, bones, it all sounds super creepy, and I don't do well with horror, as you very well know . . ."

Hamra sat up and stared at him.

"What?" he said warily.

"Say that again."

"I said it all sounds super creepy, and I *hate* horror, absolutely hate it . . ."

Super creepy. Horror. A screaming woman . . .

"You know what happened when everyone wanted to watch *The Conjuring* that time and I had that *accident* and needed new pants and . . ."

"I know."

"I know you know, and it was *super* embarrassing . . ."

"No, Ilyas," Hamra said. "I mean, I know who we're looking for."

He stopped. "You do?"

"I do." She grimaced. "But you're not going to like it."

14

THEIR BOAT SKIMMED across the water, slicing white-capped waves in its wake, and the nighttime air was filled with the steady hum of the engine and the smell of gasoline. Hamra sat at the helm, directing the nose toward their destination.

"Are you sure you know what you're doing?" Pak Belang yelled over the noise of the engine, gripping the edges of the boat tightly with his front paws.

"You seem a little nervous," Ilyas said to the tiger, barely containing a snicker. Hamra thought this was a little rich coming from Ilyas, who had spent the night before alternating between pacing the clearing anxiously and asking Hamra things like, "Are you *sure* we have to do this?" and "Don't you think you may be *completely wrong* about this?" and "Does it have to be *her*?"

"I don't like the water," the tiger snapped at him. "And if you mock me again, boy, I'll bite off your fingers."

Ilyas blanched at this threat. "All right, all right, calm down. You don't need to worry. If anyone knows their way around a boat, it's Hamra."

Hamra smiled a proud little smile to herself. Sure, maybe some people might have been worried about going out on the water at night; maybe some people would have been afraid of getting lost, or of not knowing how to operate the boat. But Hamra was not some people. She'd been going out on this boat with her father ever since she was a baby, and she'd learned to drive it as soon as she was old enough to understand what each button and lever did. She'd spent weekend after weekend helping her father wipe down its wooden flanks, flecks of bright blue and white peeling from its worn exterior; cleaning the blue canopy that protected the flocks of tourists that came to him for their island tours; counting out the neon orange and yellow life jackets to make sure none were missing. Even when the pandemic stole all their business and kept tourists from coming, even when nobody was allowed on the water, Hamra and Ayah had made sure to keep the boat clean and tuned and ready to go, something she was very grateful for now.

"We're almost there," she called back. "I'd give it another five minutes."

"Great," Ilyas muttered. "Juuuust great."

Once they'd left the night market and entered the real world again, she did feel creeping concern that the next police officer they encountered wouldn't be as easily fooled as the first. But as it turned out, all it took was Pak Belang making an appearance, baring his sharp teeth, and throwing in some growls for good measure for everyone in the vicinity to very quickly disappear, usually with a lot of shouting and screaming.

"Couldn't you just have used magic or something?" Hamra asked, feeling a little guilty at the terrified looks on people's faces.

"Sometimes the fastest solution is the inelegant one," the tiger said smoothly. Then he leaned in a little closer. "Also," he whispered in her ear. "It's more fun."

It was hard to believe that it was the same tiger who was now cowering on the floor of her boat, hissing at the wind that ruffled his fur.

Pulau Dayang Bunting loomed ahead, and as they got closer and closer it became easier to make out the shape of the pregnant handmaiden that gave the island its name. She remembered her father pointing it out when she was little:

"She's lying on her back, do you see? There's the point of her chin, then just a little farther down, that big curving belly. Do you see her?" It had taken her a minute, but when she'd finally seen, she'd clapped her hands in glee, so happy to finally be in on the story.

The island was dark when they approached. Without the teeming masses of tourists that used to descend by the boatload daily, the place was inhabited only by animals, bugs, and . . . other things. Approaching at night, without even the memory of a day's worth of visitors, it was hard not to think about those other residents of the island—the things that that locals whispered to each other about when the tourists were out of earshot.

The Langsuir was one of them.

Now, as the boat sputtered into silence and Hamra nudged it as close to land as possible before handing the rope to Ilyas, who leaped out to anchor it to the dock, the darkness felt almost suffocating.

"Are you sure this is where we need to be?" Ilyas whispered for the millionth time. Knowing what was coming, his anxiety had only grown since their journey began.

Hamra nodded. "There's only one screaming lady in the stories, you know that."

From the floor of the boat, Pak Belang let out a long

groan. "Is it over? Have we arrived?"

"We have."

"Praise be." He pulled himself up and made his way off the boat on shaky legs. "I never want to do that again."

"We're going to have to on our way back," Ilyas pointed out.

Pak Belang's only response was a string of colorful expletives that made Ilyas click his tongue in disapproval and Hamra blush.

"That's quite enough of that," she said firmly. "Let's go." She began walking, then stopped, causing Ilyas to bump right into her back.

"Oof." He adjusted his glasses and glared at her. "What are you doing?"

"I'm not sure where to go," Hamra said.

"I thought you knew this place!"

"Everything looks different at night!"

"Be quiet," Pak Belang said, and illuminated by their flashlights, Hamra could see his ears perk up as he listened intently. Then he nodded. "The cave is this way. Follow me."

"Can you at least tie your laces?" Ilyas asked Hamra, fidgeting restlessly as he gazed out into the shadows. "It's going to be hard enough without you tripping over things in the dark."

"Fine."

The moon had slid behind some clouds, so that their only respite from the relentless night was the gleam of the flashlights that Hamra and Ilyas carried.

"Good thing these have fresh batteries," Ilyas said as he adjusted his backpack. "You know me, always have to be prepared."

Hamra rolled her eyes. "We know, we know. You've said that already. You say it all the time."

Ilyas coughed. "Maybe I'm just trying to convince myself I'm prepared for this too."

Hamra wasn't sure anything could prepare them for what they were about to face, but she decided it was best not to say that kind of stuff out loud. They were walking through dense jungle now, following closely behind Pak Belang, and the humidity made the air around them sit on their skin like wet blankets; beneath her hijab, Hamra could feel sweat pooling and dripping down her neck.

"So is anyone going to explain the screaming lady to me?" said Ilyas.

"You do not know the tale of the Langsuir?" Pak Belang's voice carried through the darkness. He seemed to have recovered from their journey on the water; while Hamra and Ilyas walked timidly, fearful of what they might step on in the dark, he seemed to glide through it, flitting in and out of shadows. Sometimes their flashlights caught the gleaming amber of his eyes or the whites of his teeth, and Hamra's heart would catch in her chest, and she would reach into her pocket for the smooth comfort of the protection charm. *You just can't trust a tiger.*

"I mean, I know *of* the Langsuir," Ilyas said. "I just want to know her story."

"Where we're going is a cave called Gua Langsuir, or the Cave of the Banshee," Hamra explained, and without even realizing it, her voice slipped into an exact imitation of her father's tour guide voice, with all the dips and peaks that came with telling a compelling story. "A long, long time ago, the cave was inhabited by three female demons. Though their true forms were hideous beyond description, they also had the power to transform themselves into the forms of the most beautiful women anyone had ever seen. And when they were hungry, which was often, they would take these forms, go to the mouth of the cave where it overlooks the water, and sing. And that song would drive passing sailors and fishermen to madness. They would be so enchanted, so drunk on the song and on their beauty, that they would jump into the roaring sea to try to swim to the Langsuir. Many would drown in their attempts, but they were almost luckier than those who succeeded in reaching them—those would just be eaten."

"Can someone please explain to me," Ilyas muttered, "why we're willingly seeking out the flesh-eating demon woman?"

"Be quiet, I'm telling the story."

Ilyas grunted, but he stayed quiet, and Hamra went on. "Legend spread and people, of course, began to stay away from the cave, not being particularly excited about the idea of meeting their death there at the hands of demons, and the Langsuir grew bored and hungry for fresh meat. And then suddenly, one day, a lone fisherman appeared. And no matter how hard the three demons tried, no matter how beautifully they sang, no matter what treasures they offered him, that man just sat in his boat and fished. They did not know that he was hard of hearing; they thought only that they had lost their charms, and their surprise quickly turned to fear. For if the humans no longer succumbed to their powers, they could just as easily turn on them, scale the cliffs to get to their cave and murder them out of revenge. And so, they flew away from the cave, never to return." She paused. "Or at least, that's the version we tell the tourists."

"And in reality?" Ilyas asked.

"And in reality . . ." Hamra sighed. "In reality, the cave

is set in a steep cliff, and very few people make it there unless they have some climbing experience. And those who do make it come back talking about the darkness, and the bats, and the strange screaming and singing sounds they hear from inside . . ."

"In reality." Pak Belang's voice came through the darkness. "In reality, the Langsuir is just another creature among the many who are made out to be demons because you need villains to justify your own goodness. Humans have always needed a story to hang their fears and anxieties onto. An explanation. An excuse."

The flames leaped, ever so slightly, in Hamra's chest. "You were human too, once. And you want to be one again. Why are we doing all of this, if humans are that bad?"

There was a long pause, and when the tiger spoke again, it was so softly that Hamra almost didn't hear him: "Because every lost thing wants to be found."

And Hamra thought of her grandmother, wandering alone through old memories, and was silent.

At last, after what felt like hours of walking through the darkness, they finally stopped. "There it is," Hamra said, pointing her flashlight upward to illuminate the cave mouth, looking for all the world as if the sheet of limestone before them was yawning.

"Ah," Pak Belang said, conversationally. "And by any chance, are you two experienced climbers?"

"Nope," Hamra said.

"Not at all," Ilyas added.

The tiger sighed. "Very well. Climb upon my back."

Ilyas let out a strangled snort-laugh. "No offense, but that seems like a very bad idea from where I'm standing."

"Why?"

"You have very large teeth!"

"They are not," Pak Belang said pointedly, "on my *back*."

"Since when did you start helping us, anyway?" Ilyas sniffed. "I thought we had to prove ourselves to you or whatever."

"Perhaps I am tired of being slowed down by incompetence," the tiger snarled.

Hamra rubbed her aching head. "Be quiet, you two. Ilyas, we're getting on his back. No, I don't want to hear it! If he wanted to, he'd have killed us by now. Might as well take advantage of that supernatural strength of his while he still has it." She sighed. "But if it makes you feel any better, I'll go first."

The tiger brought himself low to the ground so that

Hamra could swing one leg gingerly over and sit astride him, gripping his soft, thick fur to keep herself steady. "See?" she told Ilyas, who still seemed pale and unsure in the harsh light of her flashlight. "Nothing to worry about. Now come on."

She reached out a hand, and though it took him ages to decide to grab it, he finally did, settling behind her as best he could.

"It is steep, and there is much loose gravel that may make me a little unsteady," the tiger warned them. "Bend low, and wrap both your arms around my sides so you can stay on."

They did as he said, and he set off, using those sharp, sharp claws to dig into the face of the cliff and haul them all up, step by step. The path to the cave was so sheer it was almost vertical, and holding on to his back required every ounce of their strength. So there was very little Hamra could do when she felt her phone begin to slip out of her pocket, centimeter by excruciating centimeter. *Please don't fall*, she thought to herself desperately. *Please don't fall, please don't fall, please don't fall* . . .

And then it promptly did, sailing down into the darkness and landing with a sickening clatter on the rocks below.

"What was that??" Ilyas asked.

Hamra sighed. "My phone." And then, in a much smaller voice: "My parents are going to kill me."

"Not if something else out here doesn't get us first," Ilyas shot back.

Hamra was quiet. She didn't want to think about it.

It seemed to her, clinging tightly as she was to the tiger's back, that the climb took hours and hours after that, surrounded by inky blackness and hearing only the sounds of Ilyas's rapid breathing and the chittering and buzzing of all the jungle creatures she could not see. But before long, the sounds were replaced by only one: a keening, high-pitched wail that grew louder and louder with each step they took. And when the ground finally leveled beneath them, Pak Belang had to raise his voice to a roar to be heard over the screaming that now surrounded them, bouncing and echoing off the walls of the cave.

"We are here."

15

THEY STOOD AT the very mouth of the cave and stared into the blackness within. At their backs, the moon had finally burst out from behind the clouds, but its milky rays did little to penetrate the darkness, as if even it were afraid of what it might see. And the screaming! It wasn't a steady, screeching thing, but a wail that floated and moved the way seaweed sways in the water, swimming its way around the cave, now louder, now softer, but always, always there.

"What's back there?" Ilyas whispered, shining his flashlight around the interior to try to get a better look. But the darkness swallowed up the light, and they could see nothing. Their flashlights would be no use here.

"So that's how it is." Hamra sighed and tucked the flashlight back into the pocket of her backpack. "Might as well have our hands free if these won't work." This time,

Hamra didn't ask if they were ready, because she was very sure none of them were. "Let's go," she said instead, and taking Ilyas's hand in one of hers and laying the other on the scruff of Pak Belang's neck, they all walked forward together into the dark.

Immediately, Hamra was hit by a force so strong that it wrenched Ilyas's hand from her grasp and slammed her to her knees, and suddenly it was as if she was being tossed mercilessly upon the waves of a churning, roiling sea. She was cold, so cold that she felt that she could barely breathe, and the weight of her soaked clothes tugged her deeper and deeper into the sea, so that she could barely stay on the surface, gasping for air. Fear gripped her heart and squeezed her lungs so that she almost choked. *Is this how I'm going to die?* Somewhere on the edges of her mind, she thought she heard Ilyas scream, and wondered helplessly if he was drowning too.

Then, as suddenly as it had begun, it stopped. Hamra was on her back now, panting hard, but—as she found from quickly patting down her clothes—dry. It wasn't dark anymore, either. Soft afternoon sunlight illuminated her surroundings, and as she pulled herself up, she realized that she was somehow no longer even in the cave, but in the middle of a jungle.

Hamra took a breath. *This, you can handle*, she thought. *You know the jungle. Whatever this is, you can figure it out.*

And then she heard the hiss.

No. No, please, not that.

Hamra turned around slowly, and then immediately wished with all her heart that she hadn't. For everywhere she looked, she saw the things she feared the most: snakes of every size and hue, slithering on the ground, regarding her from the branches of trees and rocky outcrops, hanging down like vines, hundreds and hundreds of them, all making their way toward her. And as they began to coil their smooth bodies around her limbs, as she felt their little teeth bite into her flesh, all she could do was open her mouth and scream and scream . . .

And then they were gone.

It took Hamra a while to stand up again. It was hard, when her whole body still shook. She could remember how the snakes felt against her skin, and the thought made her want to throw up. But once she was finally able to think again, the sense of relief that came over her was so intense that she felt like crying. Because she recognized where she was now: she was in her garden, and that was her front door. Hamra was home.

Home.

She broke into a run, hands outstretched to push open the door. *If I'm quick enough,* she thought, *I can make it back in time for tea with Opah and Atok.* And she was still thinking of steaming hot milk tea and freshly fried keropok lekor when she reached the door and discovered that it wouldn't open. No matter how much she jiggled the knob, how hard she pushed the door, it simply wouldn't move. Hamra began to bang on the door with all her might, pounding on it with her fists. "Atok!" she yelled. "Opah!" until her throat was sore. But still, nobody came.

Tired out, Hamra walked to the window to peer inside and see if anyone was there. *Maybe they've fallen asleep,* she thought to herself. *Maybe they're just resting. And won't they be so happy to see me? Won't we be so happy to be together again?*

The window was closed. But through the clear glass, Hamra could see everything on the other side. And what she saw turned the blood in her veins to ice.

Opah sat in her usual chair, looking up at the tiger, who loomed over her, bigger and more menacing and terrifying than ever. As she watched, Opah smiled that wide, open smile, and the tiger smiled back, displaying each one of those terrible sharp teeth.

"My," Opah said softly. "What big teeth you have."

Hamra could no longer bear it. And as the tiger opened his mouth and pounced, Hamra turned away, her legs giving out so that she slid to the ground and sobbed and sobbed as if her heart would break.

This time, Hamra didn't want to open her eyes. She didn't want to know what she might see when she did. And if Ilyas had not said quietly beside her, "Hamra, wake up, it's all right," she really might have kept her eyes shut forever.

As it was, it took her a while to work up the courage to pry them apart, and when she did, she discovered she was sitting between Ilyas and Pak Belang once more, leaning against the cool stone wall of the cave. All around them, candles burned, keeping the dark at bay. For once, she realized, there was no more screaming. Everything was quiet.

"Are you all right?" Ilyas asked, his eyes raking her face for signs of how she was feeling.

"I'm fine," she lied, her voice barely a croak. "Just fine." She felt crumpled and worn out from the tears she was so unused to shedding.

"Good," Ilyas said quickly. "Me too." But Hamra knew him, and she could see every mark the darkness had left on him all over his face, in the twitch of his mouth and the shadows under his eyes and in the way he fiddled with his glasses, now taking them off, now putting them on, now taking them off again and adjusting the nose pads.

On her other side, the tiger sprawled on the floor, his eyes wide open but staring at nothing; Hamra laid a cautious hand on him, if only to check that he was still breathing, and was relieved to feel the rise and fall of his belly. At least he was still alive.

"He's been like that for ages," Ilyas whispered. "He hasn't moved at all. What do you . . . what do you think that *was*?"

"I don't know," Hamra said grimly. "But I didn't like it."

"That was the point," a voice said, and they both jumped. "You aren't supposed to."

From the shadows emerged a tall figure, deathly pale, with long, long black hair that trailed along on the ground behind her. Her eyes were black from side to side, and each one of her teeth ended in sharp points that glinted in the flickering light of the candle flames. As they watched, gripping tight to each other, Hamra's heart beating so hard she thought it might give out altogether, the ghostly figure began to glide, moving closer and closer to them, hands outstretched . . .

. . . and then she promptly tripped on the hem of her

long white robe. "Ouch," she said quietly. "Oooh, I think I stubbed my toe."

Somehow, it didn't quite fit the nightmare vision that had been playing in Hamra's head. "Er, sorry?" she said.

"Not your fault, is it? It's my own fault for choosing to wear this." The apparition bent down to rub her hurt toe, mumbling quietly to herself. "That's what you get for choosing things for *effect* instead of *practicality*, isn't it? Silly thing."

Ilyas cleared his throat. "Sorry miss, but, uh . . . who are you?"

She straightened up to look at him. "Why, I'm the Langsuir of the cave, of course."

"So you're real." Hamra watched as a host of emotions crossed Ilyas's face, from surprise to awe to fear to the dawning realization that those sharp teeth could very well be used to eat them alive.

"Of course I am. And this is my home." The Langsuir came and sat cross-legged before them, settling her robes around her and taking great care to make sure she didn't sit on her own hair. "The real question is what are *you* doing here? This cave is not for the likes of children."

"You can say that again," Hamra muttered, then let out a muffled shriek when a bat suddenly flew from the darkness into the Langsuir's lap.

"Shh," she cooed at it softly, stroking it behind its furry ears. "I know they disturbed you. But they will be gone soon." She glanced up at them and grinned. "One way or another."

Hamra gulped. Suddenly, it seemed very hard to breathe. "That doesn't sound good."

"What?" The Langsuir looked confused for a moment, then laughed, a bright, lilting sound that wasn't at all like the screams they'd heard before. "Oh, I see! I just meant that you'd either climb down or we'd have to find another way. It's awfully steep to be climbing about in the dark."

She sent the bat off with a pat on its rump, then turned to the children and their still-silent tiger companion. "Now. What are you doing here?"

"We came to see you," Hamra told her.

"Me?" The Langsuir clasped her hands together in delight. "Why, nobody ever comes just to see me!"

Ilyas coughed. "Not to be rude, but it's not like you make it easy . . ."

"Oh, that." The Langsuir had the decency to look embarrassed. "That's because people don't usually come to see me, as I say. They usually want to make a spectacle of me. Or kill me. So my shroud of darkness is meant to serve as a deterrent, you see . . ."

"What is it?" Hamra asked, remembering the visions she'd experienced. It had all seemed so real. "The things I saw . . ."

"One of my cleverest little inventions, that," the Langsuir said, beaming proudly. "Took ages for me to weave it just the way I wanted. You see, what happens in the dark? When you wake up in the dead of night and all around you is quiet and still? When you're waiting to fall asleep and the shadows seem to grow just a little darker? All your fears seem a little bigger, a little scarier, yes? My darkness just takes that and amplifies it. It sees all the deepest fears in your heart, the ones you try to bury away and never think about, and it makes them real."

Hamra thought about the weight of water dragging her down; the feel of scales against her skin; the way the tiger's teeth had hovered, ready to tear into Opah's flesh; and she shivered. "It's monstrous," she whispered.

"Well, they call me a monster," the Langsuir fired back. "So it seems only right. Anyway, most people don't venture too far into the dark. They stay on the fringes, listen to my scream songs, get some heebie-jeebies, a little hint of the nightmares within, a shiver down their spines, and then they know to leave well enough alone. Unlike you lot, just launching yourselves headfirst into it." She sniffed. "You only have yourselves to blame, really. All I want is to be left alone with my bats. I don't hurt anyone." She scratched her head, then added quietly: "Well. Not often, anyway."

Hamra rubbed her aching head. "Sorry to bother you," she said as politely as she could, being rather too aware of the Langsuir's pointed teeth, no matter how nice she seemed to be. "We came to ask you a question, if you would be so kind as to answer."

"Oh! Is that all?" The Langsuir fluffed out her skirts and looked rather pleased at this attention. "Then yes, you may ask me . . . what's the usual? Ah yes, three questions. Though if you start pulling out any stakes or knives I'll have to dispose of you quite quickly, I warn you in advance. Don't get any ideas."

Ilyas let out a squeak of terror, and Hamra quickly nodded. "We won't."

"Very well. What is it you wish to know?"

Before Hamra could reply, Ilyas blurted out, "Do you really eat humans?" before quickly clamping his mouth shut as if he couldn't believe he'd even asked.

"Ilyas!" Hamra hissed. "Don't waste our questions!" *And don't give her any ideas*, she added to herself.

"Sometimes," she said slowly. "As a treat. You do taste good, you see. But you're such tricky things to capture, and you are so loud, and so messy, and there are so many bones. It's not really worth it, to be honest with you." She reached out a long, thin finger and poked Ilyas in the ribs. "Why, are you volunteering?" she asked, then burst into peals of laughter at the dire look on his face. "Only joking," she sputtered between giggles. "Next question?"

Hamra had been waiting for this. "Why do you scream?"

The Langsuir tilted her head back to stare at the roof of the cave as she contemplated the question. "Because I remember, and I am angry, and I am sad, and all that anger and sadness must be released somehow. For those big, billowing emotions cannot be contained by one body, not even that of one with powers like mine, and even monsters can be haunted. Do you understand?"

"Not really," Hamra said honestly. "But I will keep trying to."

The Langsuir smiled and bent down to stroke Hamra's cheek; her hand was cold as ice, but her touch was tender. "You will, eventually," she said gently. "When you are meant to. All in good time, Little Red."

"How do you—" The question was almost out of her mouth before Ilyas planted his elbow firmly in her ribs and made her stop short. "What?" she hissed. "She never leaves the cave, right? How would she know who I am?"

"Don't waste questions, remember?" he whispered.

The Langsuir smiled. The light gleamed oddly off those sharp little teeth.

"Please," Hamra said. "The tiger—he is haunted, just like you. Except instead of being haunted by his memories, he's haunted by the fact that he can't remember them. And he needs to find himself again. Can you help us?"

The Langsuir glided over to where Pak Belang lay, still staring at nothing with those large tiger eyes. She knelt on the ground beside him and, putting one finger under his great chin, tipped his head so that he looked directly at her.

Pak Belang blinked as if he'd just been woken from strange dreams. "Hello," he said. "It has been a long time."

The Langsuir smiled. "Hello again, old one. It was not so long ago that we two terrorized this jungle, you on land, me in the air. What is it you are seeking now?"

The tiger paused for a long time. "Peace," he said finally. "I seek peace."

The Langsuir patted his head as if he were a mere house-cat. "It is a long way from the power you have spent your life chasing."

"I am tired of the chase."

The Langsuir nodded. "I suppose everyone tires, eventually." She stood up and addressed all three of them, looking at each one in turn. "Listen here, my travelers three. The tiger's powers are a wall he has built around himself, much like the shroud of darkness I weave each night. I will help you remove one part of it—the keenness of his hearing—but by our rules, there must be payment for this service. Fair is fair, after all."

"I knew it," Ilyas groaned softly.

Hamra braced herself. This script was familiar by now. "What can we give you in return?"

"Nothing much." The Langsuir tossed her long, long hair away from her face. "I want a memory."

Hamra gaped at her. "A memory?"

"Well of course." The Langsuir leaned in close, so close that Hamra could breathe her in. She smelled like damp earth and sweet rot. "How else do you think my shroud is made?" she said quietly, running one sharp nail softly along Hamra's jaw, and Hamra shivered. "Dreams and memories and ghosts and nightmares, Little Red, that's how I weave my magic."

"Don't do it, Hamra," Ilyas said warningly. "It's some kind of trick."

"There are no tricks here," the Langsuir snapped. "Only knowledge beyond your puny human understanding."

"What if . . ." Hamra gulped. "What if you take something important?"

The Langsuir looked affronted at this suggestion. "As if I would! Why, I'll only take the smallest, most insignificant little thing. And really, what does it matter? You lose memories all the time, shed them like snakes shed their skin. What harm does it do to give one to me?"

"Hamra," Ilyas said again. "Please. Remember what Pak Belang said?"

"I remember," she bit back. "But tell me what choice we have." And so she stood straight and tall and looked the Langsuir straight in her dark, dark eyes.

"Okay."

"Then so be it." The Langsuir moved her nail from Hamra's jaw to the side of her head and began scraping gently against the cloth that covered Hamra's right ear.

"What are you—"

"Shh." The scraping continued, a soft *scrtch scrtch scrtch* that made Hamra squirm. "Come out, come out, wherever you are," the Langsuir whispered, her face intent, eager, *hungry*, and Hamra felt goose bumps rise one by one on her skin.

Out of the corner of her eye, she saw a single smoky tendril waft slowly from her ear; it felt like something warm was being pulled out of her. Quickly, the Langsuir wrapped it around her finger, then shoved it somewhere into the depths of her robes.

"Right," she said, suddenly businesslike. "Let's get to work."

"Wait!" Hamra glanced at Pak Belang to see if he was okay with this, if he was ready, to wonder briefly if she was too. But it was too late. The Langsuir clapped twice. There was a great fluttering, and bats began to fly from every corner of the cave, dozens and dozens of them, so many that the air was thick with them and it was impossible to see. The bats began to circle Hamra and Ilyas, drawing closer and closer.

"Hamra!" she heard Ilyas yell. "Hamra!" But soon she heard nothing more; the bats became an impenetrable cocoon, within which Hamra was completely alone, gasping and trying to fight back the rising tide of panic threatening to engulf her completely.

"Do not fear," a tiny voice said in the darkness, and a friendly bat nuzzled her cheek. "Do not fear. Our mistress is about to scream, and she does not wish you to be hurt. We will protect you."

"Thank you, little friend," Hamra whispered. "Will the tiger be in much pain?"

The little bat's expression turned somber. "Yes," he said sadly. "It will be almost too much for him to bear. But pain is part of every journey. Our mistress knows this better than most. Now shush, for it is about to begin."

Hamra steeled herself, but nothing prepared her for the sound when it came. Even within the protection of the bats, she could hear it: a scream so terrifying, so raw, so completely soul-eviscerating that she could feel it bleeding into her brain and echoing in her bones. She gasped, clasping her hands over her ears. Dimly, she could feel tiny flutters as the bats pressed even closer, desperately trying to help her block it out. "Just a little longer," they pleaded. "You must stand it for just a little longer."

"I don't think I can," she managed, forcing each word past trembling lips.

"You must."

So Hamra gritted her teeth, and kept her hands firmly clamped over her ears, and tried to think only of happy things—Sunday morning nasi lemak breakfasts with her family; bike rides along the coast of the blue Andaman sea; the way the cool waters of the Telaga Tujuh falls felt against her skin; Opah, happy and warm and welcoming and herself, truly herself, once more. She could still feel the scream tearing away at the edges of her brain, but the thoughts just about kept it at bay, until at last, the bats fell away and she looked up to see two things: Ilyas, looking just as pale and crumpled as she felt, and Pak Belang in a heap on the floor, paws clamped over his ears, fur damp with sweat and tears, still whimpering.

She didn't realize until then that there were tears falling down her own face too.

Ilyas and Hamra quickly ran to the tiger, and they crouched beside him. Hamra's legs felt too weak to do much more. "What did you do to him?" she whispered, looking up at the Langsuir. "What happened?"

Pak Belang whimpered. "I cannot hear them anymore," he panted, his voice cracking on every word.

"Hear what?"

"The stars." He shut his eyes. "I cannot hear the stars."

The Langsuir smiled a sad, sad smile. "To bring down a wall so strong," she explained, "one must use great force. My scream was that great force." With that, she reached into her robes and pulled out a small glass jar, which she held out to Hamra. "Take this," she said.

The jar was ice cold to the touch, and inside was filled with an inky black mass that writhed and wriggled as

Hamra watched. "What is it?" she asked.

"Some of my best work," the Langsuir said. "Not nightmares, but pure darkness. No light can penetrate it, not even the rays of the sun; why, I dare say if you had enough, you could smother that old star completely." She patted Hamra lightly on the head. "Now, you may rest here a while until your companion regains his strength. But it's best not to wait too long. Your journey is far from over, Little Red."

Then she turned and melted into the shadows, leaving nothing but the chittering of bats behind her.

16

THEY WERE SILENT on the ride back[,] Ilyas and Hamra gazing out at the m[...] Belang with his eyes fixed on the sky, a[...] the stars once more.

Hamra was more tired than she care[...] didn't dare blink for more than a second[...] a boat to drive. But for another, more p[...] the reason she refused to speak aloud—t[...] greatest fears were burned into the back o[...] every time she closed her eyes, they jump[...] vivid and so real that they made her want[...] glanced over at Pak Belang, who sat on the[...] back of the boat, looking back at Pulau Da[...] it steadily shrank from sight. She thought o[...] the look in his eyes as he stood over Opah, r[...]

t have.

ned into her pocket and gripped

ght, the warm smoothness of it a

esn't do to trust a tiger.

Ilyas called, yelling to be heard over

_,_ and inwardly, Hamra sighed. He'd

very five minutes since they'd left the

at's what it felt like. She bit her lip,

_t_ familiar fire leap from her chest to

ached out and briefly brushed against

d so hard over the steering wheel that

white, making sure she heard him. "Do

e over?"

in, Ilyas's constant need to interfere. She

itably. "I'm fine," she snapped, immedi-

when she saw his expression. For just a

es inside her receded. "I really am okay,"

ng her tone. "Don't worry. We're almost

Ilyas murmured, stepping away and set-

the peeling vinyl cushions of one of the

along either side of the boat.

Hamra turned her attention back to the

view in front of her. *You and your big mouth. When will you ever learn?*

Pak Belang had said he knew a safe place within the jungle where they could spend the night, so they stashed the boat and followed along behind him as he led the way. The nightmares that had haunted Hamra in the cave seemed to cling to her like bad smells or worse luck. Pak Belang and Ilyas seemed to feel it too; in their wake, every shadow seemed just a little darker, every sound just a little more ominous, every step just a little less sure.

Beside her, Ilyas stumbled and quickly righted himself. "Is it much farther?" he asked, and Hamra could hear her own exhaustion mirrored in the edges of his voice.

The tiger slowed. "Are you tired?"

Ilyas squared his shoulders. "No," he lied.

Pak Belang sighed. "I forget. You are children, after all." He padded back toward them and bent low. "Come, ride upon my back again. It will be much faster this way."

Ilyas climbed up without a second thought, but for a moment, Hamra just stood and stared at the tiger, a million thoughts racing through her mind. *How much can you really trust him, Hamra? How can you be sure he isn't just waiting to tear you to pieces, to tear everyone you love to pieces?* She reached into her pocket for the smooth amber of the protection charm once more. The fire moved inside her, restless and unsure.

"Are you coming?" Pak Belang's low rumble dragged her out of her thoughts.

"Yes," she said finally. "Yes, I am."

Once she was securely on his back, the tiger broke into a trot, so fast that the wind blew in their faces and messed up Hamra's hijab. She bent low, hugging his neck tight to make sure she didn't lose her balance. But the steady rock and sway of his gait and the gentleness of the breeze and the softness of his fur made her eyes grow heavier and heavier. . . . Was that snoring she heard from Ilyas? How could he sleep? How could she? One of them had to stay alert. One of them had to make sure they were safe. One of them had to . . . had to . . .

Hamra was asleep.

And then she wasn't.

It was a fairly rude awakening; one minute she was dreaming of a picnic by the blue, blue sea with her parents, unmasked and free, and the next minute she was almost tumbling headlong off Pak Belang's back, if not for the fact that her arms were still wrapped around his neck.

"What? What's going on?" Ilyas sat straight up, his

glasses askew, quickly wiping away the trail of drool on his chin. Then, in a small voice: "Oh."

"Oh?" Hamra turned to look in the direction his gaze was fixed, straight ahead.

"Oh."

The reason that Pak Belang had stopped so abruptly, as it turned out, was because of the long, sharp end of a spear that was currently pointed directly at the center of his forehead. The other end of the spear was in the hands of the most beautiful man Hamra had ever seen, except for the five other beautiful men who surrounded them, their faces both bright and somehow terrible in their majesty, like gazing into the sun only to realize how much it pains you. Each man had ears that tapered off into points, like the elves she'd seen in her books; each wore a black baju melayu and a sampin threaded in gold silk; each held a spear; and each spear was pointed right at them.

"Oh." Hamra said again, and swallowed very hard.

"I would not move, if I were you," the tiger said quietly. "They seem quite serious about this."

"Children," the man—should she call him a man, Hamra wondered? He seemed like so much more, and the word seemed so paltry and inadequate—said, "Children, you are keeping some unsavory company. Come away, and let us rescue you from the clutches of this foul beast."

His voice was so creamy, so musical, so enticing, that it was hard to think about the actual words he was saying.

"Do not listen to them," Pak Belang said. "The Bunian know nothing but trickery and deceit."

"Bunian?" Ilyas whispered, and Hamra knew he was thinking, as she was, about all the stories they had grown up with. The Whispering Ones, the old folks called them, or the Slight Ones, or the Hidden Folk; the ones who stole children away for their own amusement, who confused errant hikers with the sound of their laughter so that they strayed from paths and were lost, only to be found days later, dazed and confused, almost exactly where they had been last seen. Hamra thought of the sunburned hiker on her TV screen. *Was it you that was whistling in the shadows?*

The Bunian man laughed, and the sound was like music; it made Hamra feel bubbles of joy rise in her own belly and pop in her chest. "Deceit? A fine joke coming from a weretiger! Is not deceit your entire existence, old one? Is it not you that hides your weak human flesh prison behind a cape of power and ferociousness?"

"I hide nothing," Pak Belang said mildly. "I merely exist

as I am. And I am merely accompanying these children on their quest."

"No doubt with your own true intentions safely hidden from their sight." The Bunian man looked directly at Hamra then, and she started; her insides felt most peculiar, as if they were melting. "Wouldn't you rather be somewhere good and safe, little girl?" he said, and his voice was like caramel. "Wouldn't you rather be done with these adventures? The jungle is such an uncomfortable place for a child; in my king's palace, you would be safe, and your belly would be filled with good warm food, all your favorite kinds, and you would find such playthings as you would never find in your own world."

Dimly, Hamra wondered what the low rumble she was hearing was, until she suddenly realized that Pak Belang was growling. "Fight it," he told them, his voice low. "Remember what I told you."

But he's only saying what everyone else has been saying all along, Hamra thought to herself, though the words took their time to amble into her brain. Opah, Jamilah, they all said the same thing. Not to trust the tiger. And this man was here, and he seemed so nice . . .

"What . . ." Ilyas seemed to be struggling to speak, and

Hamra understood why; it felt like she was in the middle of a pink fog, very pleasant and deeply comfortable. "What kind of playthings?" he managed to ask.

The Bunian man grinned, and if Hamra had been able to see, really truly see, she would have noticed the way it seemed to stretch up just a little more than usual at the edges, so that his face contorted in strange ways in the flickering lamp light. "Oh, all kinds of things, my boy," he said, and this time his voice was a purr. "Clockwork wonders that flip and fly, dolls that dance and sing, whole cities of intricately made buildings and castles peopled with the most magical creatures . . . and the food! All manner of the most delicious treats and delicacies, all for you."

Food. What had Atok said about food?

"Don't let them win, Hamra," the tiger said warningly, and something about the way he said it made the flame inside Hamra move, so that the heat of it burned through the pink fog, just enough that she could finally find her tongue. "We are too old for toys," she said groggily, shaking her head slightly. It was starting to ache. *Atok said something about food, Hamra, what was it?* "And we don't take food from strangers. Especially nonhuman strangers."

"That's it," Pak Belang said. "Fight back."

The Bunian man's smile faltered. "Nobody is ever too

old for toys, dearest," he said smoothly. "Not these ones. You must see them. If you would come with me . . ."

"They are going nowhere," Pak Belang said, and his growl was a warning, and an invitation.

There was something struggling to make its way through the fog, a statement that seemed terribly important, if only she could get the words out. . . . "Don't you guys steal children?" she finally asked, and the asking earned an immediate scowl from the Bunian.

"We used to," he said, quickly trading the scowl for a charming smile, though it faltered a little at the edges. "We don't do that anymore. Too much trouble trying to figure out the care and feeding of them. The results were a public relations *nightmare* for us in the jungle, let me tell you. And also because, you know, human rights, of course," he added hastily.

"What do you want with us then?" Hamra said loudly. The flame was burning brighter now, and she was starting to feel less heavy-limbed, more clearheaded. "Why do you want to take us away?"

"It's not you they want," the tiger said. "It's me."

"You?"

"Of course it's him," the Bunian man spat out, all pretense gone. Without the charm and the glamour, all their faces seemed to grow sharper in the dim light, all edges and angles. "What would we want with two useless children like you? We just want him. And not even all of him either, oh no, not that useless rag bag of a body. Just his teeth."

Hamra gulped. "But why?"

"Do you know how much power one can draw from a tiger's teeth, child?" The Bunian laughed, but this time it wasn't the sound of music; it was the sound of nails being dragged across a chalkboard. "Just one of those teeth can grant their wearer all the strength and powers of the were-tiger himself, if one knows the right way to use them. Our king would pay a handsome reward for a necklace of the old one's pretty white chompers. So either get off his back willingly, or we'll make you. Either way is fine with me. Although—" And here, he sighed as he examined his perfect, shiny nails in the firelight. "I do hate to get messy."

"In that case," the tiger said, his voice dangerously even, "I'll try to keep it neat when I destroy you."

With one movement, he reared up on his hind legs so that Hamra and Ilyas slid off his back and onto their butts with a thump.

And then he pounced.

For a moment, all was confusion. There was yelling, and fearsome roars that rang through the trees; there was a flurry of fur and silk, claws, and metal. Hamra stayed where she was, bending close to the ground, clutching Ilyas's hand, breathing hard, trying to get a better view of Pak Belang, trying not to think of those sharp metal spears and what they could do to tender human flesh. Or tiger flesh.

"Should we help him?" Ilyas whispered, his eyes glued to the scene before them, his brow furrowed.

"How?"

"I don't know!" he shot back. "We have to do something! There's six of them and one of him! He's going to get hurt."

"I know," Hamra said, gritting her teeth as she heard the tiger roar in pain. "I know. But we're not fighters. How are we supposed to help him?" She began rummaging helplessly through her backpack. "With this stupid feather duster? With a container of pineapple tarts? With this jar of . . . of . . ."

It was the Langsuir's gift. Hamra's eyes met Ilyas's.

"With this jar of darkness," he breathed.

She nodded. "Right. Come on."

They crept closer to the melee, trying hard to remain unnoticed—though it wasn't that difficult, considering how everyone else was focused quite intently on killing each other. "All right," Hamra whispered as she reached into her bag and pulled out her pile of hijabs, working quickly as she spoke. "Here's the plan. I'm going to tie these together to make a rope, then I'm going to tie one end to you and one end to me. Then, you're going to wait and watch for an opportunity to grab Pak Belang's tail. As soon as you get it, tell me, and then yank on it as hard as you can. Got it?"

Ilyas wiped beads of sweat from his forehead. His chin quivered, and for a moment Hamra thought he was going to protest. But all he said was "Got it."

"Okay." She tied the end of a scarf of rich royal blue to his belt loop, then tied the other end of the rope, a scarf of deep emerald green, to her own, tugging to make sure the knots were secure. "Ready?"

Ilyas nodded.

"Go."

Quietly, Ilyas began to creep around the perimeter of the scuffle. The tiger growled deep in his throat, swiping at the arm of one of the Bunian and ripping through both silk and skin; blood dripped from the open wound, but the man barely seemed to care as he advanced once more. Then there was a yell, and another attacker sprang on Pak Belang's back. In his hand, he held the distinctive, wavy blade of a keris; on his face, he wore the happiest of grins.

And as Hamra watched in growing horror, he plunged the wicked blade straight into the tiger's back.

Hamra screamed, but the sound was drowned out by Pak Belang's terrible roar, one filled with anger and fear and so much pain that the sound brought tears to Hamra's eyes. As he reared back on his hind legs to toss the Bunian off his back, another shoved him hard from the side, so hard that he lost his balance and fell to a crouch—with his tail flailing just within Ilyas's outstretched grasp.

Ilyas looked up at Hamra and nodded grimly. With one quick move, he reached out both his hands to grip the tiger's tail, then pulled hard.

Pak Belang looked around him in surprise, then in a flash of understanding as soon as he saw the jar in Hamra's hands. "Now!" he roared.

There was no time to breathe, no time to think. Hamra grabbed the jar, unscrewed the lid—curse those trembling fingers!—then, quickly as she could, tossed the contents into the middle of the unsuspecting Bunian men.

Immediately, the entire clearing was plunged into complete darkness, every single point of light completely snuffed out. All around her, Hamra could hear the Bunian, their voices tinged with terror: "What happened?" "Where are they?" "I cannot see anything!" "How have they done this?

How have they taken our sight?" "Someone light a torch!"

But it was not for long. Because all at once she felt a tug from the rope at her waist, and then Ilyas's arms scooping her up onto the tiger's back, and then nothing but the breeze caressing her face as they bounded away into the night.

17

IT SEEMED TO Hamra that the tiger ran for hours, even though his breath ran ragged, even though his feet stumbled and they almost fell off his broad back, even though blood still flowed from the wound that she tried feverishly to clamp shut with her fingers, trickling between them and soaking into the sleeves of her T-shirt.

When he finally stopped, he was barely able to let them off his back before he collapsed onto the ground, panting hard, eyes shut. Quickly, Ilyas reached into his backpack and pulled out a T-shirt, which he began to tear into strips.

"It is not that deep," Pak Belang said, eyes still closed. "My powers are such that it shall be healed in an hour or two, with enough rest. Just bind it to stop the bleeding."

"I'm working on it," Ilyas said. Hamra knew that T-shirt

well. It was one of his favorites, soft and worn from so many washes; it was dark gray and printed with all the birds of Langkawi. As she watched, he tore right through the sharp profile of a brahminy kite, and she felt the inexplicable prickling of tears in her throat.

Not now, Hamra, don't be such a baby. She knelt down by Pak Belang's shaggy head and smoothed the fur between his eyes. "Don't worry," she said softly as Ilyas began to wrap the makeshift bandages around the tiger's wound. Pak Belang winced. "You'll be okay."

The tiger's eyes met hers, and among the hurt she saw a spark of familiar regret. "I should have heard them," Pak Belang said hoarsely. "They should not have been able to sneak up on us like that. I should have known they were coming from miles away. I should have protected us better." He closed his eyes again, as if he couldn't bear to think of it anymore.

Hamra swallowed hard. "It wasn't your fault," she told him. "You don't have that ability anymore. You can't beat yourself up about something you can't even do."

Somehow, she didn't think he was convinced. "If I had heard them, we would be safe right now and well on our way. As it is, now we must move as the hunted do—always one step ahead, always one eye behind."

"Hunted?" Ilyas looked up, suddenly alert. "What do you mean?"

"You think the Bunian will leave us alone?" Pak Belang got to his feet and began to pace up and down the clearing. "We have hurt their pride. They may lay low to lick their wounds for a little while, but now more than ever, they will want to harvest my teeth, and probably torture all three of us in the doing, just to prove a point. Bring us back to their king and make us dance to their enchanted rhythm as entertainment for the fine Bunian folk."

Hamra remembered the spark in one of the Bunian's eyes, the malicious glee in the crook of his grin. "We can't let that happen."

The tiger nodded. "Then the only thing we can do is outrun them."

"You have to rest," Ilyas told him firmly. "You've already run for hours. And that wound—you might want us to believe that it's nothing but a scratch, but it's deep enough, and fresh too. It needs some time to heal."

Pak Belang glanced at him, the ghost of a smile playing on his lips. "So you care about me after all, boy?"

Ilyas blushed. "I'm just saying," he mumbled, gathering

up what was left of his T-shirt. "You're no good to us hurt or dead."

"And if we keep going like this, we'll all end up that way, not just you," Hamra said, straightening up. "We need to rest, even if it's just for a couple of hours. The question is, where can we do that and be safe?"

The tiger sighed then, long and deep. "I know a place," he said reluctantly. "I fear I will regret it. But I know a place."

The little hut was so much a part of the jungle that it seemed to Hamra that if she didn't know to look for it, she would have simply walked right past as if it were just another tree or bush. Creepers wrapped themselves around its stilts and grew upward to meet the vines that tumbled from its tin roof, and here and there bloomed the pale purple blossoms of what looked to Hamra to be morning glory. Even though it was as if the jungle had simply decided to swallow the entire structure whole, it was clear that this was someone's home, if only because of the way the windows glowed with warm light. On the roof, a dusky leaf monkey sat silently watching them. The white circles around the dark gray of its eyes made it look like it was wearing glasses, and gave it a rather wise air.

"Who lives here?" Hamra asked, tripping on her laces as they walked toward the house.

Ilyas rolled his eyes. "Will you please just tie your shoes? How are we going to outrun anyone when we have to worry about you tripping all the time?"

She pulled a face at him. "You sound like my dad."

Pak Belang sighed. "Children," he mused quietly, as if to himself, "are terribly exhausting." He directed his gaze to the little monkey on the roof. "Tell your mistress we have come."

The monkey chittered something back, and Pak Belang sighed.

"No, you little rat, I'm not paying you a thing. And if you don't do as I say, I'll bite your tail off."

Hamra wasn't terribly familiar with monkey language, but even she could tell that the choice stream of words the monkey let off as it bounded away would definitely have earned the chili-mouth treatment from Atok.

Then they were left in a silence broken only by the usual murmurings of the jungle around them; the crunch of leaves as animals wandered past, the buzz of insects, the hoots of monkeys and trills of birds. Hamra scratched at a mosquito bite on the back of her hand and wondered who in the world they could possibly be waiting for. Someone who lived in this strange, overgrown house, who even Pak Belang was reluctant to meet.

Then a door slammed open, and a three-legged silhouette appeared, the light streaming from behind it making it hard to figure out who it could be. "Well," a quavery old voice said. "Look what the cat dragged in. Itself, at last." There was a sniff. "Come along inside then, before I change my mind."

The shadow turned and shuffled into the house, and with another soul-deep sigh, Pak Belang walked slowly up the steps and in through the open doorway, beckoning the other two to follow.

Inside, kerosene lamps lit up the corners of the tiny little house, and Hamra could finally see that the three-legged silhouette was a little old woman, bent nearly double; the third leg was actually the stout wooden cane she used to maneuver herself about. Her hair was pure white and straining to free itself of the bun it was pulled back in, and the monkey sat on her shoulder, eyeing them suspiciously. The outfit she wore reminded Hamra of Opah, with the loose, faded top covered in flowers and the batik sarong tied neatly around her waist, but just like with Jamilah, the tapping of the cane reminded her of Atok.

The old woman settled herself onto a rattan rocking chair in the corner, hooking her cane onto the back, and the monkey ran from her shoulder down her arm to settle in the pillowy depths of her lap. Then she turned to the three travelers. "Well?" she said expectantly.

Hamra and Ilyas looked at each other. *What does she want from us?* But Pak Belang merely cleared his throat. "It's been a long time, Nenek."

"She's your *grandmother*?" Ilyas blurted out.

The old woman burst out laughing, her eyes lost in a mass of deep-set lines and wrinkles. "Would you listen to the child?" she hooted at the little gray-furred monkey, who was rolling on his back and chittering in amusement. "His grandmother! No, no, child, he calls me this because that is what I am. I am Nenek Kebayan."

She shouldn't have been surprised—she'd met all manner of fair folk already on this journey, after all—but Hamra still couldn't help the gasp that escaped her, like air pushed out of a balloon.

Nenek's eyes landed on her face, knowing, amused. "You know of me, then?"

"I do, Nenek," she answered.

"And what is it you know?"

"I know that in stories sometimes you are very good,

and very helpful. And sometimes you . . . you . . ." Hamra's throat suddenly felt bone-dry. "Sometimes you aren't," she finished lamely.

"Sometimes I steal children, isn't that what they say?" Nenek grinned a wide grin, one that showed all her yellowing teeth. "Hide them away, crunch on their little bones as snacks like handfuls of keropok? Ha! There's even a song about me, isn't there?" And she leaned back and began to croon:

Cucu cucu tak dapat lari
Nenek tua banyak sakti
Sekarang juga nenek ku cari
Siapa kena dia yang menjadi

Grandchildren, you cannot run from me
Grandmother's magic you must face
I'll find you now, just wait and see
And when I do, you'll take my place.

Hamra and Ilyas had played this game with the other neighborhood kids so often, in the before times, when being with other people was more than just a memory. You sat in a circle, she remembered, and whoever played the role of the grandmother would sit in the middle. They'd be blindfolded, and everyone would sing: *Nenek nenek, si bongkok tiga . . .* And when the song was over, all the other children in the circle would sit, quiet as a grave, hearts pounding, hands clamped over their mouths to keep from giggling, while the "grandmother" would bend over, hunched as in the song, and reach out to touch their faces and hair. If they were certain, absolutely certain, that they knew who it was they were touching, they would say the name, and if they were right, that child would take her place and become the grandmother. And then it would begin all over again.

Cucu cucu tak dapat lari
You cannot run from me

Was this a warning?

Was this a trap?

Had Pak Belang led them to their doom?

From the corner of her eye, Hamra saw Ilyas's hand slowly move toward the side pocket of his backpack, where she knew he kept his whittling knife, the sharp little blade encased in its pouch of soft brown leather.

"That's quite enough of that," Nenek said mildly, and with a wave of her hand, Ilyas's knife slipped from his own hand and fell to the floor, where it burst into a dozen bright blue butterflies that fluttered out of the window and into the night.

The tiger rolled his eyes. "Show-off."

Ilyas's face fell. "My knife!"

"I'll get you another," Nenek said. "When I'm certain you won't try to stab me with it, that is. Now, please stop being so silly, children. I don't mean to hurt you, and certainly don't mean to eat you. What bad manners, to invite you into my home as guests and then turn around and make a meal of you! And I'm certain he wouldn't let me, would you, man-cat?" She grabbed her stick and prodded the tiger where he sat on the floor before her. "Now tell me what it is you're doing here, you feline menace, and why you've dragged two innocent children into your shenanigans."

Pak Belang yawned. "We required a safe place to rest," he said. "The Bunian are making trouble again."

"Oh, those fools." Nenek huffed as she hung her cane back in its place. "Never did know when to sit back and be quiet. What is it they want with you?"

"My teeth."

She clicked her tongue. "That'll be that king of theirs again, power hungry as ever."

"Not to interrupt," Hamra said. "And the king definitely doesn't seem to be a very nice person, but . . . what kind of terrible things would he do with the teeth, exactly?"

Nenek paused as she considered this question. "Those of us of magical blood in these parts, well, we care for the jungle, you see? Our relationship with nature is one of deep love. What we take, we give back in equal measure; we draw from its deep wells of old, old magic, take nourishment from its springs and boughs. But we also protect it." She sniffed. "Not that you humans make it easy. But we do our best. The Bunian, on the other hand . . . they're takers. Greedy as children, if you'll excuse the expression. They will leech magic from every source there is, sucking it all out and leaving only dried husks and ash in their wake, and all while the king expands his territories the way he's always threatened to. Felled trees, animals sacrificed to their rituals . . . The jungle would not survive their reign, and neither would any of us who dwell in it." She leveled a steady gaze at Pak Belang. "See that they don't get their hands on those teeth of yours, won't you?"

"I'm trying my best," he growled. "But I need rest to make sure of it. As do they." He nodded toward Hamra and Ilyas.

"He's hurt," Hamra supplied timidly. It was hard not to feel intimidated in Nenek's presence. "Do you . . . do you think you could help him?"

Nenek's eyes crinkled up again as she smiled, and Hamra decided she quite liked the old woman, even if she was somehow still terrified of her at the same time. "The old fleabag will heal just fine with a little time. But if he will let me, I can speed that process along," she said.

"I'm fine," said the tiger from the floor, and then yelped when it earned him another sharp prod with the stick.

"You were always a terrible liar." She turned to the monkey. "Bring me my ointments." It ran off and quickly returned with a wicker basket full of little glass jars that rattled and clinked as they moved against each other. "Ah, good, good. Let me see . . ." Nenek pored over the jars like they were treasures, a pleased smile on her face. "No, no, not that one . . . oh definitely not, that will just burn . . . this one might make all his fur fall off . . . this'll add a curl to those fine whiskers . . . ah!" She pulled out a perfectly round jar of clear glass, filled with a pale green ointment. When she unscrewed the lid, the entire room smelled of pandan and ginger, morning dew and daydreams. "That'll do," she said, with a firm nod. She handed the basket back to the monkey, who scampered off with it (though not before sticking its tongue out at a startled Ilyas).

Then she turned her attention to Pak Belang and raised an eyebrow. "Who fixed you up?" she asked.

Ilyas swallowed audibly. "That was me," he said. "I'm sorry, it was really all I had, I . . ." and he trailed off as she waved his words away.

"You did a wonderful job," she said firmly. "Magnificent. Now help me take it off so we can get some of this on him, though he probably doesn't even deserve the help, truth be told . . ."

Ilyas and Hamra knelt on either side of Pak Belang and began to remove the blood-soaked strips of cloth from his body. It was hard not to balk at the sight of the wound itself, a jagged wet gash the length of Hamra's palm.

"Not to worry," Nenek said. "We'll clean that right up." The monkey brought her a bowl of clear water—"from the stream that runs behind the house," she explained—and she began gently wiping away the worst of the blood with a washcloth soaked in its cool depths. "Stop complaining lah," she said, prodding Pak Belang with her toe when he winced and moaned at her ministrations. "Sikit tu pun nak sakit! They just don't make weretigers like they used to back in my day." She straightened up and gave him a light smack on the side. "There! That's better. Should be all healed by morning."

Then she turned to the two children. "Now you two, you had better—" and then abruptly stopped as Hamra suddenly yawned a yawn so large she thought she might split her in two. "I was going to ask you some questions," Nenek said, "but clearly, you need some sleep."

Hamra quickly stifled another yawn. "I'm so sorry, I'm really not that tired, we can talk if you like . . ."

But Nenek was adamant. "Nonsense. Go and wash up in the stream, both of you, then come in here and get some rest."

The shallow waters of the stream felt like bliss against Hamra's skin, and she sighed with relief as she and Ilyas cleaned off the worst of the day's grime. "Do you think we can trust her?" Ilyas asked her, unhooking his glasses from his T-shirt where he'd put them for safekeeping and setting them back on his face.

"I'm not sure we have much of a choice," Hamra told him. "But also, weirdly enough . . . yes." She paused. "How do you think they know each other?"

"I have no idea." Ilyas grinned. "But I do love watching her push him around."

Inside, Pak Belang was already curled up in a corner, snoring gently.

"Rude," Nenek muttered to herself. "So rude. Ingat orang lain tak payah tidur ke? Oy, you! Quiet down over there!" But the tiger slept on, completely oblivious to her complaints.

Nenek sniffed. "Typical. Right, to bed with you. It's far too late for children to be up and about. I'm sorry there's naught but a bit of tikar for you to sleep on, it's not the hotel Shangri-La-Dee-Da over here, you know."

"That's all right," Hamra said as Ilyas settled himself on the thin mat woven from screwpine leaves and tried to get comfortable. "Nenek, I know the rules in this world mean that we've got to trade you something for being able to stay here, and well, I just wanted to know what I should be ready to give up, or what kind of payment you'd like—"

"Hush, child," Nenek huffed. "No need for that. The old tiger did me a favor once, long ago, and I am merely repaying my debts. Think no more of it."

"Oh." Hamra was silent for a moment. "He keeps talking about the bad things he's done. What . . . what exactly were they?"

"Hmm." Nenek stared at her for a moment. "Not sure you really want to know."

"I do."

"Wounded men who seek power rarely do it for the best of reasons," Nenek said, massaging her calloused feet. "He was no different. He sought revenge and called that purpose. He's terrorized villages and stolen livestock, he's hurt humans and fae alike who have gotten in his way. At his worst, when he forgot who he was and slipped further and further into his tiger self, he hunted and killed a man, a lost hiker, as if he were nothing but prey. After that we called him man-eater and stayed away in fear." Nenek began to rock back and forth, the little chair creaking with every movement. "I think the killing was the undoing of him. Somehow, somewhere deep down, he recognized how lost he truly was, and he hid himself deep in the jungle as though he—we—would forget. But memories seep into the jungle's bones; they burrow their way deep beneath the earth and get absorbed by our roots. We don't forget around here."

Hamra stared out of the window, into the inky darkness of the jungle beyond. She wasn't sure what to think, how to feel. She was in the presence of a murderer—which made her fears for her grandmother all the more real—and yet somehow she still wanted to help him. *Can people change? Can tigers?*

"Does it change anything?" Nenek was watching her

intently. "Now that you know, will you go home? The jungle holds many dangers for children so young, as you've already seen for yourself."

Hamra thought of Opah, whirling around the kitchen, stirring this and chopping that, smiling and warm and happy. "No," she said. "It doesn't change anything at all."

"And why not?"

"Because." She paused to find the right words, and Nenek waited patiently. "Because he made me a deal. And I need to keep my end of the bargain so that he will keep his."

Nenek leaned forward, sharp eyes never leaving Hamra's face. "Is it so important that you see this deal fulfilled?"

"It is. He said he can get my grandmother back to the way she was, and that's worth everything." It seemed to her as if Nenek's face changed just then, but Hamra couldn't be sure it wasn't just the shadows that flickered across her face. And as she was trying to figure it out, she yawned suddenly, then clapped her hands over her mouth. "Sorry, I don't mean to be rude. I just . . ."

"Not at all, Little Red," Nenek said kindly. "Sleep. You need it."

"Do you think we'll be . . . do you think they'll . . ."

"Don't you fret about those nasty Bunian; they know better than to come looking for trouble on my turf. Now

sleep, and in the morning we will talk as long as we must."
As Hamra lay down between Ilyas and Pak Belang, Nenek
sat back and began gently stroking the monkey who had
returned to its place on her lap as she rocked. And as Hamra's eyes grew heavier and heavier, she heard the old woman
crooning tunelessly, so softly it was almost as if she were
singing for herself alone:

Cucu cucu tak dapat lari
Nenek tua banyak sakti . . .

18

"YOU HAVE TO tell her."

Hamra stirred in her sleep, frowning. *Please stop talking.*

"Why would I do that?"

That was the tiger's voice, she knew, low and rough. But who was he talking to?

"It's lies you've fed her, you felonious feline!" Nenek Kebayan, Hamra realized, eyes still shut tight and barely sealed with leftover sleep. "Your quest is built on naught but empty promises, and without trust your whole journey amounts to nothing!"

Your journey. *Our journey?* Hamra opened her eyes and struggled to a sitting position, hair poking out of the hijab that sat crooked on her head. Pale early morning sunlight was streaming through the windows, but it was hard to see it thanks to the tendrils of sweet smoke that curled through the air.

She struggled to a sitting position, coughing as the smoke hit her lungs. "What is this?" she said aloud.

"Protection," a voice said, and she twisted around to see Nenek sitting exactly as she had been when Hamra fell asleep, for all the world as if she'd never moved at all. The smoke, Hamra now realized, was wafting lazily from five brass pots that had been placed in a circle around the sleepers on the floor. She scooted over to the nearest one to take a look. Inside were the charred remains of two or three blackened lumps.

Hamra glanced at Nenek, one eyebrow raised. "What are they?" she asked.

"Kemenyan," Nenek said, still rocking slowly. "I burn some when I have a great need."

"And what was your need last night?"

Nenek's face creased into one of those wide, wide smiles. "To keep you all hidden from sibuk, prying eyes."

Hamra turned her gaze to Pak Belang, who sat on his haunches by Nenek's chair, staring out of the window. "What were you talking about?"

"Hmm?"

"Our quest being built on nothing but empty promises.

That's what she said," Hamra said, gesturing to Nenek, who had stopped rocking and now sat perfectly still, save for her eyes, which flicked from Hamra to Pak Belang and back again.

Hamra's throat felt incredibly, fearfully dry. "What was she talking about?" she asked again, and her voice sounded like it was being dragged over sandpaper.

Pak Belang just looked at her for a long moment, until Nenek leaned over to poke him in the side with her cane. "Go on then, tell her."

He cleared his throat. "I may have . . . allowed you to believe I was capable of more than I really am," he said carefully.

"He lied to you," Nenek said baldly, earning a glare from Pak Belang. "He can't bring your grandmother back. There's lost, and then there's *lost*. The way she's gone, there's no path home. All he can give you is jambu and niceties, moments in time, and those'll get shorter and shorter, until there'll be none left, no matter how many pieces of fruit you shove in her mouth."

Hamra whipped her head around to stare at the tiger, open-mouthed. She could feel her eyes filling with tears, and she hated herself for it. "Tell me that isn't true."

Still, the tiger would not meet her gaze. "I said I would

bring her back. I did not promise forever."

"You made me believe it!" Shock and anger brought Hamra to her feet, and Ilyas sat up, rubbing his bleary eyes.

"What's going—" He stopped short at the sight of Hamra's face, hands clenched in trembling fists by her side. "Hamra? You okay?"

It took her a long time to reply. "No."

Then she walked out of the little house in the jungle, slamming the door behind her.

They left her alone, and the solitude was a small mercy to her aching head, the rivulets of fire that ran through her veins, threads of hurt and rage and sadness all woven together. She sat and stared at the stream that made its merry way past the back of Nenek's house, and let the early morning jungle fog cool her hot cheeks.

I want to go home, she thought, and felt an ache in her chest.

All this time, she'd kept her head down, gritting her teeth through the pain and the challenges, the endless nightmares and the fear, just for the promise of getting her grandmother back. Truly back. And to learn it was all a lie made her feel like she was drowning.

I'm going home, she thought sullenly, dragging a twig

through the dirt, scratching patterns in the earth. *I'm going home, and he can stay a tiger for all I care. He bound me to a promise that he has no way of keeping, and that can't possibly count. I'm going home, I'm going home, I'm going home.*

And the more she thought it, the more it became a mantra, a rhythm that pounded in time with her own heartbeat.

Finally, Hamra gathered up the energy to get back onto her feet. *I'm going to tell them*, she thought. "And I don't care what they say," she added belligerently aloud, as if anyone was listening.

As it turned out, someone was.

"Bravo, little sissster," said a low, sweetly sibilant voice from the other side of the stream. "Nor should you. The opinionsss of othersss can be ssso inconvenient."

There was a rustling, and as she watched the shadows gathered themselves into a sinuous mass that flowed gracefully through the underbrush until it reared itself up and Hamra found herself face-to-face with the largest cobra she'd ever seen in her life. Its girth was easily the same size as one of her thighs, and with just half its body raised as it was, it was already halfway to the treetops.

Hamra immediately felt herself break out into a cold sweat. *Cobras eat small animals*, she remembered her father telling her, *and they usually only bite if they feel threatened. Just stay calm and keep a wide berth.* But it was hard to stay calm when the cobra looked like it could very well eat her whole and had slithered right up to her. She remembered her vision in the Langsuir's cave, and shuddered. *I hate snakes.*

"What'sss the matter?" The cobra regarded her with its head cocked to one side, amusement glinting in its eyes. "Did you not know that it'sss rude to ssstare?"

"I'm sorry," Hamra said quickly, surreptitiously trying to wipe her clammy hands off on her jeans. Even the smallest snakes freaked her out; it didn't seem like a smart idea to annoy a snake this large.

"That'sss quite all right. I am after all quite a magnificent sssspecimen." The cobra beamed and swayed, letting the morning light that filtered through the trees catch its gleaming brown-black scales. "I do not blame you for being captivated. But though I sssay ssso with great reluctance— enough about me." Its mouth curved upward in a wicked smile. "It'sss you I have come to sssee. Or rather, your travel companion."

"My what?"

"She means me," Pak Belang rumbled from behind her, and Hamra nearly jumped out of her skin.

"There you are!" The cobra's eyes lit up. "That makesss my job much easssier. I wasss going to sssnatch up the girl and have you come looking for her—" At this, Hamra let out an involuntary squeak and moved just a little closer to Pak Belang, forgetting for a moment how mad she was at him. "But thisss isss far more convenient. Come along and be captured, there'sss a dear."

The tiger narrowed his eyes at her. "What do you want with me, you worm?"

"Now that hurtsss." The cobra wore an injured expression. "Can I be blamed for trying to earn a little extra money? The Bunian king hasss made hisss demands, and even a sssnake musssst make a living in thisss dreadful economy."

Hamra gaped. "He's done what now?"

"Oh, yesss." The cobra wriggled, clearly enjoying the spotlight. "Word hasss it that he'sss sssimply desssperate for anyone to bring in the man-tiger, and the one who doesss will be rewarded quite handsssomely."

Hamra wrinkled her brow. "What does a snake want with money?"

The tiger sighed wearily. "She is not simply a snake."

"Quite right." The cobra smiled again, and as Hamra watched its body shimmered and shifted and moved until the thing standing before her was not a snake at all, but a woman with dark hair tied neatly back in a low ponytail, wearing a loose tunic and pants in shades of brown and black, the exact color of a cobra's scales.

Hamra stared, wide-eyed. "She's like *you*."

The cobra-woman snorted. "Please, enough with the insults. I, at least, am smart enough not to *forget how to change back*."

"ENOUGH." Pak Belang's roar was so loud it seemed that the ground shook, and in its wake the jungle was terrifyingly silent and still. "Get away, snake, or I shall tear you apart with my teeth. You are no match for me, whatever your form, and you know it."

The woman across the riverbank stood and looked at them for a while, her arms crossed as she contemplated his words. Then she smiled, and Hamra noted the sharp points of snake fangs in her mouth. "I shall leave you to your business, weretiger," she said, still lingering ever so slightly on every *s* as if she couldn't help herself. "But not out of fear. This is the most fun there's been in the jungle in a century. Why, the last time I was so entertained was when that mousedeer convinced everyone he was an adviser to Solomon himself."

"You're . . . you're just letting us go?"

"For now." The werecobra, which is what she was, shrugged gracefully. "Money is nice, but once you live a few hundred years, you realize how easy it is to get bored. Human lives are so repetitive. I may change my mind later on, but as of now I shall look forward to seeing the kind of havoc you two wreak on this place." She licked those red lips as if she relished the prospect. "You may want to watch your back, however. I am hardly the only creature on the hunt for your little party, and you'll see that I'm by far the most merciful. And the prettiest, of course," she added as an afterthought. As Hamra and Pak Belang watched, the woman shifted and morphed until once again the cobra was coiled on the ground. "Sssalutationsss, Little Red," it said, before wending its way through the grass and into the shadows once more.

Hamra licked her suddenly dry lips. "I can't go back," she said, the realization crashing over her. "I can't do anything but keep going, because otherwise I'll be hunted. I'll bring danger into my own home. Is that it?"

It took the tiger a long time to reply, and when he did, it was so softly that Hamra barely heard him. "Yes."

She gulped hard, trying to swallow her tears, the lump that had suddenly lodged itself in her throat. "Fine. Let's go."

Nenek's house smelled like curry, warm and inviting and familiar, and though Hamra felt chilled all the way to her bones, her stomach still rumbled as soon as the aroma hit her nose.

"It seems you have caused quite a commotion, Little Red," Nenek said briskly as she stood at the stove stirring the contents of an earthenware pot. The sight of the white-haired figure in the kitchen reminded Hamra of Opah, and she had to take deep, deep breaths to keep herself together. *Keep calm, Hamra, keep calm.*

"I didn't mean to," she said.

"Didn't mean to what?" Ilyas looked up from the table where he'd been put to work peeling potatoes, suddenly alert.

"What are you doing?" she asked him.

"What does it look like?" Ilyas gestured to the potato pile before him. "Remember the rules? If you take something, you have to give something back? I figured it also works the other way around, so I'm doing some chores for Nenek and in return she'll give us some things that can help us with our tasks. I've swept the house and cleaned the oven, and now I'm doing . . . this."

"Oh." Hamra blinked. "That's . . . really smart."

"It is," Nenek said from the stove, her back still to them, and they jumped.

"I didn't realize she could hear me," Ilyas whispered.

"I can," Nenek said, and he sighed. "But your friend is correct. It was smart to strike this bargain. You have learned much in your travels."

Ilyas blushed and ducked his head. "Paiseh. It's no big deal. Now what's she talking about? What commotion? What happened?"

"We're being hunted," Hamra said shortly. "The Bunian king has apparently promised a reward to whoever manages to catch us and bring us to him."

"Oh." Hamra watched as Ilyas's Adam's apple worked its way up and down furiously. "What do we . . . do about that?"

"There is nothing that can be done," Pak Belang said from behind Hamra. "Nothing except to keep moving as fast as we can, and to complete our quest before anyone can catch us."

"Stop calling it *our* quest," Hamra snapped. "It's yours. You just brought us along for the ride."

"Nevertheless," the tiger said evenly. "Each of our fates is now tied to the outcome of our journey. We must go on. We have no choice."

I had a choice, Hamra though bitterly. *I was robbed of it.* She looked at Ilyas, his hair sticking up here and there from his night of sleep, working so hard to ease the path ahead, and she felt a sharp pang in her stomach. *And I dragged Ilyas into it too, just because I wanted something I should have known was impossible.* Guilt nibbled at the edge of her nerves, and suddenly she wasn't hungry anymore.

"So what do we do now?" Ilyas asked, his head whipping back and forth as he looked first at Hamra, then at Pak Belang, then back again. "What's the next move?"

Hamra sat next to him at the table. "We have to find the praying man."

"Ask the praying man why he prays," Ilyas murmured, wiping his hands off on a rag and grabbing his notebook. His nose scrunched as he flipped through its pages. "Where do you think we can find the praying man? A mosque? A shrine?"

"Do you know how many of those there are on Langkawi? That's going to be impossible to narrow down," Hamra said, scooching closer so she could get a better view of his notes. "Also, your writing is terrible. All chicken scratches, look, how am I supposed to read that?"

Ilyas snatched the book away and scowled. "Sorry, I

didn't know I was being graded—OW!"

"OW!" echoed Hamra indignantly, as they both received twin raps on the head courtesy of Nenek's cane.

"I like a nice, *quiet* breakfast," she said, setting a steaming bowl of curry filled with chunks of chicken and potatoes on the table, along with a plate of roti jala. "So quit your bickering and eat and drink your fill. Then get out of here and leave an old lady in peace."

Hamra and Ilyas exchanged glances. "The thing is," Hamra said, trying very hard to choose her words as carefully as possible, "we've already had one encounter with magic food, and so if you don't mind, maybe we'll just skip breakfast."

Nenek snorted. "Children oughtn't skip their meals, particularly not breakfast and especially not if they're about to go questing. I give you my word that no harm shall befall you should you eat my food, and don't go questioning my word either, or I shall truly be angry." She poured herself a cup of tea and sat back down, swearing as she spilled some down the front of her baju kurung. "Anyway, if it's a praying man you seek, there's only one worth speaking of, and it's that ol' pile of rocks."

The tiger paused in between licking his paws and face clean. "Ah, him. I'd forgotten about him."

"Who's him?" Ilyas asked, grabbing a cup of tea and then yelping when he realized how hot it was.

"Him that's on Pulau Tuba," Nenek replied, slurping her tea noisily.

Hamra paused. Oh.

Oh.

"Gua Wang Buluh," she breathed.

Nenek nodded and chuckled. "It's to the caves you go, Little Red," she said softly.

19

BEFORE THEY LEFT, Nenek gave them three gifts, payment for Ilyas's hard work. To Ilyas, she gave a bottle of water from her stream. "You'll know when you need it," she told him. "And mind you don't waste it."

To Pak Belang, she gave a small vial of pale violet liquid that, when ingested, would hide them from prying eyes for at least five hours. "Prying *human* eyes," she'd been sure to mention. "There's not much I can do about them nonhuman ones, so don't dawdle."

To Hamra, she gave a lump of pale yellow kemenyan. "Burn it," she said, "when there is somewhere you need to be. Remember, the intent is the key." Hamra didn't understand what that meant at all, but she knew better than to ask for explanations.

Before they set off, Ilyas drew Hamra aside. "Are you

okay?" he asked softly. "You look . . . different."

Hamra frowned. "Different how?"

"I don't know." Ilyas shuffled his feet. "It just feels like something's changed. Are you sure you're okay?"

"I'm fine." Hamra shrugged. "Let's go." And it was true. Hamra didn't feel any different. She felt as she had since this morning. She felt angry.

But she walked with her companions through the jungle anyway, back to where her father's boat waited for them, with a head full of restless thoughts and a heart full of restless flame.

They'd left the boat docked at the jetty, the path to which was now blocked by police officers, patrolling for rule-breakers.

"It's time." Pak Belang took the vial from where it hung on a leather cord around his neck and tugged hard so the cord snapped, taking care not to break the glass between his strong teeth.

"Won't they just get confused when a boat with no driver just, like . . . drives off?" Hamra asked. "Won't that just give us away?"

"By the time they get over their fear and confusion and figure out what to do, we will be long gone." Pak Belang offered the vial to Hamra, who gingerly unscrewed the cap. As soon as it was opened, a small puff of purple-tinged smoke wafted into the air.

"It smells like fart," Ilyas observed quietly.

"You know what they say about beggars and choosers." She swirled the purple liquid in its glass prison, watching the way the colors glinted oddly in the light. "Here goes nothing."

"Three sips," the tiger said. "No more than that, or there won't be enough for all of us."

Hamra nodded, held her nose, and brought the liquid to her lips. She tried her best not to taste it as it went down, but the feeling of it as it slid down her throat was enough to make her gag; it was viscous, like raw eggs, and hot enough to burn a trail as it went, though it was cool to the touch.

Ilyas, watching her closely, sighed. "That bad, huh."

She handed him the vial. "Enjoy."

Invisible as they were, it only took a few minutes to sneak past the milling police officers and make their way to the boat. Hamra hopped in and took her usual place behind the wheel, ready to go.

Except she suddenly realized she had no idea where to go.

The realization was a punch in the gut. Hamra knew

these islands like the back of her hand, had explored them over and over again from when she was a baby. Langkawi was in her blood. Yet no matter how hard she tried, how much she racked her brain to think of what she needed to do to get to Tuba Island, when she tried to picture it, her mind simply went blank, as if someone had plucked it right out of her.

Which, she realized, someone had.

The Langsuir.

"Well?" Pak Belang said, irritable from the bobbing of the boat on the water. "Are we not going to move?"

"In a minute," she snapped, trying to quell the wave of panic rising from her belly. *How can I not remember? What do I do now?*

And then: *Is this how Opah always feels?*

"Hamra?"

She snapped back to attention to see Ilyas staring at her, concern written all over his face. "Are you . . . okay?" he asked, and it was only then that she realized her hands were gripping so hard to the steering wheel of the boat that pain was radiating through her fingers.

"I . . . I don't . . ."

"What is it?" The tiger was looking intently at her now. "Tell us."

"I don't remember the way," she whispered.

Ilyas's face was a mask of shock. "How can that be possible? We've made this trip so many times . . ."

Hamra didn't say anything. She couldn't. She felt perilously close to tears.

"So this is the memory the Langsuir took from you," Pak Belang said, and his voice was incredibly sad.

"She said she'd take one that wasn't important!"

"The thing about memories," the tiger said, "is that you never know which of them are important until you really, truly need them."

Ilyas touched her gently on the arm. "Hey. It's okay. I'll tell you which way to go. I'll sit right here beside you and guide you the whole time. Like a human GPS." He smiled at her, and she was somehow both endlessly grateful for his kindness and resentful of his willingness to swoop in and save the day.

"Okay," she said, not trusting herself to say more.

"Okay then. Let's go."

And so over the water they sped, heading toward Pulau Tuba, leaving yelling, gaping police officers in their wake on the dock, the flame inside her burning with shades of regret and anger and embarrassment and frustration all at once.

"So what exactly is the praying man?" Ilyas shouted over the noise of the motor.

"It's what they call a rock formation," Hamra yelled over her shoulder. "It's inside a cave called Gua Wang Buluh."

"We're going to ask for help from a pile of rocks?" He stared at her in disbelief. "Are you sure about this?"

"We've done all sorts of weird things already, Ilyas." She clung to her hijab, trying to make sure it didn't fly off her head. "I guess we'll see when we get there whether we were right or wrong."

The tiger said nothing. He'd said very little since they left Nenek's house; though the gash on his back had mostly healed, he still walked gingerly, as though it pained him. He just lay on the floor of the boat, eyes closed tight, wincing whenever they swayed a little harder than he liked. Once or twice, Hamra thought to feel sorry for him; instead, she hardened her heart and nurtured the flames within a little bit more. *You cannot trust him. Just tolerate him until this is all over and you can walk away safe and sound.*

Instead she stared ahead at the looming shape of Pulau Tuba before them and watched, and wondered.

Their adventure on Tuba started with an argument.

Pak Belang wanted them to ride on his back, but Hamra

refused. What she said *aloud* was that this would only hurt him more, no matter how much he insisted that he was fine. What they all knew she *meant* was that she absolutely would not touch him with a ten-foot pole right now. Not after his lies. The truth of what he'd done. The fact that he was a *murderer* and a *liar*.

Hamra, on the other hand, wanted to steal . . . er, borrow, that is . . . one of the many unused motorcycles lined up near the docks waiting for tourists who would not come. But Ilyas was against this. "We're not thieves!" he protested.

"It would be faster upon my back," Pak Belang pointed out again.

"Two against one," Ilyas said smugly, and Hamra felt her control slipping even more. *Am I not who the story was intended for? Was Ilyas meant to be the hero? Can I trust my mind to remember the things I need it to when the time comes?* It was hard to describe how strange and sick it made her feel, the sensation of losing what had once come so naturally.

There was no time to think any further. "Come on," Pak Belang growled, and she climbed up upon his back behind Ilyas, gripping tightly to his fur and trying hard to forget the forgetting.

The cave didn't make itself easy to find.

Wang Buluh was one of the two caves that the villagers of Pulau Tuba escaped to when the Japanese military arrived to plunder their homes, all those years ago. It was, by design, not meant to be easy. Even Hamra, who knew the islands by heart from years and years of following her father on his tours, almost missed the narrow, leaf-strewn road that took them through the towering trees of the rubber plantation and the entrance to what the sign called the Permanent Forest Reserve, and in the missing, almost spiraled into panic—*Did I forget that too? Is it lost to me too?*—until there it was, as it had always been. It was a beautiful, sunlit day, and a pleasant ride through the green, Hamra thought to herself, if you could only make yourself forget what awaited you at the end of it. Then she remembered what it was to forget and caught herself. *No, Hamra. You never want to forget again, not a single thing, not even if it's something bad.*

They walked past the roaming police officers whose eyes slid right over them, thanks to Nenek's potion; pushed past the red-and-white tape crisscrossing the path and the lone piece of A4 paper bearing the words CLOSED DUE TO COVID-19; and began walking up the cement steps until they came upon the wooden walkway that led through the jungle. With every step, Hamra thought to herself: *What comes next? Turn left? Turn right? What color is the railing up ahead? Where's that tree where you saw the hornbill that one time?* It was like a constant test of her own memory, a reminder that she still knew who she was.

It was exhausting.

"What's that sound?" Ilyas whispered.

All they could hear, wafting through the air, was buzzing. The walkway took them through the jungle, between jutting rock formations and steep limestone cliffs, and from those rocks and cliffs, Hamra noticed as she stared all around them, hung dozens and dozens of beehives.

The bees hummed, and the air hummed along with them.

"The Valley of the Bees," said Hamra grimly. It wasn't normally this bad, but then normally you'd have people trekking up and down this path all day long, and now that you didn't, perhaps the bees had figured it was the ideal place to turn into their very own neighborhood. "It's fine," she said, seeing the anxiety blossoming on Ilyas's face. She was almost relieved; it felt good to be the one knowing things again. "Bees won't bother you if you don't bother them. Just keep walking, and don't swat at them. Keep your arms to yourself and you won't get them mad."

But apparently, the bees had other ideas. They didn't come all at once, but in little swarms of five or ten at a time, and at first they did nothing but hover around the three travelers, as if they were merely curious about these intruders.

And no sooner had they gone ten steps along the walkway when Ilyas's voice made Hamra stop in her tracks.

"Hamra."

Hamra turned and saw him, completely frozen, as first one bee, then two, then five, began crawling on his arms and face. "Ilyas, don't—"

But it was too late. Ilyas reached a hand out and swatted desperately at a bee that had begun making its way into his left nostril.

Immediately, the buzzing stopped.

The silence was so loud it felt like it had swallowed them all whole, and Hamra's heart was beating so fast she was sure it was about to pop out of her chest.

When the buzzing began again, it was deafening. The bees began to pour out of their hives, so many of them that they blotted out the sunlight, and the jungle grew dark in their shadow. They hovered in front of Hamra and her companions, creating a thick wall between them and the rest of the path, blocking the way to Wang Buluh. Pak Belang growled low in his throat, hackles raised.

Ilyas's face was a mask of horrified embarrassment, and something inside Hamra pinged faintly with satisfaction. *You see? You're not useless. He still needs you.* "Sorry," he whispered. "I'm sorry. I didn't think—"

"No, you didn't," Pak Belang cut him off, his words low and vicious, and Ilyas subsided without a word.

"What do we do now?" Hamra could feel hopelessness begin to unspool in her chest, thick and black and completely smothering the fire that usually burned bright within her. Before her, the wall of bees quivered with the beating of hundreds of tiny wings.

"Think," the tiger said firmly. "Think. How do bees perceive the world around them?"

Hamra fought her rising despair and racked her brain for all she knew about bees. "Smell," she said. "They see the world through smell, the way lots of insects do." The humming of the bees was making her itch; she longed to take off her hijab and scratch her scalp.

"Correct. So it stands to reason that if we were to mask our smells with something strong enough—"

"OH!" Hamra said suddenly. "Oh!" And she slid her backpack off her shoulders, bent down, and began hurriedly rummaging around in its depths. Out came two or three T-shirts, a little pouch that rattled as it landed on the dirt, a little pot of Tiger Balm ointment that went rolling off into the shadows, a box of Salonpas . . .

"Why," Pak Belang said drily, "are you unpacking here, in the middle of the jungle, faced by what can only be described as a fearsome quantity of bees?"

"Because I was looking for this," Hamra said breathlessly, as she emerged from the bottom of the backpack brandishing a clear brown spray bottle, small enough to fit comfortably in the palm of her hand.

"What is that?" Ilyas asked, wrinkling his nose.

"Eucalyptus oil!" she said jubilantly. "Already diluted so it's safe for the skin. I always keep some with me when I go into the jungle because it's good for keeping away mosquitoes and other bugs, because it . . ."

"Because it smells so strong!" Ilyas finished for her.

"Right! In fact . . ." She reached over to grab the Tiger Balm where it had rolled off. "Even Tiger Balm could probably work. Maybe both together? We'd smell so strong, no bee would possibly want to be near us." She thought about it for a second. "Or people either, come to think of it . . ."

"It will have to be both," the tiger said. "There is not nearly enough for the two of you."

"And you," Hamra said.

Pak Belang shrugged. "I have no need for your repellents," he said. "What are a few bee stings to a weretiger?"

Hamra thought of the barely healed gash in his back, the way he winced when he thought nobody was looking. *Pain*, she thought to herself. *You will be in pain*. But she said nothing. If she were honest with herself, part of her thought: *Maybe pain is what he deserves*.

"Well?" Ilyas glanced at her. "Should we do this?"

Hamra glanced once more at the buzzing wall before them. Then she nodded.

"Let's go."

Fifteen minutes later, Hamra felt as thoroughly uncomfortable as she'd ever felt on this entire journey so far. Working as quickly as they could, she and Ilyas had taken turns spraying themselves as much as possible with the eucalyptus spray, from top to bottom—Hamra made sure they did this next to Pak Belang, so he could catch any leftovers. Then they dipped into the little jar of Tiger Balm, taking out great big glops of the white ointment and covering as much of themselves as they could. The smell of camphor and menthol, cassia and clove, reminded Hamra of so many things: Opah gently rubbing a pea-size scoop on Hamra's belly, trying to help her soothe a tummy ache; Atok massaging it into Ayah's shoulders after a long day herding tourists around the island; Ibu adding the smallest touch of it to her temples, trying to ward off a headache. The Tiger Balm made her skin tingle; when she was little, she thought it was called that because of the way it nipped her skin, like tiny little tiger teeth.

The thought of teeth made her remember both the Bunian that were hunting them and the Langsuir's nightmare. *My, what big teeth you have.* Neither one was particularly fun to think about, and in the afternoon heat, she shivered.

Around them, the buzzing of the bees grew louder, and the wall began to quiver even harder, as if the smell was enough to set them out of sorts.

As a final touch, Ilyas pulled on a long-sleeved hoodie over his T-shirt, Hamra shoved her arms into the lone cardigan that she'd packed—thicker layers would be harder for bees to get through, she reasoned—and then they both reached into their pockets for their face masks. When they were done, and with Ilyas's hood on, you could see nothing of them but their eyes.

In all that time, the tiger paced restlessly around them, sneezing every once in a while from the smells. "You missed a spot," he would say, or "Do you have nothing thicker than this?" (To which Hamra retorted, "This is Malaysia, if I had something thicker than this, I would die of heat-stroke").

"It's almost as if you're worried about us," Ilyas said, adjusting his hood. Hamra could see rivulets of sweat dripping down his forehead beneath the thick material. "Like you care or something."

"I am worried about *me*," Pak Belang bit back. "If you die, who is to aid me in my quest? Your corpses would be of little use to me but as dinner, and a paltry one at that."

Ilyas bristled. "I'll have you know that I would make an excellent dinner!" He paused. "Wait, I didn't . . . that didn't come out right . . ."

Hamra rubbed her aching head. Was this what it was like to have kids? *When I get home*, Hamra thought to herself, *I am going to be a lot nicer to my mother*. "Once again, I am asking you both to please be quiet and just follow me."

She turned to face the wall of bees. It seemed to her as if the buzzing quieted, as if they were all holding their breath, waiting to see what would happen, what she would do.

Hamra took as deep a breath as she could through her mask.

Then she began to walk.

Before her the bees parted like water before a boat's prow. They didn't fly away entirely, but hovered inches away from her body, buzzing angrily, as if she was surrounded by an invisible force field. *Which I guess I am*, Hamra thought. *A force field of eucalyptus and Tiger Balm.* Somewhere in the back of her mind, she wanted to laugh at the idea of being protected by a tiger in more ways than one.

She glanced behind her. Through the thicket of bees she could just about make out Ilyas, who gave her a quick thumbs-up; beyond him, she could see Pak Belang not at all. So maybe she was only protected by one tiger.

All right, Hamra. Time to keep moving.

And so they kept on going, step by step, for what seemed like hours, carefully stepping over loose floorboards as they went. Eventually, the wooden walkway with its white fencing gave way to a path of rough-hewn stone steps, which made the journey even trickier; some of these were slick with moss, and there was no fence, which meant nothing between Hamra and the sizable cliff drops just inches away from her. And though the bees tried valiantly to stick close to them, only moving a little farther away to make room for the noxious trio, they finally were forced to disperse, little by little, until most of them had made their way back to their hives, leaving only one or two behind, still stubbornly trying to find their way through the scent.

"We made it," Ilyas said as he caught up to her, barely audible through his layers. "They're gone."

"We did." Hamra looked around. "Where's Pak Belang?"

"I am here," the tiger said, and Hamra couldn't help but notice that he walked a little slower than usual, and that his gait was less fluid than before as he moved from step to step. It was hard to tell just from looking, given how thick and luscious his fur was, but something in her gut told her he'd been stung.

"Did they get you?"

He stayed silent.

"How many times?"

Still he refused to answer, and the flames that had stayed dormant for a moment, dampened by fear and anxiety, began to flicker once more. "We're a team right now, whether we like it or not, and if you're in pain you need to tell us so that we can help you. So please: Were you stung? And do you need help?"

"I was stung," Pak Belang said, his tone even and dangerously calm. "And I am fine. I do not now, nor will I ever, need to be tended to by children. Let us go and finish this fool errand." And he stalked off ahead, his tail waving to and fro, just as an angry cat's would.

20

THE CAVE MOUTH yawned ahead of them, a gaping hole in the rockface, with its jagged teeth of stalactites and stalagmites visible even from where Hamra stood.

"Which is which, do you remember?" Ilyas took off his glasses to wipe them on the sleeve of his hoodie. "I mean, the stalag-thingies. Which one grows from the floor and which one grows from the ceiling? I can never remember the difference."

"One's got a *C* in it and one's got a *G*," Hamra said absently, picking her way carefully along the rocks, trying not to slip. Ahead of her, Pak Belang moved on sure, quiet feet. "That's the only difference I know." She pulled her mask down and filled her lungs with cool jungle air, desperately grateful for the feeling of the breeze on her skin.

Ilyas was still staring at the cave mouth. "I really don't

like caves," he said quietly. "Especially after the last one we had to go into."

Hamra remembered the darkness of the Langsuir's cave and shivered. "Neither do I," she said. "But if we're together, maybe it won't be so bad. Come on."

So together, they walked in.

Inside wasn't as dark as you might expect. Holes that periodically punctured the walls of the cave flooded parts of it with light, illuminating the twisted figures of rock formations and stalag-thingies that might have appeared far more sinister in darkness and shadow. In the darker, more sheltered spots, bats roosted, wrapped in their own wings and oblivious to the three who walked beneath. Ficus roots from trees above had fought their way through the cracks and crevices in the limestone and now hung in twists and turns and tangles all the way to the ground. And there, at the very end of the cave, silhouetted against the harsh glow of the afternoon sun, was a dark figure.

The Praying Man.

You could see him clearly from a distance, hands outstretched in prayer. But the closer they got, and as their perspectives changed, the figure simply . . . disappeared.

Ilyas squinted. "It's just . . . a bunch of rocks." Hamra could tell he was trying to hide his disappointment, but it wasn't hard to notice the way it bled into the edges of his voice.

"Have you learned nothing on this journey thus far?" Pak Belang's voice echoed through the cave, and a couple of swiftlets flew from their nests in the eaves, fleeing the cave as if they knew something was coming. "Nothing is as it seems upon first glance. Tigers are not just tigers, birds are not just birds, snakes are not just snakes, old ladies are not just old ladies, and a bunch of rocks can still be everything you seek. You merely have to change your point of view."

Ilyas screwed up his nose. "Okay. I still don't get it, but okay."

Hamra flopped herself down on the floor of the cave, adjusting her view so that the rocks became the praying man once more. "What do we do now?"

"You have a question for it, do you not?" The tiger sat beside her. "Ask what you need to."

Hamra cleared her throat and tried not to feel incredibly foolish for talking to a rock pile in a cave. "Dear Praying Man," she began, and Ilyas snickered.

"It's not an email," he pointed out. "You're not in BM class trying to compose a letter for your karangan home-work. Ke hadapan kakanda yang dirindui . . ."

The rest of his sentence was quickly muffled by one of Pak Belang's large paws.

"Continue," the tiger said, ignoring Ilyas's dirty look.

Deep breaths, Hamra. Let's go. "Praying Man," she said, trying her hardest to find just the right words. "Praying Man, we come to you for help. We were told that we need to ask you a question, and that your answer is what will aid us in our quest. Please, will you speak to us?"

There was no response.

"Try again," Ilyas said quietly.

Hamra clasped and unclasped her hands. *Please let this work.* "Praying Man, please hear us. We need help. We don't know where else to go. Please, can you answer us?"

Nothing broke the silence but the twittering of swiftlets in the shadows above.

Ilyas sighed. "Maybe we got the wrong place after all."

"We followed what Nenek Kebayan told us!"

"Well maybe she was wrong!" Ilyas grabbed a rock and flung it across the cave; the clatter it made echoed like a slap, and more swiftlets burst from their nests and fled in a flurry of angry tweeting. "Maybe sometimes adults are just wrong! No matter how magical they are."

"Perhaps the boy is right," Pak Belang said gently. "Nenek has many gifts, but perhaps in her advancing age, she is less accurate than she used to be."

"I'm going outside," Ilyas announced, picking up his backpack and slinging it over his shoulders. "I've had enough of caves. And rocks. And all of . . . this." And he turned and walked off, the tiger following slowly behind him.

Hamra was alone. And for the first time, she *felt* alone.

Hamra was never the type of kid who cried all that much. She often envied her mother, who cried when she was sad, when she was happy, when she was angry—whenever she felt any strong emotion, really. It seemed to Hamra like a better way to be than the alternative, which was Hamra's way: forcing all the strong emotions down until she could pretend they were no longer there, and then dealing with the consequences later. That was part of why the flames that flickered within her burned so bright these days. They fed on all the feelings that festered inside her, longing to get out.

But now she could feel a burning in her throat, and that familiar prickling feeling rising up behind her eyelids. So she knelt at the feet of the praying man, and when she closed her eyes and bowed her head tears began to fall as easily as if they'd just been waiting for her to open the dam. And once she began, she could not stop. She sobbed so hard her whole body shook; she sobbed so hard her whole body *hurt*. And in between sobs, she spoke. "Please," she said, her voice ragged and raw. "Please. I need to do this. I need to get back to my grandparents. I need to keep them safe. I just want to go home. Please, speak to me. Tell me what I have to do to just go *home*." And when she grew too tired to speak, all she could do was say "Please" over and over again, until her voice gave out altogether, and there was not a sound in the cave but her own heaving, hiccupping breaths.

Then there *was* a sound, and it almost made her heart stop.

From the figure before her came a great grinding sound, so loud it made her grit her teeth. Then as she watched, round-eyed with equal parts wonder and terror, the Praying Man opened its eyes to look at her, and its mouth to speak to her, and it said: "You are getting my feet wet."

Hamra blinked. "Pardon?"

"I said, you are getting my feet wet." The praying man's mouth twisted in displeasure. "Bad enough down here in the damp and cold and the droppings without that sort of thing adding to the experience."

"I'm . . . sorry."

"Your apologies are noted." His voice was rough and gravelly, just, Hamra supposed, as talking rocks should sound. "Now what is it you have come to ask me? Why do you disturb my slumber? I was having such a nice dream too . . ."

"What do rocks dream of?" Hamra asked, interested in spite of herself.

If the praying man had eyebrows, he would have raised them. "Is that really your question?"

She felt herself blush. "No," she mumbled.

"Then what is it, daughter of the Island?"

"I was sent on a quest," Hamra said. "And I was told to ask the praying man why he prays. So here I am. Why do you pray?"

The praying man regarded her for a long time. "A prayer is a wish," he said at last. "And as even a rock has its dreams, so too does it have its desires. But prayer alone is not enough. Desires are fulfilled only when efforts are made, and as my feet are affixed to the stone floor of this cave, so too do my prayers remain nothing but dreams and dust."

Hamra frowned. "I don't understand how this can be what I'm looking for."

"You will," the praying man said, very definitely. "Sometimes things only come into focus from a distance. Me, for instance."

"I see," Hamra said, though she most definitely didn't. "I put in the effort, but my desires still haven't been fulfilled. What more should I do? I need help."

"Then ask for it."

She bowed her head. "Please, Praying Man," she whispered. "Please, can you help me?"

She waited and waited for an answer that never came. But when she looked up, the praying man was looking down on her with a tenderness she didn't think was possible for a bunch of rocks.

"It shall be done," he whispered.

And then he opened his mouth wide, so wide it distorted his face into a grotesque caricature, and out of the gaping hole poured a swarm of bees, so many of them that they seemed to fill the entire cave. Hamra threw herself on the floor and clapped her hands over her ears; the buzzing was so loud she was sure it rattled her very bones. But the bees didn't care about her. They began moving as one out of the cave, a dark, shimmering cloud of yellow and black. And then from outside came a long, solitary scream (*Ilyas*, thought Hamra, panic seizing her chest), and then a roar so terrified, so full of pain, that it pierced straight through her heart (*Pak Belang*, thought Hamra, getting to her feet. *Oh, Pak Belang, what has happened to you?*).

She looked up at the praying man, his mouth now shut so that you could barely believe there had ever been a mouth there at all, though one bee still crawled over where it should be. "What have you done?"

But he did not answer. After all, he was just a bunch of rocks.

Hamra dashed outside, slipping and tripping and skinning her knees as she went. "Ilyas!" she called. "Pak Belang!" In her head, a constant refrain played to the rhythm of her pounding heart: *Please be okay, please be okay, please be okay, please be okay* . . .

When she saw them, she stopped dead in her tracks. Ilyas stood with his back flat against the cliff wall along the path, and steps away, mere inches from the steep drop beyond, the tiger lay. Only it was hard to see him because he was covered in bees, so many bees that you could barely see the orange-and-black beneath them.

As Hamra watched, transfixed, the bees suddenly rose from Pak Belang's body in one huge cloud and dispersed, so quickly that in a minute or two it was as if they were never there at all.

The tiger lay heaving, so perilously close to the edge that Hamra felt her heart drop into her shoes. "Come on!" Ilyas yelled as he bent down to try to pull him away from danger, loose rocks and pebbles slipping and sliding down the cliff beneath his feet, and Hamra ran over to help. Together, though he was so heavy they thought their arms might be pulled right off, Ilyas and Hamra dragged Pak Belang to safety, then lay together on the ground in a panting, sweating heap.

Hamra quickly turned to check on the tiger, who hadn't made a sound, and cried out in shock and horror.

The bees had gotten his eyes.

They were swollen shut, so red and purple and so raw that even looking at them hurt. "What did they do to you?" she whispered.

But Pak Belang said nothing in response; he just lay there, taking in shallow, rapid breaths.

"They came out of nowhere," Ilyas croaked. "We were just out here talking, trying to figure out the whole praying man thing, and then suddenly they were all over us. All over him. And I couldn't get them away. I . . . I . . ."

"It's okay," Hamra said gently. "There wasn't anything you could have done. It wasn't your fault." *It was mine*, she thought to herself grimly. *It was all mine.*

In front of them, the tiger groaned.

"We have to do something," Ilyas said. "He's in pain. Maybe if we put something cool on his eyes? Maybe . . . maybe . . . wait!" And he put a hand in his backpack and drew out a plastic bottle filled with water.

"Nenek Kebayan's gift to me," he whispered. "Water from her stream, for when something needs cleaning or soothing. She said I'd know exactly when to use it, didn't she? And now's the time, I just feel it in my gut."

Hamra blinked back her tears as she stared at the bottle in Ilyas's hands. She remembered Nenek's cryptic instructions, remembered thinking to herself: *I'm getting really tired of creatures with much more power than me telling me that I'll know what to do or think or say when it's time*. It was getting harder and harder to bite her tongue, harder and harder not to say out loud what she was thinking, which was: *Easy to say for someone with nothing to lose*. People who had everything to lose couldn't depend on "when it's time." People who had everything to lose needed directions. They needed guidance. They needed *plans*.

She reached out and took the bottle from Ilyas. The three of them still had none of those things—no directions, no guidance, no plans. But they had a bottle of water, and Hamra had a prayer in her heart, and in the absence of anything else, they would have to do.

"Bismillahirrahmanirrahim," she whispered, then gently, she began to wash Pak Belang's eyes with the water from Nenek's stream.

She tried not to touch him too much—she didn't want to hurt him any more than she had to—but she did try to make sure the water got to all of the worst, most painful-looking bits. It was cool and smooth, and Hamra couldn't help but be soothed by its touch herself. *Let's hope it's working the same way for him.*

So intent was she on making sure the water got everywhere it needed to that she didn't even realize what was happening until Ilyas said, his voice trembling: *"Look."*

And when Hamra looked, she saw that the swelling was beginning to go down, and that the tiger's coloring was returning to normal. And when the bottle was empty, she sat back next to Ilyas and they both waited until Pak Belang lifted his damp head to look at them, red-eyed and blinking.

"Are you all right?" Hamra asked him. There was a long silence. For some reason she felt like she could barely breathe.

"They have done it," the tiger said, finally.

"What have they done?"

"They have taken my gift of sight," Pak Belang said, and his voice was weighed down by sadness. "I can still see, but not with that keenness bestowed by magic. I will never again see the silken patterns woven by the tiniest spiders, nor the dust settling on a moth's wing, nor, on certain nights when the moon is full, the dancing of the dead upon their graves. . . ." He sighed. "I had forgotten how limiting true human sight is. How can you stand it, I wonder? How will I?"

"We don't know anything else but this," Hamra reminded him. "We've never tasted magic like you have. We don't know what we're missing."

"I suppose you are right." The tiger laid his head down upon his paws, tired out. "Perhaps it is better that way, than to live the rest of your life remembering all you have lost."

And all around them, the trees waved and nodded in the wind as if they agreed.

21

THEY SPENT A long time afterward just sitting at the mouth of the cave, eating snacks from their arsenal of containers and resting. Or at least, that was what Hamra and Ilyas did; Pak Belang refused all offers of food and simply walked back toward the praying man, to the platform beside him that looked out over the jungle, and now sat there silently, staring at a sea of green as far as his newly mortal eyes could see.

"I wonder if there's any way to make him feel better?" Ilyas asked softly.

"I doubt it." Hamra knew what it felt like to lose something irreplaceable. She lived with Opah every single day, after all.

Around them, the jungle air was starting to cool, and it

seemed to Hamra as if a mist had begun to rise from the earth, in slow wisps and whirls. "Sunset'll come before we know it," Ilyas said. "We should get moving. Or at least find somewhere to rest for the night, if he"—and here, he jerked his head in Pak Belang's direction—"if he doesn't feel up to moving on quite yet."

"We should figure out the next clue first," Hamra said. "What's the point in moving if we have no idea where we're going?"

Ilyas grabbed his notebook and scanned his notes. "Ask the bones why they weep." He sighed. "I wish magical quests came with clearer instructions."

"Yeah, well, me too, but we both know by now that's not how it works." Hamra leaned back against a nearby rock. "The bones . . . where could the bones be?"

"Mahsuri's tomb, maybe?" Ilyas said, popping the last karipap into his mouth. "That's definitely got bones in it, and if we're going by the previous clues, she's a pretty famous legendary figure around here. The most famous one, probably." Bits of pastry and potato flew out of his mouth as he spoke, and Hamra wrinkled her nose in disgust. She didn't know why he was irritating her so much right now, but it seemed like every single thing he did just made the flames within her jump a little bit higher, burn a little bit hotter.

"Don't talk with your mouth full. And why would Mahsuri's bones be weeping?"

"Because . . . because . . ." Ilyas's eyes lit up. "Because the curse came back! Remember, when she was killed, Mahsuri cursed Langkawi to seven generations of bad luck. And then after those seven generations, what happened? The curse lifted and we got our tourism boom. And now, thanks to the pandemic, it's like we're cursed all over again! No tourists, no income, and the virus spreading everywhere . . ."

Hamra snorted. "Please. That's kind of a stretch, don't you think?"

Ilyas's face fell. "What? Why?"

"I don't know." Hamra frowned. The flames were all over now, needling her just beneath her skin, making her feel hot and angry in spite of the cool mist that now surrounded them. "Mahsuri cursed the island because she was betrayed. The pandemic is a curse on the entire world. What does one have to do with the other?"

Ilyas sighed. "Maybe you just don't like the idea because it came from me."

What was Ilyas doing? Why wasn't he listening to her? Hamra could feel her control slipping again, and in its place anxiety begin to gather itself, hard as a rock in her chest. "What are you talking about?"

He wouldn't even look at her now. "Face it, Hamra. You like it when I'm the bumbling sidekick. When I always say yes. When I follow your plans. And you're always a little less enthusiastic when I'm the one with the ideas. In your mind, you're the leader and my place is behind you. And sure, I go along with it a lot of the time. But that doesn't mean I'm useless. And it doesn't mean I'm not smart enough to work things out on my own."

"That doesn't even make any sense." The flames in Hamra's chest began to leap before she could even move to control them. "I've done nothing but listen to your ideas since this whole thing started. I followed the bird, didn't I?"

"Yeah, but you make it pretty clear you hate hearing what I think," Ilyas bit back. "And speaking of birds— that's exactly why it was so easy for you to give my present away, wasn't it? I worked on that thing for *hours*, but you never care about what I'm feeling, so it was easy to cast aside. Because it came from me."

The fire was a storm now, raining flames in her veins.

"Would you get over the bird already? I needed it to get us out of a jam, I *told* you."

"No, you needed it to get yourself out of a jam. One that you *caused yourself.*" Ilyas's voice practically dripped with disdain. "Every problem we've found ourselves in—the whole reason we're in this mess at all—is because of you. You're so full of yourself you don't even realize when you're screwing up." He stood up and dusted crumbs roughly off his jeans. "I've had enough of this," he barked. "Until you can recognize what an important member of this team I am, I'm leaving. You can figure all of this out on your own. You and your *tiger pal.*"

"Fine!" Hamra yelled at him, so angry it was as if all she could see was tinged in red. "Fine! Go get lost in the jungle, go break your bones, go get eaten by wild animals. What do I care? You were just slowing us down anyway."

She crossed her arms and turned away, panting hard, and Ilyas began marching off down the stone steps. With each step he took, something tugged at her heart, begging her to say something, call him back. And she was about to do it, she'd actually opened her mouth, when . . .

. . . when a hand clapped itself tight over it, smothering the words she was about to say.

"What's the matter, love?" a voice whispered in her ear,

sending cold fear rippling through her body. "Tiger got your tongue?"

And then there was a pain in her head, and darkness, and nothing more.

22

HAMRA WOKE UP to a frog on her face.

She didn't realize it was a frog at first. As she fought her way through the fog of unconsciousness, she felt a sticky wetness on her face that she was fairly certain didn't belong there. And it was only when she pried her eyes open and saw it perched on her nose that she realized what that sticky wetness was.

"Ribbit," the frog said quietly.

Hamra shrieked and sat bolt upright, sending the frog flying off with another strangled "ribbit."

Ilyas and Pak Belang lay unconscious beside her in the middle of a clearing in the jungle surrounded by rocky out-crops. Hamra winced as she moved, and reached up to feel a good sized lump on the back of her head that still ached faintly.

"That was my doing," a voice said, and she whipped her head around. "I suppose I should apologize, but I . . . don't really feel like it."

There, standing before her, was a . . . girl? Hamra wasn't sure if that was the right word for the creature who stood before her. She was no higher than Hamra's waist, with long, long black hair that glinted with gold highlights as she moved, pulled back in a dark ponytail that showed off ears tapering to slender points at the tips. She had dark skin that seemed to glow in the warm light of dusk and dark eyes that stared intently at Hamra as she moved. She was dressed in soft shades of green so that she almost melted into the jungle shadows. On her shoulder perched the frog, who was staring at Hamra with a rather injured expression; in her hand, she held a long, stout stick. It looked to Hamra as if she knew very well how to use it, however small she seemed, and that whoever she used it on would end up hurting for quite a long time.

"Give me your name," the girl said.

It took her a minute to find her voice and answer; her head felt like it was stuffed with cotton wool. "Hamra," she said, her tongue feeling thick and fuzzy in her mouth.

"Hamra." The girl patted the frog's head as she sounded the name out, as if she were testing how it felt in her mouth. Then she nodded. "Why do you walk with him?" And here, she swung her stick around to point at the tiger's slumbering head. Pak Belang let out a little snore. Somewhere through the fog in her head, Hamra finally noticed that his feet were bound together, though Hamra and Ilyas remained free. *Why . . . ?*

The girl narrowed her eyes; Hamra's hesitation seemed to displease her. "I warn you. Speak only the truth in my jungle, for lying tongues get nothing but punishment here."

"Your jungle?"

The girl clicked her tongue. "Do not test my patience."

"Sorry." Hamra cleared her throat. "We are on a quest. We don't mean to trespass on anyone's territory. If you let us go, we can—"

"Let you go?" The girl threw back her head and laughed, showing off strong white teeth. "How can I let a weretiger roam loose in my jungle? And with the Bunian after you? You'll do nothing but destroy our peace."

Hamra frowned. "How do you know the Bunian are after us?"

The girl rolled her eyes. "The whole jungle knows by now. Humans aren't exactly known for their discretion and subtlety, are they?"

Hamra had thought she had the flames of her anger

under control now, but it felt like this girl was really doing her best to stoke them again. "What does it matter if the Bunian are after us? That has nothing to do with you."

"It has everything to do with me," the girl snapped. "You have no idea what you've done. None."

"Ribbit," the frog said indignantly.

Hamra's head ached, and she suddenly wanted nothing more than to curl up and go to sleep. "Look, I really don't know what we did," she said honestly. "I apologize if we've done something wrong. We can move on, get out of your hair, if I can just get my friends to wake up . . ."

The girl shrugged. "They will in a bit. My potions aren't intended to last all that long."

"Your potions?" Hamra remembered the strange mist in the jungle, the way she'd felt rage course through her whole body, right before she and Ilyas argued. Realization dawned. "You did something to us."

"Just a little bit." The girl smiled smugly.

"You made us fight with each other!"

"I made you do nothing." Again, that careless, infuriating little shrug. "All I did was amplify what was already there. People do the rest on their own."

Hamra rubbed her face, so tired she could barely move. "Who *are* you?"

Before the girl could answer, Ilyas stirred beside Hamra, muttering, "no kacang in my nasi lemak, please," and rubbing his eyes sleepily.

"Ilyas," Hamra said, elbowing him in the ribs. "Get up. Now."

"Ow!" Ilyas glared at her, rubbing the sore spot her elbow had left behind. "What was that for, bossy pants? I—Oh." Whatever he was about to say trailed off at the sight of the girl, who was now holding her stick rather too close to his head for comfort. Ilyas gulped. "What have we gotten ourselves into now?"

"We're about to find out."

Beside them, Pak Belang finally opened one large amber eye. As soon as he realized what was happening, he tried to leap to his feet—then let out a huge, terrifying roar when he figured out that wasn't possible. The frog let out a panicked "ribbit" and jumped straight into its owner's pocket, where she cooed at him soothingly. "It's all right. I won't let the bad cat hurt you."

"Who are you?" Pak Belang growled. "How dare you tie me up like this?"

"My name," the girl said, planting her hands on her hips and glaring at them, "is Melur." There was a stirring in her pocket, and Melur rolled her eyes. "And he says to tell you his name is Katak."

"Katak?" Ilyas coughed. "You named your frog . . . frog?"

The stick swung menacingly in his direction again. "Shut up, Ilyas," Hamra hissed. "Maybe don't go making fun of people *holding weapons.*"

Melur began to pace around them, her steps slow and steady, her eyes never leaving their faces. "So you are the heroes on your epic quest to save the weretiger." She laughed. "You're the ones the king is so desperate to catch. You're the ones he's so willing to pay for."

"Is that what this is about?" Hamra swallowed. "Are you going to bring us to him?"

Melur snorted. "As little love as I have for a weretiger— you are not welcome in these parts, old cat—the last thing I would want is for more power in the hands of the Bunian king. For he will do nothing but take and take and take from the jungle for his own, whereas I work hard to preserve it and nurture it and watch it grow." She reached out a hand to caress a nearby tree lovingly. "I will not see my friends sacrificed for his gain." Then she turned and glared at them. "And now you have brought him here, to my part of the jungle. You have doomed us all to ruin." And from her pocket came an emphatic "ribbit."

"We didn't mean to do it," Ilyas said, his eyes wide. "We only meant to complete our own quest. We didn't think—"

"No, you didn't," Melur snapped. "The heroes of the story rarely stop to think about what their actions mean for the rest of us, do they? Let trees burn, let battles be fought, let weretigers roam, as long as you aren't the ones who will face the consequences."

"What can we do?" Hamra asked. "How can we fix this?"

The girl drew herself up and stood straight and tall—well, as tall as she could. "Give me the teeth," she said loudly, her words echoing through the clearing. "Give me the teeth, that I can make sure they remain out of the king's greedy clutches. Give me the teeth, that I can make sure every non-Bunian in these jungles remains free."

Hamra's mind was moving so quickly she could barely keep up. "I see your point," she said carefully. "But . . . and just hear me out here . . . how do we know that you won't do with the teeth what the Bunian king wants to do? How do we know that, if we were to give them to you, you wouldn't be hoarding them for power too?"

Melur bristled, and Hamra wavered for a second. What was it she'd told Ilyas earlier? *Don't upset people holding weapons. You've done it now, Hamra. She didn't like that,*

272

not one bit. "Do not liken me to the Bunian king," the girl said, scowling. "I have no love of power as he does. I merely want to be able to live in peace."

"Yes, but I'm a stranger to you, you see," Hamra explained apologetically. "And I have no way of knowing that that's true. So here's my proposal."

"What are you doing?" Ilyas whispered.

"Shut up," she hissed back. "Just trust me." She turned her attention back to Melur. "Look, I'm more than willing to give you the teeth." She could feel Pak Belang's outraged glare on her; she didn't dare meet his eyes. "I have no real attachment to them, after all."

"I do," the tiger growled. "Given that they are quite literally attached to me."

". . . but there is one condition," Hamra continued, ignoring him.

"You are in no position to set conditions here."

"You are in no position to refuse them."

The two girls stared at each other. Even though Hamra's eyes watered at the intensity of Melur's gaze, she knew she couldn't look away.

Eventually, Melur nodded. "What is it you ask?"

Hamra blinked. "As we said, we have a quest to complete," she said. "We could use some help." She stopped and took a deep breath. "If you help us finish what we set out to do, we will gladly surrender the teeth to you when the time comes."

"What?" Ilyas blurted out.

But Hamra ignored him. She ignored everything but Melur, who stood before her watching her every move. "What do you say?" she asked. "Do we have a deal?"

"Hold on." Melur reached into her pocket for Katak and whispered in his ear—or where Hamra supposed a frog's ears ought to be. Then she held the frog to her own ear, listening intently and nodding along.

"This is by far one of the weirdest things I've seen yet," Ilyas whispered. "And I've been on a boat with a talking tiger."

It seemed to Hamra that years went by before Melur finally stuck out a small hand.

"Deal," she said.

Hamra's relief was boundless. "Okay," she breathed. "Okay. Deal."

And they shook on it.

23

"SO WHERE DO we go from here?"

Hamra, Ilyas, and Melur sat around the fire the small girl had built. The two humans were eating the last of the food they'd brought from home, Hamra trying her hardest not to worry about what they were going to eat beyond this as Ilyas pondered their next steps. Melur had looked over the food they offered her, wrinkled her delicate nose, and muttered something about disgusting humans. Hamra took it that meant "no thank you."

"We've rid him of his magical sight, his magical hearing . . . what's left?" Ilyas asked.

"Strength," Hamra supplied. "And teeth." Pak Belang stalked around their perimeter, ostensibly to protect them from harm, but mostly, Hamra thought, because he was still so annoyed about the whole thing. *I know they weren't my teeth to promise*, Hamra thought to herself. *But what else could I have done?* But she couldn't stop the pangs of guilt that kept beaming through her insides, the little voice that kept asking her *when will you stop giving away things that matter? When will you stop sacrificing your friends' feelings for your own gain?*

Anyway, it was too late now. The only way they could go on was by figuring out the next clue. Ilyas sat back and rubbed his belly, now full of cold noodles and stale keropok lekor. "Trust yourself. Trust another. Ask the bones why they weep," he mused aloud. "Do you think my Mahsuri theory holds any water, Melur?"

Melur shrugged as she patted Katak, sitting sleepily in her lap. "No clue. How am I to understand your clues? This is your quest, after all."

Hamra sighed. "Is there anyone you can think of that might be able to help us?"

It took a long time for Melur to reply, and when she did, she studiously avoided looking at them. "I . . . might," she said carefully, and Katak opened one beady eye and glared at her as if she'd said something terrible.

"Ribbit," he said warningly.

Ilyas frowned. "Is that a yes or a no?"

"It's both." Melur sighed. "The pari-pari at Telaga Tujuh can help you."

"Sorry, what?" Ilyas frowned. "The ikan pari? Who wants stingray at a time like this? Although the idea of some asam pedas or ikan bakar sound really good right now . . ."

"I'm not talking about seafood, you dolt," Melur said, and Katak croaked. Melur picked him up and settled him in the hollow of her collarbone. "I'm talking about the fairies at Telaga Tujuh. You know, the waterfall that—"

"I know it," Hamra said quietly. The Telaga Tujuh waterfall, with the famous seven wells for which it was named, was one of her father's favorite places to bring both out-of-towners and his own family. Hamra had spent dozens of happy days there over the years, struggling up the many, many steps to the falls, splashing in the cool water, eating nasi lemak that Ibu had made and carefully packed into plastic containers.

"Yes. Well. The fairies always have a good idea of the goings-on in the jungle, both magical and non. If anyone would be able to get you any answers, it's them." Melur smoothed a stray hair back from her eyes and grimaced. "They're not really known for being terribly friendly to humans, however. And I don't know how happy they'd be to see *me* again either . . ."

"Sorry, did you say 'again'?" Hamra crossed her arms and looked at Melur. "Meaning you've encountered them before?"

"Meaning, er . . ." It was the most flustered that Hamra had seen the cool, collected Melur since they'd met. "Meaning I . . . used to be one of them . . ."

"You *what*?"

"Technically, I still am," Melur continued hurriedly. "One does not simply stop being who one is. Only I left long ago due to some . . . irreconcilable differences, and so I no longer make my home at Telaga Tujuh."

Ilyas narrowed his eyes. "What *kinds* of differences?"

She waved away his words with a quick gesture. "No matter. They will have information that can help us, of that I am sure."

It was better than nothing, Hamra supposed. "All right. At least it's a plan." She didn't want to talk in circles anymore; her head still bore traces of the earlier ache, like the last echoes of the fog remained trapped within.

"Still hurts?" Melur asked, and for the first time a guilty look crossed her face. "I suppose I should apologize. I really didn't mean for it to be that bad."

"What did you *do* to us?" Ilyas asked. "That fight came out of nowhere. It was nothing like our usual disagreements.

I knew we were being awful, but somehow I couldn't stop myself from saying all kinds of nasty things." His eyes slid over to Hamra for a second. "Things that weren't even *true*."

Hamra stayed quiet. She wasn't sure he meant it, or, more importantly, that she could say the same about herself.

"Ah, well." Melur rubbed her hands together and smiled gleefully. "That was my Cari Gaduh Charm. My Irritability Enhancer Elixir. My Quarrel Cordial."

"That's a lot of names."

"It's a work in progress."

Hamra thought about the red mist in her head, the way it drove the flames inside her even higher, the way her head and heart still hurt from it even now. "What's in it?"

Melur's expression grew guarded. "I can't just *tell* you," she said, caressing the bag of soft brown leather that was slung around her shoulder. Inside, Hamra could hear the clink of glass on glass. "That's my *work*."

"Okay, but can you at least tell us there won't be any particularly long-lasting side effects?" Ilyas frowned, rubbing his head. "That's what my mother says we need to know about medications. Even though this technically isn't a medicine . . ."

"More like a menace," Hamra muttered.

Melur shot her a look. "It should wear off in an hour or so," she said firmly. "And really, you should thank me. You deserved much more for the kind of upheaval you've brought to the jungle."

"It's not like we meant to." Hamra paused, considering her next words carefully. "You must know the fairies pretty well. Do you really think they'll help us?"

Melur turned away and busied herself rummaging around in her bag. On her lap, Katak stirred sleepily. "Hard to say," she muttered. "Could go either way, really."

"Either way?" Ilyas narrowed his eyes at this. "Can you maybe spell out both ways for us? Just so we know what we're getting into."

Melur sighed. "It's like this. When you think of fairies, you think of pretty, dainty little things, right? Flitting about on gossamer wings, like delicate butterflies?"

"Well yeah, kind of." Hamra nodded. "Like Tinkerbell."

"Whoever that is." Melur waved a hand dismissively. "Real fairies are not like that. They are beautiful and charming, but they can also be cold, and vengeful, and calculating, and cruel. If you do anything they see as crossing them, they won't hesitate to make you pay. But they don't tell you what it is that will make them angry.

And their prices can be high."

Ilyas gulped. "They sound . . . terrifying."

Katak peeled open his eyes and let out a ribbit that sounded a lot like agreement.

Melur shrugged. "They also have a scrupulous sense of balance and justice, and they have been known to assist humans in their quests. It just depends how they're feeling, and if they decide they like you right in that particular moment."

"The fairies do not like me," Pak Belang's deep voice boomed from behind them, making them all jump. "No matter what the moment." He shook his great head so that his thick fur swayed back and forth in the breeze. "This is a bad idea."

"You need their help," Melur shot back. "And as not liking you aligns with the views of most of the jungle-dwellers, I do not think this is something that needs to be taken into consideration."

"Of course it is." He began to pad back and forth, and it seemed to Hamra that he was almost . . . nervous?

Then realization dawned. "Are you . . . scared?" she asked. "Of the fairies?"

Beside her, Ilyas let out an incredulous snort-laugh and immediately tried to cover it up by coughing. "Sorry," he choked out. "Just . . . something caught in my throat."

"I am not scared!" The tiger stopped in his tracks and scowled. "But . . . they are rather intimidating. Do not mock me!" he said quickly, as Hamra tried to stifle a smile and failed spectacularly.

"Sorry, sorry."

"As funny as it is to think of a weretiger being scared of fairies—and it is, admittedly, just a teensy bit *hilarious*—" Melur grinned as the tiger growled in her direction, though Katak let out a panicked squeal. "My point still stands. There are no creatures of the jungle more equipped to aid you in your mission than they, and you know it."

Hamra looked at Pak Belang and shrugged. "As much as I hate the idea of not knowing how things will go . . . what choice to we have?"

The tiger let out a noise that sounded remarkably like a snort. "Get some rest," he said. "I will stand guard, and we will leave in one hour. We must move carefully, since Nenek's potion will have worn off, but the darkness will hopefully provide the cover we need."

"Oh, masking magic's easy," Melur said with another airy wave of her hand. "I can ensure our protection, don't worry."

"Let's hope this one involves less head trauma," Pak

Belang growled under his breath as he moved off to prowl restlessly through the shadows around them.

All was quiet and still in the clearing. Ilyas slept on his back beside her, one arm flung over his face as if to block out the world; Melur was curled into a tight little ball, Katak slumbering peacefully in the crook of her elbow; even Pak Belang, who had tried to stand guard as long as he could, was lost to the onslaught of his own exhaustion, his face frozen in a frown as if he resented every moment of his rest. But sleep eluded Hamra, and all she could do was stare at the stars that glinted just beyond the rain forest canopy above her, thinking about the day's events. She thought about how it had felt to be so lost without the memory the Langsuir had taken, and then to find her way back, but worrying, always worrying, about what other ways she could lose herself again. Losing her hold on her emotions as she had done when she cried in front of the praying man. Or in her fight with Ilyas.

And then, just as she was finally about to turn over and go to sleep, she heard it—a snuffling and scratching and the occasional soft grunt coming from Ilyas's feet, where she'd casually tossed her backpack next to his.

It's just some animal, Hamra thought sleepily. *Something small and harmless. It'll go away soon enough.* But no sooner did she think it then she was hit by a sudden stench, so pungent, so putrid, that she gagged quietly. And as she watched, she saw her backpack move as if someone— something—was trying to make off with it.

Hamra sat up and almost without thinking, slipped off one of her sneakers, aimed carefully, and tossed it as hard as she could.

"OUCH!"

She wasn't quite sure what "it" actually was. It looked like a large rat, except that its pale pink snout was long and pig-like, its feet were webbed, and its fur was coarse and long and white; in the watery moonlight that straggled through the branches, it almost seemed to glow. At the moment, it was mostly preoccupied with trying to chew a hole through the canvas of her backpack and glowering at her.

"Blast it all," it resumed muttering to itself, spitting bits of string from its mouth and rubbing its head with one webbed foot. "The indignity of it. A shoe to the head of so noble a creature as I! A thousand curses heaped upon the thrower of this foul footwear, and upon the head of the so-called king who demands a bounty just to restore what's rightfully mine. May every one of both their pantaloons be filled with hundreds of furious fire ants."

"What," Hamra said, "do you think you're doing?"

The rat-thing scowled, its long tail whipping back and forth. "Nothing," it said, its voice high and peevish. "Nothing, not that it's any business of yours, mind you. Just out for a walk in the woods, see?"

"And snacking on my stuff?" Hamra crossed her arms and glared right back.

The rat-thing hissed at her, and the nauseating smell of decay that emanated from him seemed to grow even stronger, so strong that Ilyas stirred in his sleep, frowning slightly. "Possessing is not belonging, you follow?" the creature said, its beady eyes gleaming as it looked up at her. "Just because you have it doesn't make it yours."

"And what is it that I possess that you're so interested in?" Hamra asked.

"Rumor has it that you lot are traveling with a bunch of tiger teeth," the rat-thing said conversationally. "And those are of par-*ti*-cu-lar interest to me, and to any number of creatures in this jungle besides."

"I am traveling with tiger teeth," Hamra said mildly. "They just happen to still be attached to the weretiger. But you're welcome to try to steal them from him, if you like."

The rat-thing balked visibly at this suggestion. "A

thousand curses!" it muttered feverishly. "A thousand curses upon you and all your descendants! May every one of your journeys be filled with bad weather and poor decisions and . . . and . . ." It looked around, casting for inspiration. "And full bladders!" it finally finished triumphantly.

"Thanks." Hamra reached over and picked it up gingerly by the scruff of its neck, trying not to shudder at the feel of its fur, coarse as wire, keeping a tight grip as it wriggled and kicked and bucked. "Now, would you mind telling me why you, of all things, are so desperate for those teeth?"

"Let me go!"

"I asked you a question." She tried very hard not to think about the disgusting, fetid stench of the creature seeping into her pores, burning into her skin.

Finally, it stopped wriggling and hung from her fingers, limp as a rag. "The Bunian king promised the wildest riches to anyone who brings him his desires," it sniffed. "He told everyone about those tiger teeth. If I get them, I could become the king I was always destined to be."

"Of the Bunian?"

"Of the animals, fool!" it snapped. "Have you never heard of the noble moonrat, king of all the animals, lord of the forests and all their denizens?"

"Not at all," Hamra said honestly. "And no offense, but you're not really how I imagine a king of beasts would look like."

The moonrat crossed its little rat arms and glowered at her. "One day, I will take back the power and position that are truly mine. And anyway, looks are not everything," it said haughtily. "As you would know," it added under its breath.

"All right, you little weasel . . ."

"MOONRAT," it snarled.

"Moonrat, whatever. Get out of here before I wake the tiger up and he skins you alive." Hamra swung the beast a couple of times for momentum before letting go, and it landed with a crash at the foot of the nearby trees. Beside her, Ilyas bolted upright.

"What's that sound?" he asked groggily, rubbing the sleep from his eyes. Then he stopped, sniffed the air, and made a face. "What's that smell?"

"That," Hamra said, pointing.

"What is that?"

"An inconvenience." Melur was awake now and glaring at the creature snuffling in the trees.

"Ribbit," Katak added accusingly from her shoulder.

"MOONRAT," it yelled at them, panting hard. "And

just you wait, you cretins. When I am king again, nothing will save you from the worst of the forest's nightmares."

Then it turned and disappeared into the undergrowth, taking its foul stench with it.

Ilyas turned to Hamra, one eyebrow raised. "Did he say 'king'?"

"Even the smallest thing can have big dreams, I guess." Hamra stared at the trees where the moonrat had been and shuddered. "We should keep moving."

"What's the rush?" Ilyas stretched and yawned. Dawn stole through the sky like a thief, painting it in streaks of pink and yellow. "Can we at least wait until the sun's properly up? Maybe eat some breakfast? Pak Belang isn't even up yet." And he pointed to where the tiger lay sprawled out, snoring gently.

"Your friend is right," Melur said, rising gracefully to her feet and retrieving Hamra's shoe. "It won't be the last thing that comes after us, not as long as we still have the teeth. And the next one might not be so easy to handle."

Ilyas balked. "You have a point."

"Here you are," Melur said, and as she handed the shoe back to Hamra she wrinkled her nose delicately. "Only perhaps you . . . might want to wash your hands first."

24

THE PLAN WAS to set out for the falls as soon as they were all done with their morning meal.

Unfortunately, they hadn't factored in a trio of wily mouse deer who had apparently trailed them through the jungle, waited for the moment Melur needed to set up a fresh masking spell, and somehow managed to slip a sleeping draught into the hot tea Ilyas had brewed to go along with their breakfast.

"You left me to fend them off on my own," Pak Belang grumbled when the three of them awoke hours later from the deepest, most satisfying sleep, faces still wet with drool tracks.

"Ribbit," Katak said indignantly.

"Except for you," Pak Belang said. He glared at Hamra accusingly. "They were irritating. And you *snored*."

Hamra blinked at him and felt a tiny pang of guilt. "But they were just mouse deer, right?"

The tiger sniffed. "Yes. But they *kicked*."

"Who were they?" Melur asked, trying to untangle bits of leaf and twig from her dark hair.

Pak Belang shrugged. "Called themselves the Sang Kancil Crew. As if those vermin could hold a candle to that wily one's legacy."

"So what happened to them?" Ilyas looked all around.

"Ah." The tiger cleared his throat. "Well, let's just say . . . it is evening, you slept through lunch and, well, I am . . . full."

"Oh." The three of them exchanged glances and then quickly got to their feet and began to pack, careful not to meet Pak Belang's eye as he let out a gentle burp behind them.

At the bottom of the falls, the water that rushed and roared and churned down the steep cliffside eventually pooled into a more still and sedate pond that was usually crowded with families; Hamra's little group bypassed this and headed behind the shuttered stalls that usually sold cheap food and gaudy, technicolor knickknacks, to the stairs that climbed up the sides of the mountain to Telaga Tujuh.

On the way to the trail, they passed two police officers, one sitting on a stone bench and the other standing, hands in pockets, as they talked. One wore his mask, but the other officer's mask dangled beneath his chin, and Hamra felt a wave of rage, thinking of the people—her own neighbors among them—who'd been handed fines for thousands of ringgit with no warning just because they'd pulled their masks down for a minute or two to catch their breath. And yet, here was a police officer breaking the rules so flagrantly.

"When do you think we'll be able to stop patrolling like this?" she heard one say as they walked softly past, doing their best to make as little noise as possible, though Melur's charms kept them hidden from sight.

"When the so-called virus is declared over, I guess," the maskless officer said, smirking.

"What do you mean 'so-called'? Surely you don't think it's made up."

"Oh come on, man. It's obviously just a conspiracy so the government can exert even more control over us! Inject us with goodness-knows-what so they can monitor our every move! I saw this video on Facebook where they're making microchips so small, bro, you wouldn't believe it. . . ."

The masked officer cleared his throat. "Maybe you

should stay off Facebook, man."

"Don't blame me when you realize you've become a government guinea pig for an experimental vaccine, is all I'm saying."

Hamra couldn't take it anymore. She leaned over to Melur. "Can't you maybe just . . . I don't know . . . give him a little present?"

"We don't have time for this," the tiger rumbled from ahead, and Hamra rolled her eyes.

"We should always have time to make sure ridiculous conspiracy theorists endangering the lives of other people get their due, but hey, what do I know," she muttered as she walked.

Melur flashed her a smile. "Do not worry," she whispered. "He shall get what he deserves." Quickly, she drew a small glass ball from her brown bag and tossed it at the maskless officer's feet, where it popped into nothingness, like a bubble. From Melur's shoulder, Katak let out what sounded suspiciously like a snicker, if frogs could do such things.

Immediately, Hamra saw the officer's face change in the dying light of the setting sun.

"What is it?" she heard the masked officer say.

"I . . . I . . . I need a toilet," the other man said hurriedly as he rushed off, dancing with every step.

Hamra and Melur dissolved into helpless giggles, and the masked officer snapped to attention, staring in their direction. "Who's there?"

The girl and the fairy immediately fell silent, gazing at each other in wide-eyed shock, not daring to move a muscle. Even Katak stayed still and silent.

"You're not meant to be wandering around here," the officer said warningly, his voice carrying loudly in the twilight stillness. "That's against the SOPs."

Hamra's heart was pounding so loudly she wondered if the officer could hear it.

"Stay still," Melur whispered. "He can't see us. He's only saying things, just in case."

It felt like an age, but eventually the officer moved off and they could run quickly to catch up with Ilyas and Pak Belang, who waited for them with twin expressions of exasperated irritation on their faces.

"Are you satisfied?" Pak Belang said, his voice dripping with sarcasm.

Melur tossed her dark hair. "Quite. Now let's go."

There were 638 steps to the top of the falls, Hamra knew, 638 steps to the highest of the still pools that gave Telaga Tujuh its name. It was a lot of work to earn a glimpse of paradise, but oh, what a glimpse it was: streams and inlets flowing into cool mountain pools; smooth rock slides and cunning little nooks and crannies carved out by years of gushing waters; and at the very edge, a natural infinity pool that afforded an incredible view of the ocean as the waterfall roared just below. Opah used to amuse Hamra—and often Ilyas, when he tagged along—with tales of the fairies who made these falls their home, and afterward they'd play pretend, imagining fairy homes hidden in the thousand-year-old trees that stretched high above them, sharp fairy eyes peering out at them from between the dense foliage.

Apparently, they'd been right all along.

Hamra looked over at Ilyas, panting as he climbed up step after step, and wondered if he was remembering all of this too.

He noticed her glance and grimaced. "Is it just me, or are your legs starting to hurt?"

"Nope," Hamra said airily, then grinned sheepishly. "They started hurting ten minutes ago."

Their laughter trailed down the mountain and floated off into the creeping darkness behind them. Hamra peeked at Ilyas, the ghost of a smile still playing on his face. "So, umm. About those things I said . . ."

His expression turned guarded. "Ya?"

"I didn't mean any of them," she said softly. "You know that, right? I couldn't do any of this without you. And I'm really sorry I hurt your feelings."

Ilyas's shoulders relaxed. "Oh, is that it? I thought you were going to tell me I smelled bad or something. Forget it, that wasn't even really us. That was magic, remember? We were fighting under the influence." He grinned at her. "I forgive you. And I'm sorry too."

That was the Ilyas she knew, always eager to help, never able to hold a grudge for more than five minutes. And Hamra grinned back, her heart light once more.

Ahead of them, Pak Belang turned back to growl. "Silence. This is not a holiday. You do not know what lies ahead . . . or behind."

Chastened, Hamra and Ilyas fell silent, and Hamra concentrated on walking up each step, trying to ignore the burning sensation in her legs. It wasn't until that moment she realized just how tired she really was, how much of a toll their adventures had demanded from her body. Now it was like it was staging a rebellion, setting off alarm systems one by one until everything shut down altogether. *Keep it together, Hamra. You can't fall apart now. You can't be the one to slow everyone down.* So she kept going, clinging to the railing painted to look like someone's idea of what wood should look like if they'd never actually seen wood in real life, an unnatural reddish-brown with shallow, wavy grooves cut half-heartedly into the surface. Every so often, they passed signs reminding them to KEEP YOUR RAIN FOREST CLEAN!

Behind them, Melur trailed along, showing no signs of tiredness, reaching out to caress trees as they passed. Some bore labels spelling out their names in stark black letters on bright yellow backgrounds, followed by complicated scientific names, and the girl said these out loud to herself delightedly so that every once in a while Hamra would hear a soft voice saying "Jejentik!" or "Panarahan!" followed by a long stretch of whispers, punctuated with enthusiastic ribbits from Katak on her shoulder.

She paused to wait for Melur. "What are you doing?"

"Oh." Melur smiled. "Well, some trees had their names written on them, and I thought it only polite to learn them since we were tramping along through their home." She scratched her neck and shrugged. "Only nobody is talking back. Not a single reply, no matter what kinds of questions I asked."

Hamra wondered for the thousandth time if she could possibly be dreaming this entire thing. "Umm. The trees here don't usually talk to us," she said.

Melur looked at her, head tilted to one side. "Have you tried talking to them?"

"No."

"Then maybe they just decided you aren't worth their time."

Hamra gaped at her. "You mean to tell me—ow!" She looked up to see that she'd walked straight into Ilyas's back, which meant colliding with the hard contours of his backpack. "What's going on?"

In front of them, Pak Belang had also gone perfectly still.

"Hamra," Ilyas said, his voice carefully, unnaturally calm. "Look. Up."

Hamra looked. And immediately bit her tongue to keep from screaming.

Because the trees on either side of them were filled with monkeys. They sat on every branch, alert and staring at the little group with wide, watchful eyes, what little light filtering through the leaves turning their gray coats silver. The sight of them wouldn't normally unnerve Hamra— monkeys were about as common as mosquitoes around these parts, and possibly even more annoying—except for one thing: The monkeys were sitting perfectly still. They were also utterly, terrifyingly silent.

They just watched, as if they were waiting for something to happen.

Slowly, Hamra felt every hair on the back of her neck stand on end.

"What do we do?" Ilyas whispered.

"They're harmless," Melur said quietly, though Katak quickly leaped from her shoulder to the confines of her pocket with a strangled ribbit. "Shush, Katak, it's all right. They're just standing guard."

Ilyas's gulp was audible. "They don't *look* harmless."

"Keep going," Pak Belang said, soft as the beating of a moth's wing, so soft Hamra had to strain to hear him. "But very slowly, and with no sudden movements. Stay close to me."

Stay close? Hamra would have clambered on his back and clung on like a leech if he'd just said the word.

Instead, she inched as close as she could to the others without making herself a nuisance and they continued their ascent. The steps leveled out now, the concrete pathway on even ground, yet they moved more slowly than ever, weighed down by a thousand gazes; Hamra tried her very best not to look up again, but she could feel the weight of their presence pressing down on her. *Please Allah, please protect us.*

The monkeys did nothing. They didn't even blink.

"Just a few more steps to go," Hamra said aloud, more for her own benefit than for everyone else.

The moment she said it, a small gray monkey on a tree just ahead of them moved, leaping swiftly, fluidly, from branch to branch, from tree to tree. The rustling he caused with his movements echoed through the stillness, so that it seemed as if the entire jungle played a fanfare to herald Hamra's group's arrival. In seconds, he had disappeared.

None of the others moved a muscle, though Hamra thought she heard a panicked croak from the depths of Melur's pocket.

"Sentinels," Melur said grimly. "They'll know we're coming."

Pak Belang sighed. "Well then, let's not disappoint them."

On they went, following the path as it swerved out of the trees and to the left, past a silent prayer room and toilets shrouded in darkness, and then there they were, just as Hamra remembered them: the Seven Wells. Here, the water was calmer, more well-behaved; it moved in graceful whirls and eddies instead of the wanton gushing and rushing of the falls just below. And just like in so many places on this island, memories awaited Hamra at every turn: Ayah scooping her up and carrying her on his broad shoulders after she whined and dragged her tired little feet along those last few steps; Ibu spreading out a feast of nasi lemak on a straw mat laid out on a sun-drenched rock; the nasi lemak itself, a wondrous meal that she rarely cooked because "leceh lah"—too troublesome with its many finicky components, the fluffy rice cooked in coconut milk, anchovies swimming in a deep red sambal that left a satisfying afterburn, crisp sliced cucumber and perfectly hard-boiled eggs; sliding down the rocks into a pool of cool mountain water and Ayah's waiting arms.

And now here the pools were, as empty and melancholy as the rest of Langkawi.

Or were they . . . ?

Because as Hamra watched, she saw lights begin to play over the water, twinkling merry dances through the darkness that had now fallen across the jungle. And as fear began to blossom deep in her belly, so too did the certainty that it wasn't just the ghosts of her past that haunted the Wells tonight.

25

NOBODY MOVED A muscle.

Pak Belang looked at Melur. "Surely you ought to make the first move. Is this not your homecoming?"

The fairy shrugged. "Not an entirely welcome one for either party, unfortunately."

Hamra elbowed Pak Belang in his side. "You go first," she whispered.

The tiger hesitated. "Perhaps it would be best if you two led the way for once," he said. "The fairies may look more kindly on humans, especially small ones such as yourselves."

Ilyas grinned. "Because you're scared."

Pak Belang bristled at this suggestion. "Not at all," he said. "I am a weretiger, after all. I wield sublime power. I have the strength of ten men. I—"

"You're scared of fairies," Hamra supplied. Not that she was one to talk. Her own heart was pounding so fast and so loud she could feel it beating in her ears.

"I am *not*!" Pak Belang hissed.

"Look, nobody blames you for it," Ilyas said consolingly. "I'm pretty terrified too. Admitting it is the first step."

"Be quiet or I will bite your finger off."

"Hush." Melur nodded toward the dancing lights. "Remember what I told you. We pari-pari are not to be taken lightly. We must approach with great respect, in a way calculated to bring as little anger down on our heads as possible."

"Okay," Hamra agreed. "How do we do that?"

Everyone else stayed silent, staring at her, until finally realization dawned, and her heart sank. "We should at least vote on it."

"Okay," Melur said agreeably. "Let's vote. All in favor of Hamra going first?"

Two hands and a paw shot straight up in the air, and Hamra scowled. "I hate you all."

"We know," Ilyas said. "But that's just how it goes when the story chooses you."

Five minutes later Hamra was leading her little procession toward the Wells, hands so clammy she had to keep wiping them off on her jeans, cold sweat pooling under her hijab. "Remember," Melur whispered from somewhere behind her. "Be respectful."

"You do it then!"

"We voted," Ilyas said. "Respect the democratic process."

Hamra was about to retort something snarky back when she felt something hard pressing against her legs and stopped short. Two long wooden staves crisscrossed before her, blocking her path; they were held in the paws of two large gray monkeys. One of them bared its teeth and hissed at her, and she stepped back, heart pounding, almost crashing into Ilyas behind her.

The other monkey just stared at her.

"Hello," she said, a small, timid little sound. "We have come to see the fairies. We are on a quest, and we think . . . no, we *know* . . . that they are the only ones who can help us."

But the two monkeys still did not speak, and the two staves still did not move.

"Please," Hamra said. She could feel the desperation begin to bleed into her voice. "Please. The fate of the whole jungle, the whole island, no, all ninety-nine islands . . . it all hangs on us. So please, can we see the fairies?"

And still, the monkeys did not stir.

Melur elbowed her way to the front and scowled at them. "Look, I know it's been a long time, but surely you remember me? Let me and my companions pass."

And still, the staves stood unyielding.

Hamra thought she might cry. "It's no use," she said, turning back to her friends, hoping they didn't hear the break in her voice. "Let's just go back. Maybe we can figure out another way to—"

And then she heard it: a sharp little click in the stillness of the night; the delicate snap of fingers echoing across the water.

"Bring them to me."

The voice was high and lilting; there was a musicality to it, but beneath that Hamra thought she could detect a hint of something hard, and sharp. Something dangerous.

The monkeys drew back their staves—though not, Hamra noted, without some reluctance and a parting hiss at Katak, who immediately drew his head back into the safety of Melur's pocket. Then they scampered off toward the water, and Hamra noticed for the first time how the mist had gathered itself until it formed shapes in the water, and then how the shapes morphed and solidified until she found herself looking at . . .

The fairies.

They were everywhere, splashing and sliding and soaking in pools, draped languidly over rocks, as the monkeys stood guard all around them. And the one who spoke, the one Hamra assumed must be their leader, sat upon a rocky outcrop, draped in batik in hues of purple and blue and green. Her hair was pulled back into a loose bun and woven with bits of gold that shimmered as she moved, just as Melur's did.

"Well?" she said haughtily, looking down her nose at the newcomers. "Come forward, do not waste my time."

Hamra came as close as she could, careful to avoid slipping on the slick rocks, and the others followed behind her. Then she stood and waited to be told what she should do next.

The fairy peered down at her, then at the monkey who stood at her side. "Can she not speak?" she said aloud. "Am I to communicate by charades?"

The monkey shrugged.

"I can speak," Hamra said quickly. "Sorry, I just wasn't sure what to say."

The fairy occupied herself with rearranging her sarong about her on the rocks, the better to show off its intricate patterns. "You can start by explaining why you disturb us," she said. "We do not take kindly to our activities being interrupted, and especially not by the likes of *you*, and *that*." She wrinkled her nose at the tiger, who looked very much as if he was biting his tongue so as to not get into trouble.

"Forgive us, er . . . ma'am," Hamra said, fumbling over the words. "We didn't mean to interrupt anything. It's just that we were told that you could help us in our quest, and we thought—"

"Ugh, you humans," the fairy sighed wearily. "One of you got it into your silly heads that we like being helpful to you, and all of a sudden everyone starts traipsing through our territories, leaving their rubbish, tramping all over our plant friends, being terribly loud, looking for answers or magic potions or worst of all, wanting to kidnap and *marry* one of us." She shuddered delicately. "Your fairy tales are really just fae propaganda. We are *not* helpful. We do not like you."

This . . . didn't seem like it was going the way Hamra wanted it to go. "Oh. Right. I guess I can't really blame you."

"Oh, stop giving the child such a hard time, Anggerik." Melur finally spoke from behind Hamra, and the fairy named Anggerik's eyes widened.

"Melur? Is that you?" Anggerik's gaze landed on Katak, who had poked his head out of Melur's pocket to see what was going on, and she snickered. "Still traipsing about with the best company, I see."

"It *is* me," Melur said firmly, pushing Katak's head down as he let out an angry croak. "And these children need help. What's about to happen is a much bigger disruption than us, or a bunch of humans trying to find fairy wives."

"Bigger than the desperation of human men?" Anggerik leaned forward, intrigued despite herself. "Go on."

"The weretiger has drafted these children's help to make him become human again," Melur explained. "To do so, they must help him shed his supernatural strength, and his teeth. And they must do it before the Bunian king catches up with them, because the old one is after those teeth, and I of course do not need to tell you what tremendous power they would give him and how—"

"How that will end up making him a nuisance and a thorn in my side, blast him to the bottom of the Mariana Trench!" the fairy exploded, and all the light chatter around them immediately ceased. "And it was you who brought all this on?"

This question was directed at Pak Belang, who drew himself up tall and proud as he answered, simply: "Yes."

"Why?" Anggerik's eyes narrowed to slits as they appraised him. "What gives you the right to throw the island so off-balance? Especially you, weretiger, with your litany of crimes—yes, we know of you. We know everything."

The tiger thought about this before he answered. "Because at the end of the day, everyone deserves to be who they truly are."

The fairy rubbed her head as if it ached. "That is human philosophical nonsense."

"'Nonsense' describes most of human existence, if you ask me," Melur mumbled.

Anggerik turned her gleaming eyes on the other fairy. "And you, Melur. Have you fallen so low as to keep the companionship of humans and weretigers? Leaving us seems to have brought you neither peace nor pleasure."

Melur lifted her sharp chin, her jaw clenched tight. "I have plenty of both. But the Bunian king gaining even greater power is a threat to us all. I cannot afford to do nothing. And neither can you."

"That's our Melur," Anggerik drawled. "Always with a cause, our very own social justice fairy. What was it that was the last straw for you? The monkeys not receiving wages, was it?"

Beside her, Hamra noticed Melur's face turning red.

"They deserve benefits and wages for the work that they do in protecting you all and the Wells besides," she muttered furiously. "I don't suppose they receive either now, even still."

"They receive enough," Anggerik snapped. "They know their place. Unlike you." The fairy leaned back and sighed, draping her batik robes around her just so. "You are a terrible bother, all of you. But nonetheless, as you have brought this headache upon us, I suppose we shall have to help you, if only to be rid of it." She clapped her hands, and two of the monkey sentinels came forward. "Take them to the Eighth Well."

Hamra's jaw dropped open; just behind her, she heard Ilyas gasp. "So there is an eighth well?" All this time she'd thought it was just another one of Opah's stories. "They say there's another well that's hidden away somewhere," she'd whispered in Hamra's ear when they were on their picnics here. "And that the fairies keep it for their very own."

She should have known. Opah only ever told her truths.

"Of course there is an eighth well," the fairy retorted. "We must keep some secrets from you humans, before your nasty polluting hands ruin them all." She turned to Pak Belang. "My monkeys will take you there, and you must bathe in its waters. When you emerge, your strength will be taken from you—one step closer to finding your true self."

Pak Belang blanched at the mention of water. "I must . . . bathe?"

"Yes." The fairy nodded. "Submerge yourself in it. Speak your desires to the moon. And you will find your strength seeping from you like blood to a leech." She waved them away as if she was tired of their presence. "Now go."

"Wait!" Hamra spoke before she even realized what she was going to say, and Anggerik immediately turned a steely glare in her direction.

"You object?" she asked, and the silky smoothness of her voice did nothing to hide the danger at its core.

"It's just . . ." Hamra wrestled with her own thoughts. "It's just . . . how do we know we can trust you?"

"You don't," Anggerik said shortly.

Ilyas edged his way forward. "The clues, Hamra," he whispered in her ear. "Nobody said they had to be in order. Trust another, remember?"

No matter how unlikely.

She looked at Pak Belang. "Will you do it?" she asked softly, and he nodded. "Are you sure?" she asked, and he nodded again.

Hamra took a deep breath. "All right," she said to Anggerik. "We accept. Thank you for your assistance."

The fairy rolled her eyes. "That's quite enough of that. Just go. And don't you dare tell anyone I was helpful. The last thing we need is more of this horrible godmother treatment."

As they were led away, Hamra leaned over to Melur. "Are they always like this?"

"Oh no," Melur said blithely. "They're often much worse. That's fairies for you."

Still utterly silent, the monkeys led them along jungle pathways beyond the seven wells that were the fairies' playground. It seemed to Hamra as if they walked for hours, the sounds of the water their only accompaniment, the shadows twisting themselves into odd, fanciful shapes as they passed.

Finally, they stopped before what seemed to be a solid wall of rock, covered in leafy green vines. One of the monkeys beckoned to Pak Belang, who slowly walked forward; when Melur tried to follow, they quickly lowered their staves and blocked her path. "I am pari-pari too," she said imperiously, drawing herself up. "I have as much right to access the Eighth Well as any other fairy. Let me pass."

In answer, the silent monkey guards simply shook their heads in unison.

Pak Belang hesitated. "I am to go alone?"

The larger of the two monkeys nodded.

"That seems dangerous," Ilyas began. "We don't know what—" He stopped abruptly as the monkey closest to him bared its teeth and growled.

"Catch me trying to help you lot again," Melur muttered darkly under her breath, and one of the monkeys hissed at her.

Pak Belang bowed his great head. "Very well," he said softly, and it seemed to Hamra that she had never seen him so small.

"Let me go with him," she said quickly. "Only me. Nobody else."

The larger monkey stared at her for a long time, as though trying to read her face. He looked at his colleague, who shrugged. Then he turned back to Hamra and extended his paw to her, palm up as if he was expecting something.

"What does he want?" Hamra looked at the tiger, puzzled, and he sighed.

"Payment."

Ilyas's face darkened. "Even in a world of fairies and magic and wonderment, cops ask for bribes," he muttered. "Hold on." From somewhere within his backpack, he withdrew a plastic bag that contained three mangos, just on the cusp of ripeness.

The monkeys' eyes widened.

"You can have it," Ilyas said firmly. "As long as you let her through."

The two monkeys looked at each other for a moment. Then the larger monkey nodded, and Hamra was flooded with relief. "Thank you," she said.

The smaller monkey snatched the bag of fruit, opened it, checked its contents, and nodded at his colleague. Slowly, the larger monkey reached to the wall and somehow—though exactly how, Hamra could never explain—he parted the rock as if it were nothing but a curtain. And behind it was the Eighth Well, a perfectly still pond that reflected the light of the full moon rising high above them, as well as the hundreds of tiny little points of light that flickered around it. "Fireflies," Hamra whispered, her breath catching as she took it all in.

"It is beautiful," the tiger said, his voice strangely heavy and sad.

Hamra took a deep breath. "Well then," she said to the tiger. "Shall we?"

And they walked forward together to the Eighth Well.

26

THE POND BEFORE them was so silent and so still that Hamra felt like she had to tiptoe toward the water. Breaking the serenity of this place seemed terribly wrong. She was almost tempted to hold her breath, lest she accidentally let out a clumsy human sound. Behind them, there was a quiet swish; when she looked, she saw that the rock curtain had been closed again.

They were completely alone.

At the water's edge, Pak Belang paused and stared at his reflection, the moon forming a halo behind his head.

"Are you ready to do this?" Hamra asked him softly.

"No," he answered, and she did not press him for an explanation.

Instead, they sat together, Hamra and the weretiger, and

stared up at the moon for a long, long time, saying nothing at all.

"What is it like?" he said at last, and Hamra looked at him, frowning slightly.

"What is what like?"

"Being human," he said. "I do not remember. It has been too long. And I . . ."

"And you are scared," she said gently.

"And I am scared."

She stared at the fireflies that danced all around them, and thought of how to reply. "I'm not going to lie to you," she told him. "It's hard. There're a lot of messy, uncomfortable feelings involved, like anger and sadness and hurt and guilt. But there are also so many beautiful moments, and there's friendship, and there's love. A lot of love." She took a deep breath. "Mainly, I guess when I think about being human, I think about trying. Trying to live a good life, trying to be a good person, trying to take care of each other. And sometimes you like the results, and sometimes you don't. But there's a lot of magic and wonder in the trying."

Pak Belang thought about this. "But you have those things," he pointed out. "Friendship and love and things worth trying for. I have spent my whole life in the pursuit of power, and I have sacrificed my world for it, sacrificed love, and friendships. And I have done so many terrible things. Things that hurt me to remember. And now . . . what if, at the end of all of this, I am left with nothing?"

"Well." Hamra drew her knees up and wrapped her arms around them, hugging them to her chest. "For one thing, you have friends now. Me, and Ilyas—we're your friends. Maybe even Melur." She paused to think about this, then quickly added, "Well. That one's a pretty big maybe."

"Really?" Pak Belang quirked one eyebrow at her. "We are friends? Even after I . . . even after the promise . . . ?"

Hamra's breath caught in her throat; even the mention of the promise sent needles of pain shooting into her chest. All that hope, all that longing, and for nothing. It took her a long time to speak again, and when she did, she chose her words carefully, oh so carefully. "My Opah is really old. And she keeps going back into her past and losing herself in her memories. And that's really hard for the rest of us, because it's like she goes back to a completely different time and place, one where we can't even reach her. But it's hard to get too mad or upset about it because . . . well, because those memories are where her true self lives, you know? Not the person she is when she's with us, all disoriented and confused. They're the best of who she is." She glanced at him, wondering if anything she said made sense to him at all. "So I guess what I'm saying is, you shouldn't think of this as what you're losing. You should think of this as all the things you gain when you go back to being your true self. The best bits." Hamra closed her eyes and remembered soft fur gripped beneath her hands, teeth bared as they protected her from harm, warm flanks supporting her exhausted frame as she walked, amber eyes regarding her over a warm fire. She took a breath. "It's hard to say we're friends right now, because I haven't seen your true self. I only know you as you are now. But for all I know and all I've seen, for all we've done and all we've been through . . . yes. Yes, you are my friend."

Were those tears in the tiger's eyes, or just the glow of the fireflies?

"That's what I think, anyway," she said softly.

They were quiet once more, a companionable silence despite the monumental nature of what they were about to do.

Then Pak Belang sighed, a sigh as soft as the wind blowing through the blades of grass. "Very well," he said. "I suppose it is time to . . . get in the *water*." He shuddered slightly, and Hamra hid a smile.

"You can do it," she said.

He got to his feet and slowly, almost unbearably slowly, gingerly dipped a paw into the pond, wincing as fur hit water. Then suddenly, as if he couldn't bear to wait any longer, he jumped straight in, disappearing entirely into the dark depths.

Hamra let out a muffled shriek. Heart pounding, she scrambled closer to the water, peering anxiously inside for a glimpse of Pak Belang. But there was nothing but the perfect reflection of the moon staring back at her.

One by one, the fireflies around her began to extinguish their lights, so that eventually only moonlight lit her surroundings.

And yet, the pond was still.

As she watched, a strange mist, tinged with hues of purple and blue, began to gather over the top of the water.

And yet, the pond was still.

The mist pulsed and swelled, tendrils forming intricate patterns and pictures in the air. Hamra fancied that she could see three children and a tiger in its delicate swirls, walking in a straight line to nowhere. The figures all melted together into one giant tiger face that came roaring toward her, baring its sharp, sharp teeth; as she steeled herself against its attack, it disintegrated into nothing but tiny drops of water against her skin.

And the pond was no longer still.

It bubbled furiously as if there were something within it that was heating it up past its boiling point, sending water splashing onto Hamra's sneakers and seeping through the canvas, wetting her toes. And then, from those roiling depths, the tiger emerged: first the tips of his ears; then his head, eyes firmly closed; then more and more and more of him until at last he walked out to stand before her.

He was completely dry, and the pond was still once more.

Hamra opened her mouth to speak, then shut it, then opened it again. She wasn't quite sure what to say. "Are you okay?" she asked. It didn't seem adequate, but it was all she had.

Pak Belang hesitated. "I think so."

"How do you feel?"

He thought about this, head cocked to one side. Then he looked at her and smiled sadly.

"Human," he said.

27

AFTER REJOINING THEIR friends, and after thanking
Anggerik profusely ("Please stop and go away," she'd said
in response, rolling her eyes), and after making sure they
had all their things, Hamra paused at the top of the steps
leading back down the mountain.

"What?" Ilyas looked up at her questioningly. "What's
wrong?"

"I just need to do something," she said. "You guys go
ahead, I'll catch up."

"Hamra!" Ilyas protested. "You can't just—"

But she wasn't listening. She'd already started walking
toward the very edge of the falls.

There was red-and-white striped tape stretching all the
way across, a warning to the more fearless traveler to stay
well away. Accidents had happened here before, she knew,

and it was hard, peering over the ledge, not to think about bodies being dashed on the rocks below. But as she stood there, wiggling her wet toes and looking at the moonlit forest below and the ocean stretching beyond, she thought she could finally understand the compulsion to stand on the edge of a precipice.

Slowly, Hamra reached into her pocket and drew out the protective charm the old lady had given her at the market what seemed like years ago. It felt warm and smooth in the palm of her hand. *You just can't trust a tiger*, they'd told her.

But maybe I can trust another human. Maybe right now that's all we can do to get through this.

And with one smooth motion, Hamra tossed the charm as hard as she could, out over the falls and into the darkness below.

Then she quickly turned and ran back down the steps to join her friends.

"Now the teeth," Ilyas said as they sat around yet another campfire that Melur had built with a pinch of powder from a leather pouch, its flames tinged with teal. "What do we do about the teeth?"

Hamra didn't reply because she was watching Pak

Belang, and Pak Belang didn't reply because he was staring into the heart of the fire, deep in thought. It seemed to Hamra as if the tiger had shrunk, and not just in size: His fur was less lustrous, his eyes less bright, his voice less rich. He was just . . . less. And even though she told herself it was part of the process, she worried about him nonetheless.

"Hamra?" Ilyas exhaled noisily, as if he could breathe out all his frustrations if he tried hard enough. When she didn't respond, he turned to the fairy, who was busily taking inventory of all the little jars of pills and potions in her voluminous brown bag. "What about you, Melur, do you have any ideas? A witch who would be willing to do us a favor? A dragon who hoards teeth? A penanggal with a head—ha, see what I did there—for dentistry?"

Melur stared at him blankly. "I don't get it."

"You know, a penanggal? The monster that detaches its head from its body and just like, flies around with entrails dangling from its neck?" Another noisy sigh. "Do the pari-pari not tell jokes?"

"Only ones that are actually funny."

Hamra choked out an involuntary laugh, and quickly turned away when Ilyas glared at her.

"That made her laugh more than your actual joke, you

know," Melur pointed out, and Ilyas's scowl deepened even further.

"That is enough," Pak Belang said wearily. "This is what I get for working with children. And one disgruntled fairy."

"I am not disgruntled," Melur said primly, bringing Katak down from her shoulder so he could eat up the crumbs on her lap. "I am quite gruntled, actually. The absolute soul of gruntledness."

Ilyas frowned. "I don't think that's actually a word . . ."

"None of this is important," Hamra said firmly. "What's important right now is figuring out our next step. What are we supposed to do?"

"We do what you said we would." Pak Belang sighed. "We give the fairy the teeth."

"Which goes back to my question of how," Ilyas said, pushing his glasses up, the teal flames reflected in their lenses making him look particularly demon-esque. "How are we going to get those teeth out of your mouth? There must be some kind of solution."

"There is," the tiger said. "We take them out ourselves."

For a moment they all just stared at him around the fire. "What do you mean, exactly?" Hamra said at last. "Because you can't mean . . ."

"I do."

"We can't just pull out all of your teeth!"

"What is stopping you?"

Hamra wasn't sure why she was so desperate to stop him, but she felt almost frantic. Surely he had to see what a terrible idea this was.

"Because . . ."

"Because what?"

"Because it would hurt you!" she blurted out. The tears were streaming down her cheeks now, and she could do nothing to stop them.

"Then perhaps that is exactly as it should be." Pak Belang let out a long sigh. "Sometimes, even in fairy tales, there are no magical shortcuts. Sometimes, you have to do things the hard way. The long way. The painful way." He knelt down to rub a soft cheek against her tear-stained one. "I have lived a life full of dark deeds," he whispered. "There was never going to be an easy way back. And I know you have been told that the story chose you, but in truth, the story chose me, and then I chose you. I am sorry I did this to you, Little Red."

She turned her face to try to hide it, but there was nothing she could do about the way the sobs made her shoulders shake, or the crying-hiccups that escaped her.

When she could finally stop and breathe again, she looked around at all three of them, staring expectantly at her, waiting for what she would say.

You just can't trust a tiger.

Even monsters can be haunted.

Desires are fulfilled only when efforts are made.

What had the bayan said? *Trust yourself.*

Hamra gritted her teeth. "All right," she said. "Let's get started."

It was a night Hamra hoped she would forget, but knew in her heart that she'd remember for as long as she lived.

For now, it lived in her mind as a series of snapshots, bits and pieces of memories and feelings rather than one continuous movie. One: the pliers from the toolkit Ayah kept on the boat, boiling in a pot of water they hung over the fire—"We need them sanitized," Ilyas said, pale and drawn in the moonlight. Two: that heart-stopping first tooth, the strength it took for all three of them to wrench it out, the way sweat streamed down Hamra's face, mingling with tears she didn't bother to wipe away. Three: blood soaking through T-shirts they fished out of their backpacks to serve as rags, blood soaking through Hamra's own top, making it cling to her skin. Four: Ilyas gently pushing her to rest and taking over, sorrowful and determined. Five: the look on Pak Belang's face as they pulled tooth after tooth.

Through it all, he didn't make a single sound—only looked up at the moon, his mouth wide open, never flinching once.

But the look. Hamra was sure she would never, ever forget that look.

Now they splayed out on the jungle floor, all four of them, barely able to move as the sun began to send timid rays peeking over the horizon.

". . . twenty-nine, thirty, thirty-one, thirty-two." Ilyas counted, adding each curved, yellowing tooth to a pouch of brown leather that Melur had produced from the depths of her bag. "Thirty-two?" He frowned. "I could have sworn I read somewhere that tigers had thirty teeth."

"He's not a tiger," Hamra reminded him wearily. "Not really. He's a human, remember?"

"Oh. Right." Ilyas handed her the pouch. "Here."

She hesitated. Part of her longed to reach out and grab it; part of her longed to make sure she had all the pieces, that everything was within her control. "You hang on to them," she said instead. "I trust you." And as she struggled to a sitting position, trying to shake off the tiredness she could feel weighing down her bones, she was rewarded with Ilyas's proud smile.

"Of course," he murmured. "Of course you trust me."

Next to her, Pak Belang stirred, and she put a hand on his side just to reassure herself that he was still breathing.

"Are you all right?" she whispered.

His reply, when it came, was soft. But not weak. "I am all right," he said.

"Does it hurt?"

His smile was almost a grimace. "No more than I deserve." The words came out all soft and mushy, as if the lack of teeth meant they had nothing to lean on.

"We need to move," Melur said, and she was almost apologetic as she said it. "We should get cleaned up and then keep going. The Bunian may appear any minute; we really need to get these teeth secure and make sure they don't fall into their clutches."

"You're right." Hamra turned back to Pak Belang. "Are you sure you can do this?" His breaths seemed so shallow; he seemed so weak.

In answer, he merely nodded, slowly, but firmly.

"Here," Ilyas said, scooting over with a bottle of water. "At least drink and eat something. It'll help recover some of your strength."

"Whatever is left of it," Pak Belang muttered, but he lapped up the water anyway, wincing slightly as it washed through his sore mouth.

In the meantime, Hamra took cover behind some dense bushes with her backpack, ready to finally change out of her blood-stained T-shirt and sweat-soaked hijab. It was hard to figure out what clothes she actually had left. There were things she'd used as makeshift ropes, things that had become bandages, things that had been used to wipe up sweat and blood and all manner of other liquids besides—she was pretty sure one bore stains of bat poop from the Langsuir's cave. But right at the bottom of her bag, she found one final T-shirt, long-sleeved, heather gray, and soft to the touch from years of washings; and she found one more clean hijab, red like her name, and the thought of that was somehow comforting. *In a world of uncertainties, Hamra, at least you still have your own name.* Only then it made her sad again, realizing that Pak Belang still didn't even have this to hang on to. *Well, that's about to change,* she told herself firmly, shoving her belongings back into the backpack. *We're going to help him, aren't we? We're the heroes here. Stories belong to the heroes.*

But as she pushed through the bushes to get back to her friends, her eagerness faded.

Because the Bunian had arrived.

As Hamra took in the terrified, defeated faces of her friends, her heart pounding painfully hard in her chest, their leader smiled at her—a wide, terrifying, familiar smile.

"Hello, sayang. Miss me?"

28

HAMRA THOUGHT SHE might actually stop breathing altogether, so hard was it to suck air into her lungs right then. Ilyas and Melur struggled uselessly against the iron grips of their captors, their mouths covered by Bunian hands, Katak leaping desperately against the walls of the glass jar they'd confined him in. In the center of the clearing, the Bunian leader held Pak Belang by the scruff of his neck, his keris pointed right at the tiger's throat. Never had Hamra seen him look so helpless.

"It's almost annoying, really," the Bunian mused aloud. "To be able to capture the old bag of fleas so easily. Where's the fun in a toothless tiger? None, I tell you."

They were interrupted by a pained yelp. "She bit me!" Melur's guard said, staring accusingly at her as he waved his injured hand in the air as if he could shake off the pain.

Melur ignored him. "I'm sorry, Hamra," she cried out. "I'm sorry. We were so busy with the teeth that I forgot the masking magic. It's my fault—" It was all she could manage before the guard slipped a cloth around her mouth, his face dark as he tied it as tightly as he could.

"No it isn't," Hamra told her firmly, doing her best to keep her voice from trembling. "Don't blame yourself." Then she turned back to the Bunian. "We're not here for your *fun*," she spat out at him. "Leave us alone. We aren't hurting you."

His expression darkened. "Perhaps. But if we don't fulfill our mission, it is our king who will hurt us. So hand over the teeth, little girl, and we'll be on our merry way."

"I don't believe you," she said, arms crossed, eyes narrowed. "I don't believe you'll just let us go, just like that. You're not to be trusted."

He put on a wounded expression, which annoyingly did nothing to diminish the handsomeness of his face. "Your words are ever so hurtful, Little Red. What can I possibly have done to earn such mistrust?" His grip tightened on the keris that poked lightly against Pak Belang's fur, and the tiger let out a little whimper. "Oh yes. That. But *besides* that . . . and really, what other options do you have? Think about it for a minute."

But Hamra couldn't think. She looked around at the faces of her friends, pale and wide-eyed in the weak light of early dawn, and the wicked, curving blade of the Bunian's keris, and the mocking curve of his smile.

And then, so quickly that Hamra barely registered how it happened, Ilyas stamped down hard on his captor's foot, elbowed him in the stomach, and stepped forward, clearing his throat as the Bunian groaned on the ground beside him. "I have a proposition for you," he said.

"What are you doing?" the Bunian leader asked, suspicion written all over his face, as another guard quickly grabbed Ilyas again and the rest moved closer, their weapons at the ready.

"Yes, Ilyas," Hamra hissed. "What are you doing?"

"Saving us." Ilyas turned to the leader. "Tell him—" He jerked his head toward the guard who held him in an iron grip. "Tell him to let me go."

There was a pause. Then the leader nodded slightly at his underling, and—reluctantly—the Bunian let Ilyas go.

Hamra watched in disbelief as Ilyas rummaged in his pocket, then held out his hand. The pouch of teeth dangled from his wrist. "I have the teeth."

The Bunian leader's eyes gleamed. "And you are giving them to us, just like that?"

From the corner of her eye, Hamra saw Melur move, and a guard immediately twisted her arm viciously, so that she cried out and sank to her knees. "Ilyas," she wrenched out. "You can't do this."

"Yes I can," Ilyas said, his jaw set, light glinting off his glasses. Hamra could hardly believe this was the boy she had known for so many years. "And I will." He turned to Hamra then, and there was a look in his eyes she couldn't quite make out. "It's the right thing to do, Hamra," he said, almost beseechingly. "It's the next *step* in our journey. Remember?"

Hamra frowned at him. "What?"

"You have to believe that I have the best of *intentions*." He kept looking at her. Why? What was he talking about? Why was he . . .

And then she understood.

"Smart boy." The Bunian leader smiled, and this time it reminded Hamra of nothing so much as a crocodile about to snap its jaws on unsuspecting prey. "Give it to me."

"Give me my friends."

The smile faded. "You are not in a position to make demands."

"Neither are you," he shot back. "I doubt your head is any safer than mine if you get back to your king and he hears you've failed. Again."

The smile was definitely gone now, and in its place was a scowl. "How do I know you will not double-cross me? Humans are not known for their honor."

"I swear to you," Ilyas said, loud and clear. "I swear to you upon my mother's life that this is a bag of teeth. You see?" And from the bag, he pulled out one tooth, one large, curved tooth that ended in a wicked point.

The Bunian leader nodded, satisfied. "Place the bag on the ground in front of you." Ilyas did, setting it down as carefully as he could.

The Bunian turned to his guards. "Let the other cretin go." The guard that held her prisoner released Melur almost reluctantly, and she ran to join Hamra at Ilyas's side.

"Now him," Hamra said, pointing at Pak Belang. "That's part of the deal, remember? Let him go."

Smirking, the Bunian leader released the tiger and sheathed his keris, and Pak Belang stumbled to where the children stood.

"And my frog," Melur chimed in, her voice shaking with fury. "Release him at once."

The guard who held Katak in his glass prison rolled

his eyes, but opened the jar without comment, and Katak bounded out and into Melur's arms with a disgruntled ribbit.

"Right," Ilyas said. "When I count to three, you get the bag, and we turn and run. Deal?"

"Fine with me, boy," the Bunian said languidly. "What do I care if you run, or walk, or slither, or crawl? I have what I need."

"Ready?" Ilyas asked Hamra quietly, and she nodded.

"Hold on to me, and to each other," she told her friends, who quickly complied, though Melur looked slightly confused about it.

Then, to the Bunian, Ilyas shouted: "All right. We're ready. One . . ."

She felt Ilyas's hand reach out to clutch her arm.

"Two . . ."

Then she thrust her hand into the dying flames of their campfire, gritting her teeth against the pain as the heat bit into her skin, just long enough for the kemenyan Nenek gave her to catch fire.

"Three!"

Hamra took a deep breath, and a step forward.

And then they vanished.

29

HAMRA OPENED HER eyes.

In front of her was her own home, shutters thrown open, lacy curtains fluttering in the morning breeze. From inside she could hear the strains of P. Ramlee. *Engkau laksana bulan . . .*

She wondered if it was a bad time to cry.

"Why are we here?" Ilyas asked, his voice thick with confusion, his hand still gripping her arm. "*How* are we here?"

"*Where* is here?" Melur sputtered; she'd somehow landed in the middle of the ixora trees and was trying to extricate herself from its dense branches.

"Home. My home." Hamra clutched the still-smoking kemenyan, trying to ignore the way it burned her skin. "What matters is the intention," she said softly. "That's what Nenek said. And more than anything, I just wanted to get us away and take us somewhere . . . somewhere . . ."

"Somewhere you feel safe," Pak Belang said. Everything about him was heavy with exhaustion and pain, from his soft voice to his drooping shoulders.

"Your hand, Hamra!" Ilyas pried open her reluctant fingers and gasped at the sight of her burned skin. "You need to treat that, you can't just . . . here, let me . . ."

"I can't let go of the kemenyan," Hamra said, brushing him off. "Not until we're done going where we need to go." She smiled at Ilyas through the waves of pain. "I'm fine."

"What happened back there?" Melur had finally made it out of the ixora trees and was now staring at Ilyas, wild-eyed and accusatory. "How could you give him the teeth? After everything we talked about? You know he'll . . . they'll . . ."

"Oh. That. Don't worry," Ilyas said.

"Don't worry? My jungle is at stake! My home!"

"But it really isn't. At least, no more than it was already." He slipped his hand into the pocket of Hamra's backpack; when he drew it out, it was filled with the familiar sight of sharp tiger teeth. "See?"

"How?" Hamra breathed out, staring at him in confusion. "How . . . ?"

"I didn't lie," Ilyas shrugged. "I said I was giving them a bag of teeth, and I did. Only it wasn't tiger teeth."

Melur frowned. "Then what . . . ?"

Ilyas grinned a wide grin at Hamra. "Atok's dentures."

And all of a sudden, she burst into laughter. "Ilyas, you're amazing."

"I know," he agreed. "Now what do I do with these?"

"Here," Hamra said, "give them to me." And she placed them carefully in a little zip-up pouch covered in tiny multi-colored hearts that she'd hurriedly emptied of the sunscreen and lip balm it usually held.

"I don't get it," Melur said flatly. "Is this another one of your so-called jokes? I swear, humans are really not as funny as they seem to believe they are."

"Ribbit," Katak said in agreement.

Hamra tried to stop laughing long enough to explain. "My grandfather has a bad habit of misplacing his dentures. I guess he accidentally slipped us the container that he keeps them in when he packed our food." Hamra grinned. "I hope the Bunian king enjoys his treasure of old man teeth."

This time even the tiger couldn't contain himself, and their whoops of laughter were so loud that Hamra had to quickly shush them before Opah or Atok heard. "We can't afford to be seen," she said quietly. "I've bought us some time, but we also can't afford to stick around; that just means we'll bring the Bunian here, and put our families in danger. I'm sorry, Ilyas," she said to her friend, who kept casting longing glances in the direction of his own home.

He straightened his sagging shoulders and gave her an attempt at a brave smile. "It's okay," he said. "I know you're right."

The kemenyan still burned, and Hamra knew there was limited time to use its power. "Come on," she said. "We've got to get these teeth to safety."

"That's the thing." Ilyas turned to Melur, a suspicious look on his face. "You never actually told us what you plan to do with them."

"That's easy enough." Melur looked at Hamra and smiled. "Take us to the Lake of the Pregnant Handmaiden."

As Hamra took a breath, as she stepped forward and the world around her tilted and shifted in dizzying ways, she thought she heard Atok's voice calling her from the open windows. But she closed her eyes so she wouldn't see. She didn't think she had the strength to stay away if she caught a glimpse of his face.

The kemenyan in Hamra's hand was now little but a sliver, still emanating that sweet-smelling smoke, still burning hot to the touch. She gritted her teeth against the pain and tried not to think about the way it felt on her skin.

"What's this?" Ilyas blinked. "Where are we?"

They were standing on the slightly-swaying pontoon of the freshwater lake Pulau Dayang Bunting was so famous for, the very same island they'd encountered the Langsuir what seemed like years ago. Whenever Hamra had come here in the past, this spot had been teeming with people struggling into rented boats, jumping off into the water, enjoying the sun. Now it was absolutely empty, the stalls nearby that used to rent out the life jackets and boats, or sell snacks and drinks to entice holidaymakers, all shuttered and silent. Kayaks lay in rows on the floating platform, dry as bones and gathering dust, while green-tented paddleboats and white ones shaped like giant majestic swans bobbed sadly on the water, tethered together with rope. The only living things were half a dozen monkeys who were lounging about on the roof, seemingly quite surprised at the group's sudden appearance.

"This is Tasik Dayang Bunting," Hamra said in answer to Ilyas's question. The morning sunlight shone through the trees surrounding them and played across the blue-green waters of the lake, and Hamra felt vaguely annoyed that she couldn't even enjoy the beauty and serenity of her surroundings, given that they were being chased by a hostile mob of magical bullies.

"I know *that*," Ilyas said. "I mean . . . what are we doing here?"

"The crocodile," the tiger said, and Melur nodded.

"The teeth will be safe with him."

Ilyas raised one hand tentatively. "Excuse me. Hi. Question. *What* crocodile?"

"How have you lived here this long and learned nothing about our stories?"

"I had other interests, okay?" he muttered. "Just answer the question!"

"A long time ago," Hamra began, slipping into her storyteller-tour guide voice once more, "there was a man named Mat Teja who fell in love with a fairy princess named Mambang Sari, and managed to trick her into marrying him. And eventually, they conceived a child together. But unfortunately, the child did not live more than seven days past its birth. And so they laid the child to rest in the depths of the lake, and a heartbroken Mambang Sari blessed its waters so that any woman who had complications bearing children would need only to drink from it to be able to conceive."

"And what," Ilyas interrupted, "does this have to do with a crocodile?"

"Let me finish, bangau." Hamra cleared her throat. "Legend has it that the child was magically transformed into a giant white crocodile that guards the lake, and only appears to those who are truly sincere at heart."

"Not to point out the obvious," Ilyas said. "But why would anyone want a giant white crocodile to appear to them? I'm very sincere at heart in my desire to not ever encounter a crocodile of any size or color. . . ."

"He would make an ideal guardian for the teeth," Melur snapped. "Let them rest in a watery grave, where nobody may reach them."

Hamra glanced at Pak Belang, who nodded reluctantly. "It's a good plan," he admitted. "Though I hate to compliment a fairy."

"Well then." Hamra took the zip-up pouch filled with tiger teeth out of her bag. "Who's going to give it to him?"

She looked up to see them all looking at her and smiled weakly. "Just kidding, I know it's me."

"I will go with you," Pak Belang said.

"Are you sure you can manage?" She was almost certain that the tiger was swaying gently on his feet where he stood. "And will he even—" She stopped short. She had been about to ask if the crocodile would even appear to them if the tiger was with her.

"Yes." Pak Belang paused. "And hopefully." He began to walk away, and she hurried to catch up.

"Where are we going?"

"The Miracle Border."

"Oh." They walked to the boardwalk that would take them to the Miracle Border, the small strip of rocky ridge that separated the lake from the sea. The walk felt longer than it really was, and Hamra had to pause once in a while to shake away a sudden light-headedness. The pain in her burnt hand was beginning to pulse like a heartbeat, but still she held tight to the sliver of kemenyan, as if her life depended on it. Which it probably did.

They reached the end of the narrow wooden bridge and stopped.

"I've never really understood why they call this a miracle," she said. "It's just a little bit of land. And yes, one side is fresh water, and then just about thirty meters away is an entire ocean filled with salt water. But to call that a miracle seems a little . . . extreme."

"If there is one thing I have learned," Pak Belang said, his words coming out even slower now, "it is that miracles are a matter of perspective. To a roaming ant, the smallest crumb is a miracle. To a dying man, each breath is a miracle. To a lone weretiger, friendship is a miracle." He smiled the ghost of a smile. "Who are we to say what is miraculous and what is not?"

Hamra leaned against him lightly. His fur was no longer soft; it was matted and clumpy and spotted with blood. But she took comfort from his warmth anyway. "I suppose you're right."

"It has been known to happen sometimes." Gently, the tiger nudged her off and walked closer to the water. "Cover your ears."

"Why?"

He sighed. "Must you question *everything*?"

She clapped her hands over them just in time. Pak Belang opened his mouth and let out his loudest and most fearsome roar, a roar that echoed through the trees and silenced the jungle's inhabitants, a roar so loud that it felt like it shook the very earth they stood on.

For a moment, all was quiet.

And then, something in the water went *glup*. And a large bubble shot up and burst through the blue-green surface, then another, then another, faster and faster each time, as if someone—some*thing*—was rapidly ascending to meet them.

I'm not scared, Hamra told herself. *Of course I'm not.*

But she found herself inching closer to Pak Belang just the same.

The tip of its snout appeared first, two nostrils like smudges in leathery white skin. Then little by little came the rest of it, emerging slowly from the water, until finally Hamra could see its entire head, from the grim line of its mouth to the sharp eyes that stared directly at them. Just the part that she could see looked to be almost as long as she was tall, and she thought about the rest of it stretching out beneath those waters and shivered.

The beast said nothing; it just watched them, and waited.

Hamra steeled herself to speak, but just as she was about to open her mouth, Pak Belang spoke first.

"Hello, Ancient One. I have come to ask for a favor."

The crocodile regarded him without a word.

"You have no reason to grant it. But I think, as you have appeared to me, you may see the sincerity of my heart, the trueness of my intentions." The tiger took a deep breath, and winced as if it pained him. "I have lived a long life on stolen time; time siphoned through magical means. I have done unspeakable things. I have sacrificed all that was good and right in my life for the sake of power, which I have hoarded as a dragon hoards treasure. And I have learned, of late, that power is a tool best wielded only by those with a foundation strong enough to withstand temptation. And those people are few."

He paused again, trying to choose the best words he could. "I cannot allow this power to fall into the hands of the corrupt and the cruel, and I cannot trust that even the best of human or fae will not fall to temptation. The world will always produce more like me—more who will try to swing the balance in their favor, for entirely selfish reasons. And so I ask for your help, Ancient One. I ask you to protect us all . . . from another me."

Pak Belang stopped then, exhausted from his efforts, and Hamra waited with bated breath to hear what the crocodile might say.

But when the crocodile finally moved, it wasn't to speak; it merely unhinged its massive jaws and opened them wide, so that Hamra could see its long pink tongue and the rows of sharp teeth within.

"What's it doing?" she whispered. She didn't want to be rude, but she was also uncomfortably aware of the fact that the crocodile could easily swallow her whole if it wanted to, and would probably have room for more afterward.

"Throw him the teeth," the tiger said.

"Are you—"

"Just do it." He sighed. "Trust me."

Hamra swallowed the anxiety and uncertainty gathering in her throat. Then she took the pouch in her hand and threw it as best she could toward the crocodile's gaping mouth.

For a moment, time seemed to stand still, and it was as if the pouch hung motionless in the air, each of its technicolor hearts gleaming in the sunlight. But the moment passed, and the crocodile leaped up and closed its jaws around it with a snap that echoed through the jungle and set off a chorus of whoops and screeches from the monkeys within, and a swell of waves rippling through the water and splashing on Hamra's shoes. Then it disappeared once again into the depths, until the surface was calm once more and not a trace of it was left but the wetness she felt against her toes.

30

THEY WALKED BACK to the others, Hamra and the weretiger, side by side, her hand on his back. They didn't talk. There didn't seem to be anything to say. Their steps were slow, but Hamra told herself that Pak Belang was in pain and shouldn't be rushed, and did her best to ignore the little voice that tried to tell her *and you, Hamra, you're in pain too.* Her hand burned with the remaining kemenyan.

They were still a short distance away from the pontoon when it happened: something struck Hamra's arm, forcing a yelp of surprise out of her and making her stop short as she looked around to figure out what it was and where it had come from. As it turned out, the culprit lay by her feet: a pebble the size of a ten sen coin, jagged-edged and mottled gray. *Probably just a monkey*, Hamra thought, except that it was quickly followed by another pebble—this time ricocheting off her knee before clattering against the board-walk by her feet.

All right. Maybe not a monkey.

She whipped her head quickly to the left and finally spotted them, Ilyas and Melur, waving frantically from the cover of the trees, fingers on lips to tell them to be quiet.

She tugged at Pak Belang's coat to get him to follow, and they quickly clambered over the railing and into the shadows of the jungle. "What's going on?" she whispered. The air felt still and heavy, as if rain was coming despite the sunshine.

"They're here," Ilyas said quietly. "The Bunian are here. It was really hot, and we thought we'd sit in the shade behind those stalls while we waited for you. And then we heard the monkeys screeching, and we saw them coming down the steps toward the pontoon. And we quickly ducked here out of sight, so we could warn you. They're probably lying in wait for us there, hoping to ambush us or something."

"How did they even *find* us?"

"The jungle is full of eyes and ears," Melur said. "And not all of them can be trusted." She glanced at Pak Belang. "Did you take care of it?"

"It has been done," he said quietly.

She nodded. "Good. Then we must go."

"The question is *where*," Ilyas said.

Hamra opened her palm; the sliver of kemenyan stared back up at her, burnt ash-black by now and somehow still smoldering slightly. "Wherever it is," she said, "it's the only trip we're going to be able to make. So we'd better be sure."

"Intention is what matters," the tiger said. "Remember? Our final clue is the bones. Tell it to take us there, and see what it does."

She glanced at him. "You think that will work?"

"You think we have any other choice?" he shot back, and she knew he was right. "Besides, if the Bunian are here, then anywhere else we can be is an improvement."

"Point taken." She made sure her pack was secure, then looked around at her friends. "Okay, everyone hang on to each other. Ready?"

They nodded, faces serious and sweaty.

"Let's go."

Hamra took a step, and the world changed again.

This time, they were on a beach. She knew it even before she opened her eyes, knew it from the smell of salt on the wind and the way her shoes sank in the soft sand.

"Pantai Tengkorak?" Ilyas sounded as confused as

Hamra felt. They knew this beach well, with its soft white sands and its clear waters; it was more secluded than the others, butting up against a forested area and a little more hidden unless you knew where to look, so that tourists skipped it in favor of the more posh Datai area, with its five-star hotels and its air of expensive exclusivity. This was a *local* beach. This was home turf.

"What does this place have to do with anything?"

"I don't know." Hamra opened her palm, which was now empty of anything but ugly red welts and blisters from the heat; the kemenyan was gone. "And there'll be no more quick getaways for us now."

Melur stared all around them, as if she was trying to find a clue to their mystery. "The bones," she murmured. "The bones. What bones?"

Hamra sank to the ground, her legs suddenly too tired to keep her upright. "I know what happened," she said dully. "My intention must have gotten the kemenyan magic confused. I asked for bones, and it brought us here—to a beach that's literally called Skull Beach."

Melur sat down beside her. "Well . . . maybe it's still right! You never know! Maybe there's something here that will—"

"That will what?" Hamra snapped. She was suddenly

entirely too tired of being hopeful, entirely too aware of the tears that were clawing at her throat. "They call this Pantai Tengkorak because supposedly, it's where the bones of sailors and pirates lost to shipwrecks or sea monsters would get washed up long ago. But there are no bones here now. And anyway, that's just a story."

Pak Belang flopped onto the sand, resting his head on his great paws. "All of this has been 'just a story,' Little Red."

"Just say I messed up." The tears were perilously close now, threatening to spill over any second. She wished desperately for her old flames; tears were so much worse than the fire in her heart. "Just say this is my fault. All of it. Just say if I never took that fruit, if I never risked my whole family, if I never made the decisions that I made . . ." She swallowed hard, and the movement made a single tear come trickling down her cheek. "Just say I'm the one who did this. I'm the one who got us all into this."

"I cannot," the tiger rumbled.

"Because you don't believe it's my fault?"

"Because," he said evenly, "I am bleeding."

Hamra's head snapped up in shock. "What?" Then she saw it. The wound on Pak Belang's back courtesy of the

Bunian leader's wicked blade had reopened. Fresh blood was oozing its way slowly down from the gap, which looked red and raw and painful.

"I thought your powers meant you heal quickly!"

"It might have escaped your notice, Little Red," Pak Belang said with a grimace. "But I have been giving those things up as we go."

"Hold on, I'll get a cloth to stem the blood," Ilyas said quickly as he began tossing things out of his backpack.

Hamra scooted closer, and Pak Belang rested his head on her lap, eyes closed as if he was too tired to think. "Please be all right," she whispered so that only he could hear. "Please don't die, not now, not when we're so close."

But he didn't speak. He just opened his mouth and licked her hand with his rough, rough tongue. And Hamra lowered her head close and let the tears she'd been holding back flow. She cried for the tiger, and for Opah, and for herself; for all the things they'd been working so hard to find, for all the things lost forever, and for all the things they were about to lose. She cried so hard that she barely noticed Melur and Ilyas as they moved to help Pak Belang; she cried so hard that she barely noticed the way the blood pooled onto the sand only for a moment before it was somehow sucked in, leaving no indication that it had been there at all.

But she did notice that the sun seemed to have disappeared behind dark clouds, and that the wind had begun to blow so hard around them that had it not been for her artfully placed pins, her hijab would have flown off her head in seconds. Still, she clamped her good hand on it just to be sure. "What's going on?" She had to yell to be heard over the howling gale.

Ilyas was too busy chasing his things to respond; the wind was sending all the items he'd excavated from his bag rolling along the beach. "Storm coming?" Melur yelled back, still trying her best to stop Pak Belang's bleeding with a Star Wars T-shirt imprinted with Yoda's face. DO OR DO NOT, THERE IS NO TRY was emblazoned below.

That seemed obvious enough. But there was no thunder, no lightning ripping jagged holes in the sky; only dark rolling clouds and this inexplicable wind that bent the trees as if it wanted nothing more than to snap them in two.

And still, Pak Belang bled, and still the wind howled, and finally Hamra started to notice that it was actually lifting the sand up and sending it swirling in torrents around them, a beach full of small sand tornadoes.

On her lap, Pak Belang opened his eyes. "The bones," he croaked.

"Bones?"

"In the sand." She had to lean in close to hear him. "The bones . . . become one . . . with the sand. Blood and bone . . . that is the strongest magic there is."

And on the wind, she began to hear whispers, whispers that she couldn't quite make out at first, but which eventually separated themselves into words. *What do you want?* the wind asked. *What do you ask of us?*

Hamra closed her eyes against the sting of the sand, and opened her mouth, and yelled as loud as she could: "Why do you weep?"

The answer, when it came, was quick: *Because we remember.* And then: *Let us show you.*

And all around them, the tornadoes went still, the grains of sand suspended in the air as if they were waiting for instructions. When they moved again, it suddenly dawned on Hamra what they were doing. They were making pictures, like elaborate sandcastles in the air, so fast that Hamra could barely catch them all: here, families laughing together, sharing food, splashing in the water; here, a little body being pulled from the water, still, lifeless, the grieving mother beside it, face contorted in pain; here, a group of friends, arms around each other, mugging for the camera; here, a father and child digging for crabs in the sand. Memory after memory, picture after picture, until at last the sand began to slow down. And now it began to linger: a little boy and a girl, holding hands as they splashed through the shallow waves. The same children, sharing one packet of nasi lemak between them, two spoons, cross-legged on a tikar. And again, a little bigger, running races up and down the sand. Building a sandcastle. Fighting over a spade they both wanted to use. Sitting side by side, watching the sun set. Shrieking as they ran away from a particularly large monkey. Whispering secrets, and crossing pinkies to swear they'd never tell. On and on, a little older each time, until the picture came when they were children no more; they were a man and a woman, and the man had a ring, and the woman had an expression of infinite sadness. And then it was just the man on his own, his face a mask of anger and hurt.

And then nothing.

The sand settled back down to the ground. The wind had shrunk to nothing but the usual sea breeze; the clouds had disappeared, burned away by the rays of the sun.

Pak Belang looked at Hamra. "That was me," he said

quietly. "That boy was me." And then, looking at her tear-stained cheeks, he asked her gently, oh so gently: "Do you know who that girl was?"

And Hamra nodded, because she did.

"That was my grandmother," she whispered. "That was Opah."

31

"I DON'T GET it," Ilyas said yet again as they made their way, as fast as they could, through the jungle. "Explain it to me like I'm five."

"The tiger and Opah were friends," she called over her shoulder, pushing branches out of her way impatiently. "Best friends. Like you and me. Only it didn't end the way either of them wanted, and they stopped being friends. Now she's probably the only person left in the world who knows his true name. It's locked somewhere in her memories. And we have to help her get it out."

"And how are we going to do that?"

Hamra flashed a grin at him. "The jambu. Remember?"

Ilyas groaned. "The thing that started it all? Really?"

"Full circle, baby."

The tiger ran alongside Hamra, his energy seemingly

renewed, his expression determined. The wound on his back was bound now, as neatly as Ilyas could manage, but Hamra caught herself glancing at it every so often, as if to make sure it really was still okay. "We must hurry," he called to them. "There is no telling where the Bunian are now, or when they will catch up to us again."

"Are we close?" The jungle was starting to blur together for even Hamra, so used to navigating its green pathways.

"Almost there."

Here in the dense undergrowth, it was as if the canopy trapped the heat and humidity in with them, making walking an even harder task. *Breathe, Hamra, that's it, nice deep breaths, fill those lungs, we're almost there . . .*

The clearing was just as she remembered it: gentle sunlight filtering through the leaves; the tree in its center, branches laden with the most perfect jambu.

The only thing that was different about it was that it was surrounded by a dozen black-clad Bunian, and one other.

This one was clad in yellow silk shot with threads of gold. This one wore his hair down to his shoulders, with a thin circlet, also of gold, atop his head, gleaming like a halo. This one too was handsome, as they all were; but he was handsome the way a diamond is, all planes and edges and angles, brilliant and hard and cold.

This one, Hamra knew with sudden certainty, was the king.

"Good afternoon, Little Red," he said, smiling a smile that never quite reached his eyes. "We've been expecting you."

32

THE BUNIAN KING reclined languidly on silks and cushions in rich hues of burgundy and gold that his guards had set up for him beneath the jambu tree, and the four friends were made to kneel before him as they awaited what he had to say. None but the tiger were restrained, and he wore thick rope that bound his paws together two by two, a situation he made clear he was mad about with the way he glowered and growled and roared at anyone who dared come near.

"Calm yourself, tiger," the king said, examining his nails for blemishes. "You do yourself no favors by maiming my guards."

"Let us go," Hamra said, trying to hide how badly her hands trembled. "We don't have what you're looking for. We're no use to you now."

"That's the trouble, Little Red." The king leaned forward now, all humor gone, leaving only a burning intensity in his eyes as he looked at her. "Not only did you trick my guards—a price they paid dearly for, I might add—and cause me severe inconvenience, you have also made it such that I cannot ever get what I want. And I do not take kindly to not getting what I want."

"What are you going to do with us?" Melur demanded, and the king smiled.

"Fairies. Always so *direct*, so . . . so . . ." He wrinkled his nose delicately as he thought of the right word, and finally settled for "unrefined." The king waved a pale hand, and a guard came forward to quickly bind a protesting Melur's mouth so that she could no longer speak. "That's better. I do hate to be interrupted." He turned back to the others. "Now. Given how much time and effort you have cost me—and truly, I abhor having to put in any sort of effort whatsoever—the only acceptable consequence here is death." His eyes swiveled to Pak Belang, and in them there was such a malicious gleam that Hamra's blood ran cold. "At least for you. The children can be put to work. There is always use for children, and after all, I am not cruel. Merely fair." His gaze slid over to a red-faced Melur, and he sighed dramatically. "I suppose I might even find it in my merciful heart to extend a place to this creature, as much as it pains me to do so. That's just the kind of king I am."

"No king of mine," Hamra said, and the flames burned sharp on the edge of every word. "Never a king of mine."

"Now, now," the king said soothingly. "Hard work is good for you, you know. Builds character. Or so they tell me; I have quite enough character without putting myself through that nonsense. Now be quiet, I've got a killing to do. Bring me my keris," he called out as he rose to his feet, and a guard quickly appeared at his side bearing a sheathed blade.

Slowly, the king walked toward them, step by deliberate step, a smile playing on his lips as if he was enjoying this moment, all eyes glued to his every move. When he reached Pak Belang he stopped and unsheathed his keris in one smooth movement. "So this is how the great weretiger of Langkawi is destined to die," he said contemptuously, sweeping his gaze over the tiger's once-proud frame, now lank and weak. "Stripped of his powers, toothless, nothing but a shell of his former self. If you were to get on your knees and beg for your life now, tiger, perhaps I would be merciful to you too."

Pak Belang lifted his great head. "Never."

The king's mouth twisted in displeasure. "Then if you

will not kneel, you will fall at my feet instead." He lifted the blade, ready to stab the tiger right through the heart.

And it was at that precise moment that two things happened at once.

One: There was a huge cry from the trees as creatures and people burst from the shadows, wielding knives and waving staves, much to the Bunian's shock.

And two: The entire clearing erupted in teal-tinged flames.

33

HAMRA COUGHED AS smoke filled her lungs as well as the clearing around her, a thick, dense smoke that made it almost impossible to see and, curiously, seemed to dampen sound as well, so that everything she could hear—admittedly, not a lot right now—seemed as though she was hearing it from behind a wall. "Pak Belang?" she called. "Ilyas? Melur?"

And then she screamed as she felt a hand clamp around her wrist and pull hard, so that she landed on her hands and knees . . .

Face-to-face with Melur. "You're okay!" Relief bloomed in Hamra's chest; she might have hugged Melur if they weren't still surrounded by smoke, flames, murderous Bunian, and other creatures besides, whose legs kept brushing against them, resulting in barely heard yelps of shock amidst the smoke above.

"For now," Melur whispered. "Katak cut me loose—what? You've never trained a frog to use a blade?"

"Not really, no!"

"Pity." Melur shrugged. "It's a useful trick." From her shoulder, Katak puffed out his chest and let out a proud ribbit.

Hamra stared at the familiar shade of teal that ringed the flames around them, and realization slowly dawned. "This was you?"

Melur flashed her a smug grin. "Of course it was. Now follow me. We're okay if we stick close to the ground; the smoke is meant to disturb your line of sight and hearing, and allows us to either attack undetected from the ground or escape undetected."

"Given that we are literally two children, a toothless tiger, and a fairy, and that there are suddenly *way* more creatures here than there were before, we're probably better off with the second option."

Melur sighed as she fingered the knife at her belt longingly. "You're probably right. Unfortunately."

"Who—*what?*—are all these people, anyway?" Hamra accidentally brushed against a hairy leg, resulting in a surprised squeal from somewhere above the smoke cloud that was soon lost in the commotion of fighting and flailing.

"My best guess," Melur said, crawling along beside her and carefully avoiding a pair of legs that ended in cloven hooves as it battled against a pair of black-clad Bunian legs, "is that some of them are here trying to get the same thing the king wants. Those teeth. And then others are trying to stop *those* people from getting those teeth."

"And none of them know we don't even have the teeth anymore." Hamra's heart sank.

"Correct. Which probably will not please anyone very much." Melur smiled humorlessly. "Which means we need to get away as soon as possible."

"Right. You get Ilyas, I'll get Pak Belang." Hamra began to move, carefully picking her way past more legs, human and otherwise, and keeping an eye out for the tiger's striped haunches. It was hard going; light barely filtered through the cloud of smoke above her, and there was so much confusion and tripping, so much clashing of steel and wood, so many yells of pain and fury. But finally, she saw him, cowering to try to avoid the smoke, feet still bound.

Their eyes met, and she saw his lips move. "Hamra."

Quickly, she moved to untie him. It seemed to take her forever to work the knots; her one hand still hurt, and she was trembling from stress and fear, and she kept looking around to make sure no black- or yellow-clad legs were near. But at last she got him free. "Now come," she whispered. "Follow me. We have to get back to Melur and Ilyas—" She stopped short then. For in front of them had slithered a familiar form—the massive werecobra wending her way gently past the sea of legs, and heading straight for them with a wicked little smile on her face.

Pak Belang grabbed the edge of Hamra's T-shirt in his mouth and yanked to get her attention. "On my back," he roared.

"But you're hurt—"

"*At once!*"

And so Hamra flung her arms around his neck and hung on tight as the tiger began to run, swerving to dodge the battles going on all around them. "What about Ilyas and Melur?"

"No time to worry about that right now," Pak Belang panted. "I'll get you to safety, and then I'll go back for them."

"I can't leave them!"

"Don't argue with me, child." The tiger seemed to forget his pain as he loped on. "Your grandmother . . . I could never forgive myself if something happened to you."

"And I could never forgive myself if I left my friends to be hurt or . . . or worse!"

All of a sudden, Pak Belang stopped dead in his tracks—so suddenly that Hamra was almost thrown off his back. "Ow! What's going . . ."

And then her voice trailed off. Because the Bunian king stood before them, blocking their path, wild-eyed and grinning. "What a coincidence. I could never forgive both of you either."

Slowly, Hamra slid off the tiger's back, and he moved to stand before her, his body between her and the king's wicked blade. "She is a child," he said, his voice low. "She has done nothing to deserve death at your hands."

"She has done nothing to deserve to be spared either," the king snapped. In the firelight, his skin took on a strange glow, and shadows played disconcertingly over his face. "Look what a mess she's made!"

"The mess is your own doing."

The king sighed. "Enough talk. More dying."

Hamra closed her eyes then. She couldn't watch the advancing blade, or the way it would pierce right through Pak Belang's flesh. She'd been carrying her backpack all this time, but now her shoulders went slack and it fell with

369

a thump to the ground. *All this weight I've been holding on to*, she thought to herself. *Maybe it's time to let go. Maybe it's time to accept that this is how the story ends. Maybe . . . maybe . . .*

Something rolled against her foot, and she blinked. It was Opah's feather duster; she'd almost forgotten she had it at all. *Bring my containers back with all their covers, or I'll whack you* . . . It must have detached itself from where she'd tied it onto her bag. She couldn't help blinking back tears at the sight of its familiar brown feathers, the way its bamboo handle curved into a hook at the end. What hero brings a feather duster of all things on a magical quest? But Opah had been so certain that it would come in useful . . .

And all at once, Hamra knew exactly what she needed to do.

She looked up at the king, his face wreathed in triumph. "You know what my grandmother always told me?"

He raised an eyebrow, bemused. "What?"

"The truth. And in your case, the truth is that you lose." And in one swift movement, she grabbed the king's leg with the hooked end of the feather duster and pulled with all her might, so that he tumbled onto his back with a yelp of shock . . .

And Pak Belang pounced.

It was like something out of a movie: the tiger looming over the king, one heavy paw pinning the arm that held the knife down to the ground; another on his chest, sharp claws hovering dangerously close to his throat; and all around them, flames, smoke, and bodies in battle.

"Yield," Pak Belang said, and his voice had never sounded stronger or more regal to Hamra.

"Never!"

The claws inched just a little closer, until they were pressing close to his neck, so close it would take nothing more than the tiniest bit of pressure to pierce the skin.

The king gulped. "Of course, you present a most persuasive argument. I yield."

"Louder."

"I YIELD!" And with that, he unwrapped his fingers from the hilt of the keris and let it hit the ground, where Hamra quickly ran to scoop it up and away from trouble-making hands.

At the sight of their king's surrender, the rest of the Bunian begrudgingly surrendered their weapons, and the rest of the creatures broke out in cheers as the smoke finally began to lift—though Hamra noticed some took the distraction as an opportunity to inch uncomfortably closer, eyeing them hungrily.

"We don't have the teeth anymore," she said hurriedly. "Stop looking at us like that."

"Blast!" she heard a shriek from somewhere close to the ground, and the moonrat turned his back and trudged dejectedly back into the forest, everyone else making a wide berth for him as he muttered something about interfering humans under his breath.

"Hamra!" Melur and Ilyas came barreling from amidst the crowd, wrapping her in the most enormous group hug. Melur had a cut over one eye, and Ilyas seemed to be wielding some kind of parang, but she decided those were stories she could get out of them later.

"Are you guys okay?"

"Us? We're fine!" Ilyas twirled his parang with exaggerated nonchalance and almost dropped it on his own foot. "Someone gave me a knife," he pointed out gleefully.

"I can see that."

"It was so cool, helping to fight off the bad guys!"

Melur rolled her eyes. "He spent most of the time hiding behind me, and at one point I had to tell him to stop waving the knife around because he was about to slice my ear off."

Hamra laughed. It felt rusty, and strange, and good.

Nearby, a stout ogre and a pair of bushy-bearded orang kerdil who barely came up to Hamra's knees were busy binding the king and his guards with iron chains. "Not so hard!" Hamra heard him whine. "My skin is delicate!"

Pak Belang came to stand next to them, watching the proceedings.

"What will you do with them?" Hamra asked.

"It is not for me to decide." He turned to look at Melur. "Justice shall be determined by you and the other denizens of the jungle, as is only right."

Melur paused. "So I could still kill him if I chose? And you would not interfere?"

Pak Belang bowed his head. "I cannot stop you. I can only warn you of how anger corrupts, like a flame that burns everything in its path. Our destinies are our own to choose, as many-pronged as the branches of a tree."

Melur walked to where the prisoners sat and stood staring for a long, long time at the king in chains at her feet, and in the curve of her shoulders Hamra saw all the love she bore for the jungle, and how angry she had been at the thought of losing it all.

"You should listen to him," the king said helpfully. "He seems to know what he's talking about."

"Be quiet."

At last, Hamra saw her straighten up and set her chin. "I have a suggestion," she said, and the whole clearing quieted down in anticipation. "Since the king and his ilk seem to have a fondness for great cats . . . it seems to me that the most fitting thing to do would be to exile them to the uninhabited Pulau Singa, where the giant lion spirit that guards the island may do with them what he wishes." Melur smiled then, a slow, satisfied smile, as the Bunian faces around her grew pale. "It has been many years. I'm sure he's just dying for a little entertainment."

And as the other creatures of the jungle raised their voices in a roar of agreement, Hamra walked up to the tiger and stood on tiptoes to whisper in his ear.

"Time to go."

34

THIS TIME, THE house was quiet. The windows were open, but no music wafted out of them; all was still within. Hamra frowned and checked her watch. "Oh, right," she said. "This is when they usually nap."

"It's not even eleven in the morning," Ilyas said. "I thought they nap at three."

"They do that too."

There were only three of them now, Hamra, Ilyas, and Pak Belang. Melur had chosen to stay behind with Katak, helping to clean wounds and mop up the messes the Bunian had left in their wake. "Besides," she'd told Hamra with a wink, "your world and mine are very different, Little Red. I should be entirely out of place among the humans."

Hamra nodded, though her heart had constricted slightly

then, at the idea of leaving her friend behind. "You'll come visit?"

Melur's grin was wide, and her embrace warm. "Of course I will," she'd whispered in Hamra's ear. "It's a lucky house that has fairies come to visit, you know?" And Katak let out a small "ribbit" of agreement as he nuzzled against Hamra's cheek.

Now Hamra began to walk toward her front door, Ilyas following closely behind, the tiger keeping up more slowly. Her steps already felt freer, lighter. *I'm home,* she thought. *I'm finally, finally home.* The doorknob felt snug and familiar in her hand. "Mind the step," she said, turning to the others. "Make sure you don't trip . . ." her voice trailed off when she realized the tiger hung back, looking awkward and uncertain. "What's the matter?"

He could not seem to meet her gaze. "What will she think of me?" he asked. "What do I say? How do I make up for all this time?"

Hamra leaned her face against his. "There are no real answers to any of this. I think the best you can do is start with 'I'm sorry' and work your way up."

The tiger shut his eyes. "I suppose you are right."

"I can't believe you just admitted I was right. That might

be a first." She tugged gently at the fur on his neck. "Now come on."

And together they all walked up the path toward the door . . .

. . . which swung open before they could even reach it.

"Hamra." Ayah stood in the doorway, his hair disheveled, clothes rumpled, face etched with exhaustion and concern.

Hamra swallowed. "Assalamualaikum, Ayah."

And then she was in his arms, and suddenly she was absolutely certain that everything was going to be just fine.

"I'm sorry we took so long," she mumbled into the crook of his neck. "I didn't mean to make you all worry about me."

"Worry? About you?" Ayah released her reluctantly and smiled as he tweaked her nose. "It's everyone else in the jungle we were worried about. Who dares cross paths with our Hamra?" His smile turned soft, tender. "Your mother and I are so proud of you, kiddo. Now go on inside. There are some people who have been waiting for you for a long, long time."

Hamra kicked off her sneakers and stepped over the threshold. After the bright sunshine outside, it took a while for her eyes to adjust to the cool dimness of indoors; when she did, she saw Atok lying on the sofa, clad in his sarong and nothing else, his chest heaving with each breath in, light snores escaping with each breath out. Tears pricked behind her eyes as she paused just to drink in the sight of him: the liver spots dotted around his skin, the round swell of his belly, the checkered sarong worn thin with use. She remembered that sarong from when she was little; he'd scoop her up in it as he sat on his chair and swing her about, crooning a little lullaby. *Getaran jiwa, melanda hatiku . . .*

Hamra knelt down beside her sleeping grandfather and gave him a kiss on the papery skin of his cheek. "Atok," she whispered. "I'm home."

For a moment, she thought he hadn't heard her. Then his eyes fluttered open and he sat straight up to look at her, blinking as if he couldn't quite believe what he was seeing.

"Hamra?"

And then there was nothing in the world but the comfort of his arms, nothing but the love she felt radiating from every pore, reaching out and enveloping her in its warmth. "Hi, Atok," she mumbled against his chest.

It didn't seem like he wanted to let her go, but eventually he pulled her away so he could peer more closely at her. "Are you all right? Are you hurt? What happened to your hand? Why is it—YA ALLAH YA TUHANKU!"

"Bawak bertenang, Bapak," Ayah said soothingly. "He's not here to hurt us." Then he stepped back and tweaked Ilyas's elbow to get his attention. "Is he?" Ayah whispered.

Ilyas shrugged. "I mean, I went through this whole thing with him, and I'm still alive. I think you guys will be okay."

"Fair enough."

"Oh," Hamra said, as Atok shrank back into the sofa cushions as if he thought they might camouflage him. "I guess I should explain why—"

"Why there's a giant tiger in my living room?" Atok gulped. "Yes, I would appreciate that very much, thank you."

"We need Opah's help," Hamra explained. "Long story."

"I'll bet." Atok stared at the tiger and frowned. "Remember what you did to me the last time we met, sir?" And he tapped his weak leg with his cane. "Never been the same since."

"Wait a minute." Hamra looked back and forth between the two of them, her mouth agape. "*Last time?*"

Pak Belang looked shamefaced and tried his best to appear as small as possible. "I do apologize," he rumbled, backing away and accidentally knocking into a side table. Picture frames fell flat on their faces, and a bowl of potpourri upended itself on the floor with a crash and a shower

379

of dried flower petals. "Er. I can help clean that?"

Ilyas patted his back. "Maybe best to leave that one to me, buddy."

Hamra shook her head and turned to her grandfather. "Never mind all of that. I have to take him to see Opah," she said softly. "Is that okay?"

Her grandfather stared at Pak Belang, his eyes narrowed. "You going to bite her leg too?" he asked. It sounded like a serious question, but Hamra could swear she saw the tiniest little tell-tale twinkle in Atok's eyes.

"N-No," the tiger replied.

"Well then. Go ahead, and I'll see if I can get up some lunch for us. Ilyas, boy, come and help me, would you?"

In Opah's room, the fan whirred overhead and the curtains were drawn to keep out the heat. Hamra's grandmother was lying as she always did, flat on her back in the middle of the double bed, same pink sheets, same pink pillow. Everything exactly the same as it was, except for Hamra herself, who was never going to be the same again, and the tiger that now filled almost the entire available space in the little room.

As if she could feel herself being watched, Opah peeled open first one eye, then the other, "What?" she mumbled.

She didn't seem at all fazed by the presence of the large wild animal in her bedroom.

Hamra smiled. "I brought you something."

Opah pointed at the tiger. "Is it him? Because you can't trust those things. I keep telling you."

"I know." Hamra slipped a hand into her backpack and brought out the jambu she'd plucked from the tree in the clearing earlier, and suddenly the air seemed a little clearer, a little brighter. "Don't worry about him. I brought you a treat."

"A jambu!" Opah clapped her thin hands together in delight. "Oh, how lovely! How did you know it's my favorite?"

Hamra swallowed a lump that had lodged itself in her throat. "You know, somebody must have told me." She sat beside her grandmother on the bed, and the worn mattress sagged under their combined weight. "Do you think you could bite into it? Or do you need me to cut it?"

Opah's mouth set in a stubborn line, like a little kid who has been told they probably can't do something. "Of course I can bite it. Watch me." And she grabbed the jambu and took a big bite.

"Good?" Hamra asked, reaching over to tenderly wipe the juice that dribbled down Opah's chin, and her grandmother nodded, her mouth too full to speak.

And then she stopped, and turned to look at Hamra, and her eyes lit up in the way they did when Opah was truly Opah again, and Hamra's heart sang. "Hello, my Hamra." Opah reached over to pull her into a long, tight hug. "Oh, my dear girl. I feel like I haven't seen you in a very long time."

"You haven't." Hamra leaned into her grandmother, taking in all of her, loving all of her. "I missed you, Opah."

"I missed you too, sayang."

They sat this way for a good while, until the sound of a tiger clearing its throat brought them back to reality.

"Ah," Opah said, gazing levelly at the tiger, who seemed to cower beneath her stare. "You."

"Hello," Pak Belang stammered. "It has been many years . . ."

"Indeed. Many years since you simply stopped being my friend, all because I wouldn't marry you, and then became obsessed with this idea of weretigers and whatever other nonsense."

Hamra was reminded sharply of all the times her grandmother had rapped her on the butt with the feather duster for her transgressions. This was giving off very similar vibes.

"I had . . . certain ambitions . . ." the tiger muttered.

"You wanted to control everything around you, particularly me," Opah corrected him. "And when you found you couldn't, you decided that the best way to gain control was to gain more power."

The tiger grinned sheepishly. "I have made some mistakes, certainly . . ."

Opah crossed her arms. "You ate all my mother's chickens," she said flatly. "You ate EVERYONE'S chickens. The whole village lived in fear of you for years. And you fought my husband-to-be! His leg's never been the same since."

"I know." Pak Belang hung his head. "I cannot apologize enough for all my misdeeds. This isn't even the worst of them. But nonetheless, I wish to tell you that I am sorry. Truly and sincerely. And that I wish . . . I wish I had been a better friend. That is all."

Opah peered at him with her sharp eyes. "Really? Is that all?"

"Opah," Hamra said, tugging at her grandmother's arm. "Opah, the tiger wants to become a human again. He's got no powers now. He just wants to get back to how he used to be. But he needs to know his name, his true name, before he can do that. Do you remember what it is?"

Opah sniffed. "Of course I do. Used it often enough for so many years of my life, didn't I?" She sighed and looked the tiger directly in the eye. "For years and years, I thought about what I would say to you," she said quietly. "I wrote down my accusations, my curses, my insults—I had some pretty good ones! I rehearsed long speeches in my head." She sighed, long and deep. "But I am old now, and so are you. And these days, I live so much in the past. And it's simply not worth holding on to the bad memories, when there is so little space for even the good." She paused. "These days, I simply want to be loved, and to be happy. And so, I forgive you. I forgive you for everything—Firman."

As she said it, the tiger's ears pricked straight up. "Firman?" he whispered, uncertain at first, then with dawning remembrance. "Firman. That's it. That's my name. That's my name!" And Hamra laughed to see his delight.

Then all of a sudden his eyes widened in shock, and he opened his mouth, and from its depths came a beam of white light so bright that it felt as if it would burn her eyeballs right out of their sockets. From behind a pillow, Opah shrieked, "What is happening?" But Hamra couldn't answer; she was too transfixed by the sight before her. For now other beams of light had begun to pierce through the tiger's eyes, and through his skin, more and more of them until it seemed the light was all he was made of, so bright and brilliant and terribly, wildly beautiful that it made

Hamra's eyes water. And then there was one final flash that made Hamra squeeze her eyes shut against it. And then . . . and then . . .

And then, when she could finally see again, there was a man. Just a man, lying on the rug of the room, old and skinny and dressed in worn garments of faded orange and black, bruised and battered and barely breathing.

Atok and Ilyas burst into the room just as Hamra and Opah dropped to their knees beside him. Opah carefully gathered his head into her lap. "Firman?" she whispered.

The old man opened his eyes, and in them Hamra recognized the tiger's amber gaze. "Good to see you again, Fatimah," he said faintly, and Opah smiled.

"Even after the tongue-lashing I just gave you?"

"Especially after." He reached up to grasp her hand. "Thank you for your forgiveness. And thank you for your granddaughter. She is a gift."

Opah smiled at Hamra. "She is, isn't she?"

Firman glanced at her. "And thank you for helping me, Little Red. You and your friends."

Hamra couldn't speak through her tears; she just reached out and placed her hand gently on his chest, right where his heart was, and he smiled. His breaths were shallower still now, little gasps like a fish out of water. When he spoke, it was slow, and labored.

"What a privilege this journey has been. What a kindness your friendship has been. What a blessing, to leave this life with so much love surrounding you."

Firman closed his eyes and took as deep a breath as he could. And then he opened them, and his smile was as deep and lovely as anything Hamra had ever seen.

"Goodbye," he whispered.

And with one last breath, the weretiger closed his eyes and was still.

EPILOGUE

THERE WAS ONCE a girl named Hamra who lived in a crooked house on the edge of the tangled Langkawi jungle, with a mother and father who told her what to do, a grandfather who told her stories, and a grandmother who told her truths. There was also a boy; he did not live there, but was there often enough—and, as Hamra's grandfather often lamented, certainly ate enough of the food there—to make it *feel* like he did. The two friends spent many happy days playing together in the garden, where flowers bloomed and vegetables grew and in one corner stood a stone marker with the name FIRMAN carved into it in block letters. They kept this clean and shiny no matter how hot or rainy it got outside.

Hamra's grandmother often lived in a place and time that wasn't quite in sync with the rest of her family. But that was okay. Because every so often, they managed to meet in a space that was all their own. And in the moments in between, Hamra never stopped trying to reach her.

Because after all, there was always magic and wonder in the trying.

ACKNOWLEDGMENTS

Before I begin, let it be known that this all started because I told my friend Margaret Owen I'd like to try my hand at a retelling or reimagining, to which she replied "I could see you taking on Little Red Riding Hood." Blame her.

As usual, heartfelt thanks to Victoria Marini, for always being open to every wild pitch and increasingly complicated project I drop into your lap, and for always fighting for my words. I am grateful to have you in my corner.

Books are made in edits, and Alice Jerman continues to help me make magic out of the messes I dump in her inbox. I am grateful for her insight and guidance—and for knowing when to step back and when to push forward.

My gratitude also goes to the team at Harper who helped make this book happen: Clare Vaughn, Vanessa Nuttry, Jessica Berg, Gweneth Morton, Chris Kwon, and

Alison Donalty, as well as Deborah Lee, who so gorgeously brought Hamra and her tiger to life for the cover.

Thank you to Alia Ali for allowing me to pick your brains on Langkawi lockdown life, and to the friends who shared their caretaking experiences to supplement my own.

Every book is hard, but this book was harder than most. It was largely written in a strange, stressful period of lockdowns and isolation, and at the very height of my burnout. It would not have existed without the friends who allowed me to slide into their DMs and texts and WhatsApp chats and unload all my concerns and fears and pettiness. You know who you are; I cannot thank you enough.

Malik and Maryam, I started this journey because I wanted you to see yourselves as heroes. Thank you for all the hugs and sticky kisses that powered me through those low, low times. I love you both.

Finally: My husband watched me struggle through the process of writing this book, flying, failing, crawling, and falling by turns, and caught me every time. Thank you for saving me.